The Outlaw's Bride

BOOK TWO
THE BRIDES OF SKYE

Jayne Castel

WINTER MIST PRESS

The Outlaw's Bride, by Jayne Castel

Published by Winter Mist Press

ISBN 9780473538736 (paperback)

Edited by Tim Burton

Cover photography courtesy of www.shutterstock.com
Scotch thistle vector image courtesy of Wikipedia Commons.
Map by Jayne Castel

Visit Jayne's website: www.jaynecastel.com

A woman desperate to escape an arranged marriage. A prisoner with nothing to lose. The promise that will change their lives forever.

Adaira MacLeod has just been betrothed to a brutal older man—a chieftain many believe responsible for his last wife's death. Adaira is desperate. She'll do anything to avoid wedding him.

Lachlann Fraser is a chieftain's eldest son, and prisoner in the Dunvegan dungeon. Captured after a bloody battle between the MacLeods and Frasers, Lachlann faces a bleak and uncertain future ... until Adaira approaches him to strike a bargain: his life for her freedom.

Lachlann agrees—he has nothing to lose and everything to gain. But some bargains come at a high price.

Historical Romances
by Jayne Castel

DARK AGES BRITAIN

The Kingdom of the East Angles series
Night Shadows (prequel novella)
Dark Under the Cover of Night (Book One)
Nightfall till Daybreak (Book Two)
The Deepening Night (Book Three)
The Kingdom of the East Angles: The Complete Series

The Kingdom of Mercia series
The Breaking Dawn (Book One)
Darkest before Dawn (Book Two)
Dawn of Wolves (Book Three)
The Kingdom of Mercia: The Complete Series

The Kingdom of Northumbria series
The Whispering Wind (Book One)
Wind Song (Book Two)
Lord of the North Wind (Book Three)
The Kingdom of Northumbria: The Complete Series

DARK AGES SCOTLAND

The Warrior Brothers of Skye series
Blood Feud (Book One)
Barbarian Slave (Book Two)
Battle Eagle (Book Three)
The Warrior Brothers of Skye: The Complete Series

The Pict Wars series
Warrior's Heart (Book One)
Warrior's Secret (Book Two)
Warrior's Wrath (Book Three)

The Pict Wars: The Complete Series

Novellas
Winter's Promise

MEDIEVAL SCOTLAND

The Brides of Skye series
The Beast's Bride (Book One)
The Outlaw's Bride (Book Two)
The Rogue's Bride (Book Three)
The Brides of Skye: The Complete Series

The Sisters of Kilbride series
Unforgotten (Book One)
Awoken (Book Two)
Fallen (Book Three)
Claimed (Epilogue novella)

The Immortal Highland Centurions series
Maximus (Book One)
Cassian (Book Two)
Draco (Book Three)
The Laird's Return (Epilogue festive novella)

Stolen Highland Hearts series
Highlander Deceived (Book One)
Highlander Entangled (Book Two)
Highlander Forbidden (Book Three)
Highlander Pledged (Book Four)

Guardians of Alba series
Nessa's Seduction (Book One)
Fyfa's Sacrifice (Book Two)
Breanna's Surrender (Book Three)

Epic Fantasy Romances
by Jayne Castel

Light and Darkness series
Ruled by Shadows (Book One)
The Lost Swallow (Book Two)
Path of the Dark (Book Three)
Light and Darkness: The Complete Series

***

For Tim, *per sempre.*

***

Map

THE CLAN TERRITORIES
OF THE ISLE OF SKYE
IN THE 14TH CENTURY
THE MINCH
SOUND OF RAASAY
INNER SOUND
MAINLAND
MACLEOD
MACDONALD
ISLE OF SKYE
FRASER
Isle of Raasay
MACKINNON
MACDONALD OF SLEAT
SEA OF THE HEBRIDES

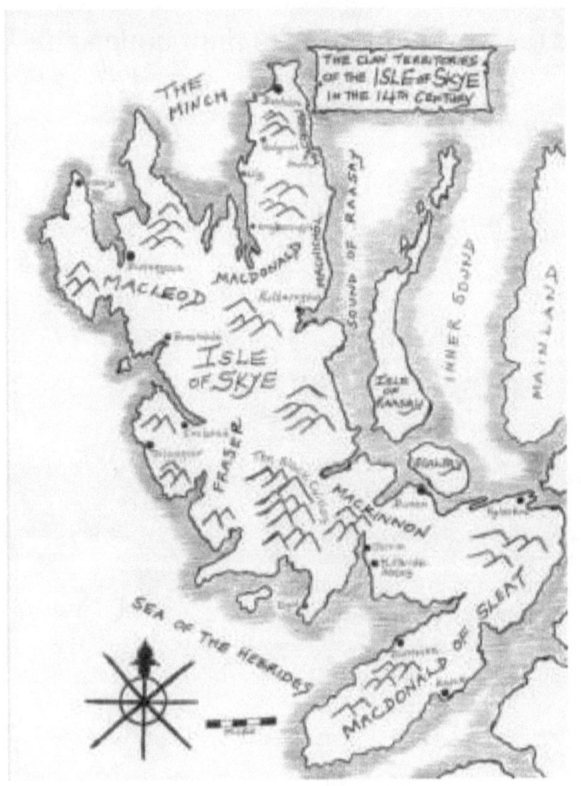

"Better a broken promise than none at all."
                                    —*Mark Twain*

Chapter One

Betrothed

Dunvegan Castle, Isle of Skye, Scotland

Early autumn, 1346 AD

"SO DELICATE AND fair ... I shall enjoy taking yer innocence."

Aonghus Budge's words brought a cold sweat to Adaira MacLeod's skin. He spoke as if they were alone and used a lover's voice. Fear clawed its way up Adaira's throat. She'd barely been able to eat a mouthful of the meal before her anyway. Now, it would be impossible.

"What's wrong?" Chieftain Budge crooned, leaning in closer. "Have yer sisters not told ye what happens between a man and a woman?"

It was shortly after dawn. Adaira sat with her kin and their guest upon the dais in the Great Hall of Dunvegan keep. It was just a day after Adaira's father had announced that Chieftain Budge would wed his youngest daughter.

Adaira was still reeling from the shock of it. She felt utterly betrayed by her father.

The Great Hall was a lofty space dominated by a huge hearth at each end and rows of tables where her father's men now attacked plates of fresh bannocks, spreading them with butter and honey.

The rumble of male voices, interspersed with laughter, echoed through the hall, masking her betrothed's words from the others at the chieftain's table.

Adaira swallowed and reached for a cup of milk, anything to distract her from Budge's love talk. Raising the cup to her lips, she took a tentative sip—a mistake, for her belly now roiled. Across the table, she caught her sister Rhona's eye.

Statuesque, with a mane of thick auburn hair, Rhona sat next to her husband, Taran MacKinnon. They'd only recently wed, but Adaira had never seen Rhona so happy. She swore her sister grew more beautiful with each passing day. Taran, whose scarred face made him forbidding to look upon, had indeed won Rhona's heart.

Rhona put down the wedge of bannock she'd been buttering and fixed Adaira with a look she knew well. Even though Rhona had been unable to discern the words that Aonghus Budge of Islay was murmuring to her, she'd guessed their meaning. There was concern in her sister's eyes.

Adaira had never been good at hiding her feelings. Her father had always said she wore them on her face for the whole world to witness.

"Demure, I see." There was amusement in Budge's voice now. "I like that in a woman ... less cause for me to give ye a beating ... although I'd enjoy that too."

Adaira made the mistake of looking at him then.

The Budge chief was a portly man with florid cheeks and greying brown hair. He was around her father's age—in his mid-forties. There was something about the warrior that had always frightened Adaira, for Aonghus Budge had been a regular visitor to Dunvegan over the years. She wasn't sure if it was the slack expression he often wore or his mean pale-blue eyes that frightened her. His thick lips reminded her of two fat slugs, and he had coarse, blunt-tipped fingers. Her heart quailed at the thought of those hands on her body.

The chieftain grinned, revealing yellowing teeth of which a few were missing. "But with a little fire in yer belly … that'll make ye fun to bed."

Bile rose in Adaira's throat, burning like vinegar.

She tore her gaze from his and stared down at the uneaten piece of bannock before her. Fear pulsed through her; she was starting to feel light-headed from it.

To distract herself, she glanced right to where her eldest sister, Caitrin, sat. Dressed in a black kirtle, a veil covering her pale-blonde hair, Caitrin was the moon to Rhona's sun. Her beauty was cool and untouchable, even more so this morning for she wore a shuttered expression.

Caitrin was in mourning for her husband, Baltair, the chieftain of the MacDonalds of Duntulm. He'd fallen in battle two days earlier during a confrontation with the Frasers. But despite Caitrin's somber clothing, Adaira knew her sister did not truly mourn Baltair MacDonald. He'd been a cruel, brutal husband. Adaira was relieved her sister was free of him, although she wondered what the future would hold for Caitrin. It wouldn't be long before their father would start looking for another husband for her.

No wonder Caitrin was planning to leave this morning and head north to the MacDonald stronghold of Duntulm. There, she'd be free from her father's scheming for a while at least.

Adaira looked to the head of the table then, to where Malcolm MacLeod himself sat. As usual, her father had the appetite of ten men; a mountain of fresh bannocks sat before him, and he feasted upon them as if he'd not eaten for days. A comely man in his youth, her father's muscular frame now ran to fat. Rhona had inherited his auburn hair and storm-grey eyes—and his fiery temperament.

The MacLeod clan-chief was not a man lightly crossed, as Morgan Fraser had recently discovered. The two clans had feuded for the last few years, ever since the Fraser chief's wife, Una, had run off with Malcolm MacLeod. As always, Una sat silently next to her husband. Dark-haired with sharp blue eyes, Una was a woman who saw much but said little. Adaira had never trusted her.

"There's no point looking to yer father," Budge's voice cut in. "His mind is made up, lass. The stronger ye protest, the more he'll dig his heels in."

Adaira swung her gaze back to her betrothed. "Rhona told me yer wife didn't fall down the tower steps," she gasped out the words before her courage failed. "She said ye pushed her."

Chieftain Budge went still. His pale eyes narrowed, and those thick lips stretched into an unpleasant smile. "Folk love to gossip," he murmured, casting Rhona a dark look. "Ye shouldn't listen to them."

Adaira raised her chin as she'd seen Rhona do countless times when confronting men. The gesture made her feel a little braver. "So ye deny it?"

"My wife was a silly, clumsy woman who should have watched her step," he growled, leaning close once more. "Mind ye take care in the tower when I bring ye home. The steps are slippery and worn with age."

Adaira pushed herself away from the table and rose to her feet. *Enough.* She couldn't stand to be in this man's presence a moment longer.

"Adaira?" Caitrin turned to her, snapping out of the dreamlike state she'd been in since sitting down at the table to break her fast. "What's wrong?"

Everything.

"I feel sick," Adaira replied, forcing her voice not to tremble. "I'm going to my bower."

"Sit down, Adaira!" Malcolm MacLeod's order thundered across the table. "I didn't give ye permission to retire."

Adaira shook her head. "I'm unwell, Da."

"No, ye are not," he boomed, crumbs flying as he spoke with his mouth full. "Ye are drawing attention to yerself. Sit down."

Adaira hesitated. At the long table, many pairs of eyes watched her. Some, like those of Caitrin, Rhona, and Taran were filled with concern. Others, like those of her brother, Iain, and stepmother, Una, were indifferent. However, Aonghus Budge's gaze was victorious. If she obeyed now, he would have won.

Adaira picked up her skirts, turned, and fled.

"Adaira MacLeod!" Her father's roar shook the rafters. "Come back here!"

But Adaira didn't heed him. She sprinted from the Great Hall, her long hair flying behind her like a flag.

Adaira's breathing was coming in sharp sobs when she reached the battlements. A cool breeze, laced with the salt-tang of the sea, feathered across her wet cheeks. It breathed in from the loch below the castle, a welcome and familiar smell that calmed her galloping heart.

She'd pay for her disobedience, but she didn't care. It had been worth it. For a few instants, she'd felt free, her feet flying as she bolted from the Great Hall and up the stairwell beyond.

Adaira gulped in the sea air and approached the battlements, leaning against the cool wall. It was still early in the morning; the sun had not yet warmed the pitted stone. Scrubbing away the tears that still coursed down her cheeks, Adaira raised her face to the sky. An eagle circled overhead in search of prey upon the wind-seared hillsides below. She envied the bird its freedom. Maybe she too could fly.

Reaching out, Adaira gripped the edge of the battlements. She leaned forward, going up on tip-toe.

How easy it would be to launch herself from here. It was a long way down to the bailey courtyard below. She'd never survive the fall.

She'd be free from Aonghus Budge then.

Adaira closed her eyes, her fingers digging into stone. Her heart hammered against her ribs, and her pulse pounded in her ears.

I can't do it.

Adaira lowered her head to the edge of the battlements and heaved a deep sob. She couldn't bear this. Her father was likely to force her to wed Chieftain Budge within the next few days. Like Rhona, who'd been handfasted to Taran on the same day that he'd won her hand in the games, MacLeod would waste no time in ensuring his daughter was shackled.

Adaira sucked in another lungful of air, forcing back the grief that thundered through her like surf upon the shore.

My life is over.

Chapter Two

My Choices are Few

LACHLANN FRASER GLARED up through the darkness. He craned his neck back, his eyes squinting at the tiny slivers of light that filtered in through the grate above. The guards had just thrown him down weevil-infested bread and moldy cheese—his third meal since he'd been in the Dunvegan dungeon.

After three sunless days, the darkness was slowly starting to break him. Lachlann could feel it, chipping away at the corners of his mind, gnawing at his self-control. He wondered how many men had gone mad down here.

The guards hadn't moved away from his cell yet. Coarse laughter filtered down.

"Do ye want some meat to go with yer supper?" A voice echoed from above.

Lachlann didn't reply. He hadn't spoken to the guards since his arrival here; instead, he saved his energy and passed the hours imagining how he'd kill them when he got out.

"Here ... eat up!"

The grating sound of metal echoed through the cell as the guards lifted the grate above once more. Something fell inside, landing with a thud at Lachlann's feet.

A heartbeat later, torchlight flooded into the cell, highlighting the filth-smeared walls and the straw-littered floor. The chunk of bread and cheese that Lachlann had not yet touched lay around him—along with the corpse of a giant rat that the guards had just thrown into his cell.

Lachlann's eyes watered, and he blinked furiously, trying to get used to the light. At the sight of the rat, his stomach clenched.

"What's wrong, lad?" Coarse laughter filtered into the cell. There were two of them up there, chortling at his fate. "It's fresh!"

Another burst of mirth assaulted his ears.

Lachlann sucked in a deep breath. Aye, he'd enjoy killing these two. He'd take the one that laughed all the time first. He'd slit his throat and watch while he choked on his own blood. His friend, the one who tormented him the most, he'd kill more slowly. A wound to his belly perhaps.

A disappointed silence fell before one of the guards gave a snort and tossed something else into the pit. It was a bladder of water, stoppered tight.

Lachlann stifled the urge to grab it, for his mouth felt like dried cracked leather, and his throat was so parched it made it hard to swallow. But he would wait until the guards had gone before he slaked his thirst.

"We've got a proud one here," the mouthy guard observed, a sneering edge to his voice. "Pride will do ye no good here, Fraser. It'll only turn ye mad. In a few days, we'll hear ye howling for yer mother."

Aye, and when I get out of here ye will be howling for yers.

The torchlight receded, the iron grate slammed shut, and Lachlann listened to the heavy thump of receding footsteps.

Inhaling deeply, he leaned forward and scooped up the bladder, bread, and cheese. As he did so, he accidentally brushed against something furry. He yanked his hand back with a shudder. *The rat.*

Lachlann retreated to a corner of the cell and lowered himself down on the floor, his back resting against the cold, damp stone. Summer had ended, the long warm days giving way to the cooler months, but it felt as chill as January down here. Once winter did come, he wouldn't last long.

I'll get free before then.

He'd been promising himself he'd escape from the moment they'd thrown him down here. He repeated the words to himself in a mantra whenever despair welled up within him—as it did now.

He couldn't let himself believe this would be his end.

He was Morgan Fraser's eldest, the heir to a vast tract of lands. Not only that, but he had three ruthless younger brothers who'd be happy to see him gone. He couldn't bear the thought of Lucas inheriting what was rightfully his if he didn't return.

None of them would come for him—none would try to rescue him from the Dunvegan dungeon.

If he was to get free, it would be by his own hand.

Lachlann unstoppered the bladder and took a long, measured gulp. The water was flat, stale, and slightly warm, but it tasted like nectar to his parched throat.

His thoughts shifted then to the reason he was here: the battle that had taken place in the Vale of Hamra Rinner, on the border of their lands. The Frasers and MacLeods had clashed violently. He'd seen Malcolm MacLeod, as fat and gouty as he was, stab his father. MacLeod had managed to get a blade under Morgan Fraser's mail shirt.

A blow to the back of Lachlann's skull had felled him an instant after he'd witnessed MacLeod strike his father down. Now he couldn't be certain if his father was alive or not.

Lachlann took another tentative gulp of water. He had to be careful not to drink it all in one go. God only knew when they'd give him another.

The Fraser defeat at the Vale of Hamra Rinner was a bitter one. If his father had indeed survived, he'd be furious. MacLeod bested him at everything it seemed. He'd stolen Morgan Fraser's wife and had now won back his lands.

But Lachlann knew his father well—he'd never let it go. If the Frasers were known for one thing it was their stubbornness. MacLeod had earned himself an enemy for life, and Morgan Fraser would never let the past lie.

Lachlann lowered the bladder and stoppered it carefully. He then took a bite of cheese. It had a rancid, soapy taste, but it was food. He chewed slowly, forcing himself to think on other things.

The sun setting on the slopes of Preshal More, the mountain just south of Talasgair, and turning it gold. The sound of the wind through the grass on the slopes before his father's stronghold. The salty tang of the sea that filled his lungs as he walked along the wide strand before the Bay of Talasgair.

Home.

I'll see it again, he promised himself as his jaw set in determination. *I won't let this place defeat me.*

"We can't let Adaira wed that man." Rhona MacKinnon looped her arm through her husband's and cast him a fierce look. "He'll kill her."

Taran met her gaze for a moment, his face troubled. They walked down the curving causeway from the castle, heading toward the gardens that lay south of the keep. It was their evening ritual these days, this stroll. However, Rhona couldn't relax this evening, not when Adaira's future was so precarious.

"I like this as little as ye," Taran said after a pause. "But ye know what happens to those who defy yer father."

Rhona drew in a sharp breath at Taran's reminder.

She knew all too well. Rhona had defied her father at every turn for years, and in the end, he'd forced her to wed. Things could have turned out badly indeed for her, but fortune had twisted in her favor.

"This is my doing," she said bitterly. "Da wasn't so inflexible in the past. I've made him this way ... he won't have any daughter stand up to him now."

Taran didn't reply, for they both knew it was the truth.

Aonghus Budge had been meant for Rhona, but she'd spurned him. After the support the chieftain had given the MacLeods of late, her father was determined to strengthen his relationship with the Budges of Islay. He'd not let Adaira stand in his way.

The couple walked in silence then, taking the path that cut south, and entering the gardens. Unlike the heavy confines of the keep, and the thick curtain walls that sometimes felt as if they hemmed Rhona in, the gardens were a place of refuge: a quiet space where she could breathe, where the scent of flowers soothed her.

The scent of the last of the summer roses enveloped Rhona and Taran. They walked amongst the riotous growth of rosemary, sage, and thyme, their boots crunching on the fine pebbles underfoot.

A damp sea breeze wafted across the garden, bringing with it a sharp, briny tang. The air was changing; the softness of summer was gone. But for now, there was warmth enough in the sun for them to venture outdoors without a heavy mantle. Rhona inhaled the sharp crispness of autumn. In just over two months' time, the solstice of Samhuinn would be upon them, and then they would begin the long winter.

Stopping next to a canopy of honey-suckle, Rhona turned to face her husband.

Taran met her eye and grimaced. "Something tells me I'm not going to like what ye are about to say."

Rhona arched an eyebrow. "Ye are right about one thing, Taran," she began, her voice low and determined. "If I confront Da about this, it'll only enrage him. We

can't change his mind so we must go around him."
Taran's brow furrowed, but Rhona continued doggedly.
An idea had been growing in her mind all day; she'd not
be thwarted. "We must help her escape Dunvegan."

Adaira hurried into the gardens, one hand clamped
over her mouth in an attempt to hold back the sobs that
racked her.

Tears streamed down her cheeks, and her vision
blurred, yet she knew the path to the gardens so well she
could have traveled it blindfolded.

And she knew Rhona and Taran would be there.

She had to see them. They were the only souls in the
keep who'd know how she felt.

Adaira entered the heart of the garden through an
arch of trailing roses and spied her sister and brother-in-
law up ahead. They were standing next to a canopy of
honey-suckle—and they appeared to be arguing.

Rhona was talking quickly, waving her hands around
for emphasis, while Taran stood before her, arms folded
across his broad chest. His expression was thunderous as
he barked out sharp replies.

Adaira slowed her pace. Despite her upset, and the
panic she could barely contain, she was suddenly wary of
intruding.

She was sorry to interrupt them, but she had no one
else to turn to.

The crunch of her booted feet on gravel alerted Rhona
and Taran to her arrival. They glanced up and stepped
away from each other, their expressions almost guilty.
Rhona turned her storm-grey eyes—so similar to their
father's—toward Adaira. The cross look on her face
softened when she saw who interrupted them.

"Adi," she greeted her. "What is it?"

Adaira stopped before them, and her defenses
crumbled. She wanted to be brave, but everything had
gotten too much. She covered her face with her hands
and started to sob.

"I've ... just come from ... Da's solar," she managed in
panicked gasps. "The wedding will be ... in three days'

time." Adaira drew in a ragged breath and scrubbed at her tears. The upset look on her sister's face, and the concerned expression on Taran's, made it difficult to keep calm. They both understood how grave this was.

"Aonghus Budge will remain here until the handfasting," Adaira continued hoarsely, "and directly after the ceremony he and I will leave for Islay."

Rhona drew in a sharp breath. She then cast an imploring look at her husband. "We must help her."

Taran stared back at his wife, his face taut. Long moments passed before he muttered an oath and raked a hand through his short blond hair. Then he turned his attention to Adaira. "Yer sister has a plan," he said roughly. "I think it's madness, but she won't be swayed."

Adaira went still, her gaze shifting back to Rhona. "Ye do?" she asked hoarsely.

Rhona favored her with a determined look. "Aye. Taran doesn't like it, but I think it's the only way."

Adaira swallowed, straightening her spine. Hope kindled in her breast for the first time since her father had announced her betrothal. "My choices are few right now," she replied. "I'd like to hear it."

Rhona cut a glance to her husband. Taran's face was set in stern lines, his ice-blue eyes hard. Seeing she'd get no support from him on this, Rhona turned her attention fully upon her sister. "We're going to get ye out through that passage in the dungeon."

Adaira's breathing hitched. She watched Taran's expression grow grimmer still. Until today, he likely wouldn't have known of the keep's secret way out. Rhona and Adaira had spoken of the passage recently, for Adaira had suggested her sister use the escape route in the summer, just days before the games when Rhona would be forced to take a husband.

"But won't Da's men catch me?" Adaira asked, her pulse racing. The fragile hope shattered, and fear replaced it. She didn't fancy being hunted.

"Not if someone went with ye," Rhona replied. "A warrior ... someone who knows how to fight, how to survive out in the wild."

Adaira's gaze flicked to Taran. *Surely not?*

"Taran can't go with ye," Rhona said sharply. She'd seen the direction of her sister's gaze. "Da would have him flayed alive for the betrayal."

"Who then?" Adaira whispered, meeting Rhona's eye once more.

Rhona drew in a deep breath, folding her arms across her breasts. "Ye know Da has a new prisoner locked in the dungeon?"

Adaira frowned. "Aye ... Lachlann Fraser." All of Dunvegan knew of the capture of Morgan Fraser's first-born son.

"I plan to free him—his freedom for yers."

This announcement rendered Adaira speechless.

Taran was scowling. He looked at his wife like she'd just lost her wits.

Rhona was the first to break the silence. "I know it's a bold plan, but I've thought it through."

Adaira found her tongue. "And ye believe Lachlann Fraser would help me?"

"Aye, his choices are even fewer than yers. Da will never let him out of that cell. He'll be desperate."

"Ye should never make an alliance with a desperate man," Taran growled. "Ye will never be able to trust him."

Rhona cast her husband a quelling look. "We will make him swear an oath."

"And do ye think it's wise to let our enemies learn of a secret entrance into the keep?"

Rhona tensed, a shadow passing over her face. "We'll make him promise never to reveal it."

Taran snorted. "Ye would take him at his word?"

"We have no choice." Rhona put her hands on her hips and glowered at her husband. "Without our help, he'll never see daylight again. We have to hope that the man has some honor." She turned her attention to Adaira then. "He must escort ye out of Dunvegan and take ye to our kin in Argyle—only then is he free to return home."

Silence fell while Adaira digested her sister's words. She understood Taran's concerns. It was a bold, reckless, and incredibly risky plan. Yet if Lachlann Fraser agreed, it might just work. Adaira knew she'd never make it to Argyle without help.

Still, a heavy weight settled in the pit of her belly at the risk her sister was putting herself, and Taran, at by helping her.

"I can't let ye do this," she whispered, tears welling as despair rose within her once more. "What if Da discovers ye helped me?"

"He won't," Taran replied, his voice rough. Adaira met his gaze and saw his expression had changed. His face was still stern although there was a determined light in his eyes that reminded her of Rhona. "Not if we are clever and careful."

Chapter Three

Just Three Drops

THE CUNNING WOMAN lived on the edge of the village of Dunvegan, in a hovel surrounded by brambles and hawthorn.

Rhona drew up her mare, Lasair, before the gate and swung down from the saddle. Glancing around, she wondered if anyone had seen her leave the keep to ride here, or if any villagers had spotted her along the way. She had a story ready for them if they had: she would say she'd visited the woman for help getting with child. She and Taran hadn't been wed long, but many a wife was anxious for her womb to quicken.

Curling mist wreathed in from the loch this morning. It was Rhona's ally, obscuring her from prying eyes. Even so, she was on edge. Dunvegan was a place where little went unnoticed and unseen. She'd deliberately taken the long way here, skirting the village, yet she still glanced around her, eyes straining as she peered into the mist.

Rhona tied Lasair to the rickety fence and let herself in through the gate. *I can't believe this mad plan is my idea.*

But as mad as it was, she knew she had to do this.

She couldn't stand by and let Adaira wed Budge.

The mist closed in around Rhona now, obscuring the white-washed, thatch-roofed cottages of the village. However, to the north, the keep loomed above the pillowy white blanket. Dunvegan Castle was a dove-grey fortress that appeared carven from the rocks on which it stood. Its curtain wall and craggy battlements stood out against the grey sky. The fortress had once been a prison for Rhona, and it now was for Adaira too.

She would help in any way she could.

Guilt arrowed through her then, for she didn't like to involve Taran in her plans. Her father's retribution would be terrible if he suspected Taran of helping Adaira escape.

Rhona hated putting her husband at risk. Yet she couldn't do this without him—and there was no way he'd allow her to venture into the dungeon and release a prisoner. He'd insisted that part of the plan was to be his responsibility.

A wave of love, so fierce that it made her eyes mist, swept over Rhona. She'd never met a man like Taran MacKinnon: brave and strong, yet with a tenderness and protectiveness that took her breath away.

Rhona made her way up the narrow path to the front door of the hovel, passing a messy garden. As she walked, her eyes picked out a number of plants: woundwort, marigold, boneknit, mint, and chamomile. Herbs were the cunning woman's trade. Locals often requested her help when a healer could not find a cure.

"Afternoon, Lady Rhona." An old woman greeted her at the door. Small and lean, with a weathered face and thick white hair tied back into a severe bun, Bradana Buchanan knew all who lived at Dunvegan—from the high to the low.

"Good day to ye, Bradana," Rhona greeted her with a smile. "I'm in need of one of yer potions. Can I come in?"

The cunning woman nodded and stepped back so that Rhona could enter her hovel. A tidy space scented with the odor of dried herbs, and the more pungent odor of burning peat, greeted her. Surprised, Rhona

straightened up. The garden was such a tangle she'd
expected the interior of Bradana's home to be in disarray
as well. Instead, there wasn't an item out of place. The
dirt floor had been swept clean, fragrant bunches of
dried herbs hung from the rafters, and a plush fur
hanging shielded the hovel's sleeping space from view. A
long worktable—where rows of bottles, a pestle and
mortar, and earthen jars were neatly stacked—sat
against the far wall.

A lump of peat burned in the hearth. Rhona warmed
her hands before it; the mist had turned the day cold and
damp.

"What sort of potion were ye after, lass?" Bradana
asked. The old woman ran a speculative gaze over her.
"Surely ye aren't worried that yer womb won't quicken?
It's too early for such worries."

Rhona smiled. "Aye, there's plenty of time for that,"
she replied. "Although if anyone should ask, that's why I
visited ye."

Bradana inclined her head, gaze narrowing. "What
are ye wanting then?"

Rhona dragged in a breath. "I need a potion to put
someone to sleep for a while."

The cunning woman gave a brisk nod. "I can make ye
a sleeping draught of valerian root."

Rhona shook her head. "I need something much
stronger than that ... a potion that will put someone to
sleep quickly and make them slumber a long while."
Bradana's face tensed, and Rhona hurriedly added.
"Nothing to cause harm."

Bradana observed her for a few long moments, dark-
blue eyes gleaming. "May I ask why ye need such a
potion, Lady Rhona?"

Rhona chewed at her lower lip. "It's best if ye don't."

The cunning woman gave Rhona a long look. "Lady
Rhona," she began quietly after a moment. "My poultices
and potions are for the use of good, not ill."

"And this *is* for good," Rhona answered quickly. Panic
rose as she realized the cunning woman thought she was
planning something villainous. "I wish I could say more,

but I'm sworn to secrecy. But please believe me when I say that this potion will save someone's life. I wouldn't ask otherwise."

Bradana Buchanan continued to watch her. It was a probing look that made Rhona feel as if the woman could see right into her soul. Eventually, she huffed out a breath. "I have something," she said. "However, ye must be wary of how ye use it."

Rhona nodded, relieved. "I will, I promise."

The cunning woman crossed to the table and picked up a small clay bottle. "This is a tincture of nightshade," she said, holding up the bottle but not passing it to Rhona. "I keep it for those who have nerve trouble. One drop in a cup of wine will relax ye. Three drops will put someone into a deep, dreamless sleep. And ten drops will kill them."

Bradana handed her the bottle. There was a steely look in her blue eyes, a warning. "Ye never received this from me, Lady Rhona, is that clear?"

Rhona swallowed, before nodding. "Just three drops then."

"Aye ... and no more."

Adaira picked up a sweet bun and took a bite. It stuck in her throat as she swallowed.

Fighting the urge to gag, she turned to the young woman with thick brown hair and hazel eyes who stood at a workbench before her. "How's Gordon faring these days?" Adaira asked.

"Much better, thank ye, milady." Greer twisted her head and flashed Adaira a warm smile. "I appreciate ye asking."

Adaira forced a cheerful smile back. Truthfully, it was difficult to concentrate, hard not to look at the two trays behind Greer, where she was setting out food and drink:

cups of apple wine and dishes of mutton stew served with oaten dumplings.

Supper for the men taking their watch in the dungeon tonight.

"I was relieved to hear he'll keep his leg," Adaira continued. She felt bad feigning conversation with Greer, although her concern for Gordon MacPherson was real. The warrior had taken a serious injury to the thigh during the battle against the Frasers.

"So was I," Greer admitted, pushing a lock of hair out of her eyes. "He'll bear a limp for the rest of his days though ... and he won't stop grumbling about it."

"Better a limp than a peg leg," Adaira replied, keeping the smile plastered on her face.

Greer snorted. "Aye, that's what I tell him when his complaining gets too much."

Adaira laughed, although to her ears it sounded like a nervous titter. Until this evening, she'd always felt comfortable in this kitchen. Greer and her mother, Dunvegan's cook, had been good to her over the years. She'd spent a lot of time with them after her mother died. Tonight, Greer's mother, Fiona, was poorly with a bad head. Greer had overseen the day's food preparations.

Swallowing hard, Adaira tried to calm herself. It was hard though as her heart was beating so fast it felt as if it might leap from her chest. She felt sick.

Maybe I should have asked Rhona to do this.

No, her sister had already taken a great risk on her behalf. Adaira needed to complete this task—no one else. She just hoped her nerve wouldn't fail her.

Next door to the kitchen, Adaira could hear the lilt of female voices and laughter. The servants in the scullery were hard at work, washing up after supper had ended in the Great Hall.

Adaira's attention shifted to the haunch of venison that hung from the rafters on the far side of the kitchen. Noting the direction of her gaze, Greer's face turned serious. "It's for the handfasting feast."

It was the reminder Adaira needed. The wedding was looming now. If she messed this up, she'd never escape it. "I imagine ye will be busy with the preparations," she said, her voice suddenly brittle.

"Aye." Greer favored her with a sympathetic look. All of Dunvegan knew she didn't want to wed Aonghus Budge. "I've got a lot of baking to do over the next two days. Hopefully, Ma will feel better tomorrow so she can help."

Taking another bite of bun, Adaira widened her eyes. "I love these, Greer … ye really are a talented baker."

Greer was, although if Adaira took one more bite, she felt as if she'd throw up.

Greer grinned, her cheeks flushing at the compliment. "Take some away with ye, if ye want, Lady Adaira."

"Can I?" Adaira took a small basket and placed four more buns inside. She cast Greer a hopeful look. "I don't suppose ye have some butter to go with them … and some of that blackcurrant jelly ye made at mid-summer?"

Greer huffed. "For a wee thing, ye have quite an appetite." She cast a glance behind her at where the trays were waiting. Adaira was interrupting her chores, although she couldn't deny one of MacLeod's daughters. "Very well … wait here. We've got plenty of butter leftover from today, but I'll have to dig out a pot of jam." She moved toward the pantry, wiping her hands upon her apron. "I'll be back in a moment."

A moment was what Adaira had been waiting for.

As soon as Greer disappeared, she set aside her basket, withdrew the bottle from her sleeve, and approached the two cups of apple wine.

This was a stressful situation. Rhona had told her a tincture of nightshade could be deadly. She needed a steady hand and really didn't want to be rushed. Yet this was the only chance she'd get. Crouching down, so her gaze was level with the cups, she unstoppered the bottle.

To her horror, Adaira saw her hands were shaking.

Calm down. If ye fail in this, it's over.

Carefully, holding her breath to catch a tremor in her wrist, she tilted the bottle.

One, two, three.

In the pantry, she heard Greer mutter a curse as she rummaged through the pots of jam for the elusive blackcurrant. Adaira knew their stores were getting low of that variety—which was why she'd asked for it. However, any moment now, Greer would locate her last jar.

Inhaling sharply, she moved to the second cup. She could feel sweat beading on her upper lip. Her pulse thundered in her ears.

One, two ... three.

It was done.

The Lord preserve her, she hoped she'd got the measurement right.

Adaira stoppered the bottle, rose to her feet, and stepped back sharply. She'd only just hidden the bottle up her sleeve and picked up her basket of buns when Greer burst out of the pantry. The young woman held a small clay pot aloft, her expression victorious. "Here it is—just one left!"

Adaira beamed at her. "Ye are an angel. Blackcurrant is my favorite."

"I know," Greer said with a wink, handing her the pot and a large pat of butter wrapped in linen. "There ye go ... now off with ye. I've got some hungry guards to feed. They'll be wondering where their supper's got to."

Chapter Four

No Place for Ladies

"I'M SORRY, PUP, but I can't take ye with me." The wolfhound puppy, Dùnglas, wriggled in Adaira's arms. He reached up with his front paws, trying to lick her face. Adaira's eyes filled with tears. She'd chosen Dùnglas from a recent litter. His name, which meant 'grey fort', had been her choice too.

She didn't want to leave him behind.

"Go on." She set him down inside the stable and watched as he scampered off to join the other puppies. Their mother lay in the corner of the stall, a long-suffering expression upon her face. The pups were getting to an age where they were becoming mischievous, their needle-sharp teeth nipping at her teats when they fed.

Not wanting to draw out the moment, Adaira turned on her heel. She hastily blinked away tears and hurried from the stables. *No weeping.* She couldn't crumble now, not when she was to make her escape tonight.

Rhona and Taran were risking their necks for her. She had to be brave.

The sun was going down, setting the western sky ablaze. Supper had been a tense affair. Adaira had sat in silence while Aonghus Budge threw her heated glances and whispered more filth. If her father heard any of the comments, he'd made no sign. Instead—his attention tonight had been fixed entirely upon the mutton stew and dumplings before him.

Adaira climbed the stairs that led to the upper levels of the keep. There was no one around; it was still too early for most folk to retire.

In her bower, she found Rhona waiting.

"There ye are!" Her sister hissed, gripping her arm and steering her back through the door into the empty corridor. "Where have ye been?"

"I was putting Dùnglas back down with the other pups," Adaira whispered back. "If he stays in my bower alone overnight, he'll howl."

Rhona's face relaxed. "Good thinking … come on. We need to get ye to our chamber up in the tower. The first of the guards will be taking up his post outside yer room shortly."

"Just wait a moment." Adaira crossed to the bed, where the satchel she'd prepared awaited. The satchel's sides bulged. She'd packed a large water bladder and the four sweet buns, with the butter and blackcurrant jam, all tightly wrapped. Grabbing the satchel, she slung it across her front.

The thump of heavy booted feet ascending the stairs below them, made both women freeze. The guard in question was early.

"Let's go." Rhona's fingertips bit into Adaira's upper arm, but she didn't complain. Instead, she let her sister drag her along the corridor, down a narrower stairwell, and down to the bottom level of the keep. By the time they reached the tower stairs, both of them were out of breath.

The guard would have taken up his position outside her door by now. Their father had recently instructed Adaira to retire directly after supper. The guard would take his place outside her door, assuming she was inside her bower. She would not be disturbed until her hand-maid, Liosa, visited her the following morning.

The sisters did not speak until they were safely ensconced in the tower room.

Shutting the door firmly behind her, Rhona turned to Adaira. Her cheeks were flushed and tense. "Did ye manage it?"

Adaira nodded. "I think so. I had to be careful."

"Ye only added three drops to each cup?"

"Aye ... Greer took some time looking for the food I requested. Even so, she almost caught me."

Rhona loosed a deep breath. "Thank the Lord she didn't. I don't know how ye would have talked yer way out of that." She crossed to the sideboard and picked up a bone-handled dirk and a slingshot. She handed them to Adaira. "Ye need to be able to defend yerself. Do ye remember how to use a slingshot?"

Adaira nodded hesitantly. "I think so," she murmured. She certainly hoped so. She remembered their father showing her how to use a slingshot when they were children. She'd be very rusty, but she was sure she'd regain her skill quickly. Especially if need drove her to it.

Adaira favored Rhona with a sickly smile. "Da watches me like an eagle these days," she murmured. "Do ye think he suspects something?"

Rhona shook her head. "I don't think so. However, those of us left behind must brace ourselves for his rage when he discovers ye gone."

Adaira wrung her hands together, squeezing so hard she heard the bones of her fingers creak. "I don't want ye punished because of me."

With a sigh, Rhona went to her and pulled her into a tight hug. "I won't be. If things go to plan, no one but the cunning woman will know that Taran and I have helped ye." Rhona stepped back, meeting Adaira's eye. "Ye are to meet him in the bailey courtyard, to the right of the front keep steps, later ... once the moon has risen."

Adaira nodded, nervousness coiling in the pit of her belly.

"Taran will take ye to the dungeon and help ye free the prisoner," Rhona continued. She started to pace the chamber, agitated. "The guards should be fast asleep by then."

The coil of nerves in Adaira's belly tightened. She hoped Rhona's sleeping potion would work, although she didn't voice her fear. Heaving a deep breath, Adaira crossed to the open window. It was almost completely dark outside now; the last of the sunset was fading from the sky.

Now we must wait, she thought. The tension was almost unbearable.

Waiting was the hardest part.

"Are ye ready, lass?" The low rumble of Taran's voice soothed Adaira's jangled nerves. She'd stepped out into the bailey and waited in the deep shadow of the keep for Taran to join her.

"Aye," she whispered. "Are the guards asleep?"

It was too dark to make out his face although she sensed his expression was grim. "We'll find out soon enough," he murmured. "Follow me."

Adaira fell into step behind Taran and drew her cloak close around her. It was a still night, and the air was damp and cold. She was traveling light, with just the satchel slung around her front. It was heavy with the food and water. The buns would stave off hunger for a short while. She imagined that Lachlann Fraser would appreciate some good food.

It was late. The keep slumbered, and a deep silence had fallen over the fortress. The stillness of the night unnerved Adaira; she'd have preferred the whisper of a wind to take the edge off it.

She followed Taran toward the entrance to the dungeon, marveling at how silent his tread was for a big man. He moved like a shadow, and she was careful to follow suit.

As she walked, Adaira glanced up at the window to the tower chamber, high above her. It was dimly lit, signaling that someone was still awake. Rhona would be up there, awaiting her husband's return.

The sisters' goodbye had been painful. Adaira's chest still ached from the tears she'd seen in Rhona's eyes.

"Promise me, ye will be careful," Rhona had whispered. "Promise me that when ye get free of here, ye will fight to remain so. Don't look over yer shoulder … don't ever come back."

Adaira had nodded, tears of her own welling.

She couldn't bear the thought of never seeing her sister again, yet she had little other choice. Once she wed Budge, and he took her off to Islay, she'd likely not see Rhona again anyway.

Taran and Adaira entered the dungeon stairwell. Neither of them carried torches, and so they were forced to feel their way downstairs in the dark, using the damp stone wall as a guide.

The glow of light ahead warned Adaira that they were reaching the guard room. Blinking, she followed Taran out into a small space with a low ceiling that had been carved out of the rock. A narrow passage led out of the back: the way to the cells.

Adaira's attention moved to where two guards sat at a table in the corner. The men lay slumped against the wall, mouths gaping. Two trays with empty clay bowls and cups sat before them.

Adaira's breathing hitched. *Are they asleep—or dead?*

Taran pushed back the hood of his cloak and approached the nearest guard. He then snapped his fingers in front of the man's nose. The noise cracked like a whip in the damp air, but the man didn't stir. He reached down and felt for a pulse upon his neck. Taran's breath gusted out. "He's alive." Taran checked the second guard. "And so is this one. They sleep deeply, but they'll live. Ye did well."

Relief swamped Adaira, making her legs go weak. Guilt assailed her then. If her father ever discovered the truth, Rhona's life would be spared, but Taran's wouldn't. He'd swing from a gibbet for this.

She stepped next to Taran, placing a tentative hand on his arm. "I haven't thanked ye properly, Taran," she murmured. "I know ye are doing this for Rhona ... ye must love her very much."

Taran turned to her. The guttering light of the torch on the wall illuminated his scarred face. "I couldn't let Rhona do this on her own," he admitted quietly, "but I also can't stand by and see ye wed Aonghus Budge. If I can help in any way ... I will."

Adaira swallowed the lump in her throat. "Ye are a good man, Taran MacKinnon. My sister is very lucky."

"Come." Did she imagine it, or did his cheeks color slightly at her praise? Turning from her, he helped himself to a ring of keys hanging on the wall and lifted the torch off its brace. Taran carried the torch over to where another hung at the entrance to the passageway. He lit it and passed it to Adaira. "Let's go find Lachlann Fraser."

Adaira followed Taran down the passageway. A few yards on, they came to another set of stairs that led down even farther underground. Adaira hadn't visited the dungeon in years. It was forever nighttime down here, a smothering darkness that made it difficult to breathe. Not that she wanted to take many deep breaths. The air smelled putrid: mold, stale urine, sweat, and worse. It made her eyes water.

"This isn't a place for ladies," Taran grumbled. "I can't believe ye and yer sisters used to play down here."

Adaira responded with a soft snort. She was wondering the same thing herself.

Moments later, they stepped out onto a wide passage. A row of iron grates lined the stone floor.

Adaira stepped close to Taran. "Do ye know where he is?"

Taran nodded. "The second last one. All the rest are empty at present."

They made their way to the cell in question. Halting before the grate, Taran passed Adaira his torch and crouched down. He selected a key and unlocked the grate before lifting it free.

"Lachlann Fraser." Taran's voice, although low, rang in the stillness. "Are ye awake?"

Chapter Five

Upon Yer Life

A RASPY VOICE broke the silence. "Aye ... what's it to ye?"

The male voice had a harsh edge to it. Adaira's spine stiffened. She hadn't given any thought as to the character of the man imprisoned down here. She hoped Rhona was right, and that he would agree to help her.

"I have someone here who'd like a word with ye," Taran continued. He then inclined his head to Adaira, indicating that it was her turn to speak.

Adaira handed Taran back his torch and moved forward. She then bent her head and peered into the darkness below. Dear Lord, the stench coming from down there was awful. Didn't he have a privy he could use?

"Lachlann Fraser," Adaira began, swallowing bile. "I come bearing an offer. Are ye interested?"

A beat of silence followed before the prisoner spoke once more. This time, his voice was gentler, edged with curiosity. "A lady? What's this?"

"Just answer her, Fraser," Taran growled. "Are ye interested?"

Another pause. "I might be."

Adaira leaned forward, squinting. She couldn't see anything in the gloom. "My freedom for yers," she said quietly, reciting the words she'd practiced with Rhona earlier. "If I set ye free, ye must agree to escort me out of this dungeon to freedom. Ye must protect me with yer life."

A soft, bitter laugh followed. "I agree readily," he drawled. "But I also point out that we stand in the dungeon, with a curtain wall and a portcullis preventing my escape."

"I know a way—a secret way—out of this dungeon," Adaira countered, her voice low, urgent. "If ye will swear upon yer life to protect me, I will show ye it."

Another silence fell, this one heavy. The prisoner was pondering her words.

"And where do ye wish me to take ye?" he asked finally, an edge of wariness to his voice.

"I must leave this isle," she replied. "We shall travel to Kiltaraglen on the eastern coast and find a boat that will take us to the mainland. Ye must escort me to Gylen Castle in Argyle. Once I am safely delivered to my kin there, ye are discharged of any responsibility. Ye are then free to return to yer own kin." Adaira drew in a long, steadying breath. "Do ye still agree?"

Another beat of silence passed before he answered. "Aye."

Relief swamped Adaira. However, when she glanced up and looked at Taran, she saw he was scowling. He wasn't happy about this. "Let's hear ye swear it then," he growled. "Upon yer life, upon everything ye hold dear, ye will protect this woman and see her safely delivered to her destination. Ye shall also promise never to tell a soul how ye escaped this place."

"I swear it." The prisoner's voice was low and steady. "Lady ... I shall take ye wherever ye desire. I will protect ye with my last breath." He paused here. "And I will tell no one how we got out ... although I suggest we stop talking and start moving."

That was good enough for Adaira. She was keen to leave as soon as possible. However, she saw that Taran still hesitated. With a jolt, she realized he didn't trust the prisoner. In truth, she didn't either. But what choice did she have? He'd made an oath, and she would need to trust him to uphold it.

"Come," she murmured. "He's sworn to me; we can't wait any longer."

Taran gave a curt nod, rose to his feet, and took hold of a wooden ladder that was resting against the wall. He lowered it into the cell. "Climb up," he ordered curtly.

Moments later, the scuff of boots on the wooden rungs echoed through the dungeon. And then a tousled head appeared.

Adaira stared at the prisoner, momentarily transfixed. This was her first proper look at him. She'd seen Lachlann Fraser from afar when they'd brought him in unconscious. But then she'd just caught a flash of his bright auburn hair and little else.

He was a few years older than her. Wild red hair framed a handsome, if pale, face. He had eyes the color of moss and beautifully drawn features that were set in a fierce expression. A dark auburn shadow of stubble covered a strong jaw. Adaira stared, mesmerized.

Even stinking and disheveled, he was the most attractive man she'd ever seen.

Likewise, the prisoner stared at her. His expression grew shrewd, those green eyes narrowing as he observed her. Then he drew a slow breath and inclined his head. "Evening, Lady ...?"

"Ye don't need to know her name," Taran growled. "There will be time enough for that later."

Holding his torch aloft, Taran stepped back to allow the prisoner to climb from the cell.

Lachlann Fraser did so. He stretched his long body, his eyes squinting as they adjusted to the torchlight. He was dressed in braies and a loose léine. Both were filthy.

Fraser's gaze settled upon Adaira once more, unsettlingly direct. "Which direction is it then?"

Adaira's breathing quickened under his scrutiny before she tore her attention from the prisoner and focused on Taran.

Her brother-in-law was watching her, concern in his eyes. "Do ye remember the way?"

She nodded her head, although her heart started to hammer against her ribs. It had finally come to this; she was escaping. "Aye," she murmured. "Go back now, and thank ye. I'll never forget this." She was careful not to use Taran's name or to mention her sister's. Once they were far from here, her escort would learn her name and identity. But not yet. Taran was right to be cautious.

Taran nodded and stepped back. Yet he didn't move away just yet. Instead, he turned his attention to Lachlann Fraser. The two men stared at each other for a heartbeat. Taran's face was as hard as hewn granite. "If any harm comes to her ... if ye fail to uphold yer end of the bargain, I'll come looking for ye, Fraser," he growled. "I'll hunt ye down to the ends of the earth. That's a promise."

The ferocity of his words shocked Adaira; she stared at Taran, struck speechless.

Lachlann Fraser sneered. "Don't threaten me, *Scar-face*," he growled.

Tension rippled through the air. Taran's jaw clenched, and he took a step toward Lachlann. Panic trembled inside Adaira as she realized the pair might come to blows.

Without thinking, she stepped in between them, craning her neck to meet Taran's eye. "We're going now," she said, her voice brittle with nerves. She then cast a glance over her shoulder at where Lachlann Fraser wore a murderous expression. "Follow me."

Lachlann couldn't believe it.

He was free. Just like that. He'd been huddled in a corner of the cell, wondering how much longer he'd be able to keep his wits in this endless darkness, when he'd heard a man calling to him from above.

That scar-faced warrior had looked as if he wanted to throw him back down the ladder into the cell and slam the grate shut. And he probably would have, if the choice had been his to make.

But thanks to this young woman leading him down a series of increasingly small passageways, it wasn't.

The girl was quite lovely. She'd been the first thing he'd seen when he'd emerged from the cell. A mane of walnut-colored hair framed a pert face that contained the loveliest pair of hazel eyes he'd ever seen. She was small, her curves hidden by the heavy woolen mantle she wore. Across her front, the young woman carried a bulging satchel. She looked like someone about to set out on a long journey.

And I am to be her escort.

A grim smile spread across Lachlann's face. He'd have gladly made a pact with the devil himself if it meant escape from that putrid cell.

"How did ye manage to get past the guards," he asked casually. "Did yer scar-faced friend kill them?"

"They're drugged," she replied, an edge to her voice. "They shouldn't awaken for a long while."

Drugged. Disappointment flooded through Lachlann. For an instant, he was tempted to leave the lass here and go find those two. He had unfinished business with them both. However, freedom was more important to him right now than petty vengeance. He'd not risk it for the pleasure of killing two lack-wits.

"A hidden passage, eh?" he murmured as they entered another corridor, this one so low they both had to stoop to avoid hitting their heads. "How did ye learn of it?"

"Please save yer questions for later," she replied, her tone sharpening. "I must concentrate now."

Lachlann's smile turned hard. He would indeed, for he had plenty of them. She and her protector had been cagey upon letting him out of the cell, but it was clear to Lachlann that the maid was high-born. She spoke and dressed like a lady. He knew that MacLeod had three daughters. Two were wed apparently, but the youngest was not.

Lachlann's gaze settled upon the girl's slender shoulders. He'd wager that this was Malcolm MacLeod's youngest daughter. He didn't recall her name, but he'd discover it soon enough.

Eventually, the passageway became so low they were virtually crawling through it. It was difficult going, for the girl insisted on carrying the torch with her. Lachlann's back was beginning to ache when they came to a rusted iron grate, much like the ones that covered the cells.

The girl sat back on her heels and looked Lachlann's way for the first time since leaving her companion. She had a shy, hesitant gaze, although he noted the lines of determination on her face. Curiosity gnawed at Lachlann. He wanted to know why this young woman was fleeing in the dead of night and enlisting *his* help to do so.

"This is the way out," she announced. "Can ye open the grate and climb down. I'll hand ye the torch."

Lachlann nodded, grabbing hold of the grate and pulling it upward. It wasn't that heavy and, fortunately, the grate wasn't locked, although the bars were covered with rust—almost entirely corroded in places. Lachlann wagered no one had come this way in a very long while.

A hidden passage under Dunvegan ... a secret well worth knowing.

He climbed down, his boots hitting iron rungs, and took the torch the girl handed him. Moments later, she was climbing down the ladder. Halfway down, she paused.

"Wait ... I need to close the grate."

He huffed. "Is there any point?"

Her tone was clipped when she replied. "I'd rather leave no evidence of our passing."

Lachlann's mouth quirked. She might appear as meek as a mouse, but the lass had a spine. He shouldn't be surprised, for a coward wouldn't have chosen such a daring escape as this.

Down in the passageway, Lachlann kept hold of the torch. The roles were reversed now. He would lead the way, and she would follow.

Nonetheless, he turned to her. "Straight ahead?"

The lass nodded. "This tunnel is long ... but it eventually comes to a dead-end." She paused here, her brow furrowing. "It's been years since I've been down here, but I remember there was an iron grate in the roof ... and I saw daylight through it."

Lachlann nodded. "Was it locked?"

Her face tensed. "I can't remember."

Lachlann loosed a sigh. "Come on then ... let's hope it isn't."

The tunnel was small and cramped, with wet stone walls and the ever-persistent sound of dripping water. It was an unpleasant space, but nothing compared to the festering cell Lachlann had left behind. He'd happily endure this place if it promised freedom. He longed for fresh air and daylight, things he would never take for granted again.

As the girl had warned, they spent a long while in the tunnel. Shortly after beginning their journcy, they ceased to speak. Instead, they shuffled along, bent double, step after step, toward freedom.

By the time they reached the end of it, the torch was starting to die. Lachlann dropped it to the ground and craned his neck to the grate above them. No light of any kind shone through it.

He cut his companion a glance. Her face, lit by the guttering torch on the ground, appeared strained. "I can't see a lock," she murmured, her face tilted up, her gaze narrowed as she peered at their escape route.

"There's only one way to find out," Lachlann replied. Climbing up the ladder, he grabbed hold of the iron bars. It wasn't easy to budge. At first, he suspected the grate really was locked. But then after a moment, he realized that it was merely a bit stuck; it was covered with rotting leaves and what smelt like pine needles. He gave a hard shove, and with a groan of metal, the grate shifted.

They were through.

Lachlann pushed the grate aside and climbed up and out of the tunnel. Rising to his full height for the first time in what felt like hours, Lachlann massaged his aching back. He stood amongst a growth of pines.

Moonlight filtered through the trees, and he breathed in the pungent scent of sap.

Freedom had never smelled so good.

"Are ye going to help me out?" An irritated female voice intruded.

Lachlann turned. He'd almost forgotten the woman; they weren't off to a good start.

Reaching down, Lachlann grasped a small, warm hand and pulled the lass up out of the tunnel. The touch of her skin caused a frisson of heat to ripple up his arm. Lachlann caught his breath, his fingers tightening around hers.

The young woman stared at him, her eyes growing wide.

Gently, she pulled back from him, tugging at his hand. Reluctantly, Lachlann let her go.

"I know this place," she observed, shifting her gaze from him. He caught the edge to her voice and knew the touch had affected her as it had him. "These woods lie northeast of the keep. Da and his men often hunt here." She abruptly stopped speaking, realizing she'd unwittingly revealed her identity.

The lass took a step back from him, drawing her mantle close.

"Worry not, Lady MacLeod," Lachlann drawled. "I guessed yer identity the first moment I set eyes on ye. It changes nothing of our agreement. However, I would like to know yer name ... if I may?"

She watched him, her face glowing pale in the moonlight. "Adaira," she said softly.

Lachlann held her gaze. He couldn't believe his luck; this girl was his angel of mercy. What a reprieve—and now he was free, he intended to stay that way.

"Can I ask how ye knew of such a passageway?" he asked. "The dungeon isn't a place for high-born maids."

She swallowed. "My sisters and I discovered it years ago," she replied softly. "We weren't supposed to play in the dungeon. Da would have been furious if he'd known. We used to dare each other, to see who the bravest was ... who could explore the farthest."

Lachlann smiled. "And who discovered the end of the tunnel?"

She looked away. "My sister Rhona."

"Well, Lady Adaira," he murmured. "Argyle is a long way off. I say we travel through the night and rest in daylight. Yer father will be after us come the dawn."

Chapter Six

Aingeal

"I KNEW YE were an angel ... the moment I set eyes upon ye."

The words were muttered between large bites of bun slathered in butter and jam.

Watching Lachlann Fraser devour his second sweet bun, Adaira smiled. "Slow down, or ye will give yerself bellyache."

He nodded but then proceeded to stuff half a bun into his mouth, chewing vigorously. "Ye have no idea how good these are," he managed when he'd swallowed. "I've had nothing but weevil-infested bread and rancid cheese since they threw me down in that hole."

Adaira's smile faded, and she suppressed a shudder at this comment. She looked around her, noting that the sky was growing lighter by the moment. After emerging from the tunnel, they'd fled like hunted deer. Lachlann had led the way east, his long legs covering the ground easily until Adaira had called out to him, begging him to slow his pace. She couldn't run great distances, especially wearing skirts and carrying a heavy satchel and cloak.

Lachlann had relieved her of the satchel, and they'd set off once more, this time at a brisk walk.

Dawn had stolen upon them quickly, arriving with startling swiftness. They now sat on the mossy bank of a creek, taking a much-needed rest. Adaira's lungs still ached from exertion, as did her legs. She'd taken off her heavy cloak and now carried it. Her léine—a long ankle-length tunic she wore under her kirtle—now stuck uncomfortably to her back.

"Ye should eat," Lachlann said as he reached for a third bun. "Or I'll end up finishing all of these."

"I brought them for ye," she replied. "I can eat once we reach the coast. I've got some pennies with me. We'll resupply when we find passage across the water."

Lachlann Fraser raised an eyebrow. "Going hungry on my account … ye truly are an *aingeal*."

Adaira looked away, her cheeks warming. "Not really," she murmured. "I'm too nervous to eat."

"Well, I'll leave the last bun for ye," he said, his mouth curving. "For when ye get yer appetite back."

Their gazes met briefly, and Adaira returned his smile.

She'd been wary of Lachlann Fraser at first, especially after his confrontation with Taran. Yet he'd behaved honorably so far. He'd carried her satchel and slowed his pace to accommodate her. When he'd taken her hand to help her out of the tunnel, heat had jolted up her arm. The feel of his strong fingers curling around hers, the warmth of his skin, had completely scattered her wits.

She'd been acutely *aware* of him ever since.

Adaira watched Lachlann now as he scanned their surroundings. The good humor faded from his face, and his moss-green gaze narrowed. "We can't stay here much longer. Very soon, someone will notice we are missing."

Adaira nodded, her belly contracting. "My maid usually comes to my bower shortly after dawn. She'll raise the alarm … if the dungeon guards don't wake up first."

Lachlann ate his third bun, although not with the ferocity of the first two. Around them, the dawn chorus of birdsong echoed through the trees: blackbirds, song thrushes, and warblers. Their chirping took the edge off Adaira's anxiety and soothed her ragged nerves.

"I love the sound of the dawn chorus," she said eventually, "but I can't hear it from my bower. Sometimes I get up early and go to the gardens at dawn just to listen to the birds."

Lachlann's mouth quirked, and Adaira wondered if her comment had amused him. Here they were, running for their lives, and she was admiring birdsong.

Finishing his meal, Lachlann dusted crumbs off his filthy braies. He sat a couple of yards from Adaira, yet she could still smell him. The man was in need of a bath and fresh clothing. However, both would have to wait.

Lachlann then met her eye once more. "Why were ye so desperate to flee Dunvegan?"

Adaira had been expecting the question, but she still tensed when he asked it.

He's my protector now, she reminded herself. *I need to trust him.*

"I'm to wed Aonghus Budge of Islay," she murmured, dropping her gaze.

Lachlann gave a low whistle. "Say no more ... I know all about him."

Adaira's head snapped up. "Aye ... he killed his first wife—and he'd kill me too, I'm sure of it."

Lachlann Fraser's eyes shadowed before he nodded. Remaining silent, he packed away the remaining food, stuffed it into the satchel, and got up. Slinging the satchel across his front, his gaze met Adaira's once more. "In that case, we'd better keep moving."

Adaira winced as she slipped upon a mossy rock and her ankle twisted.

"Can't we rest for a while," she panted. Holding her skirts high, she splashed across the creek bed after Lachlann. Cold water soaked through the soft leather of her boots. Adaira glanced down at them with dismay. The boots were new and made of costly chamois, but they'd be ruined after this journey.

They'd been traveling all morning, without respite. The sun beat down on them; it seemed that summer had returned after days of colder weather. The heat was both a blessing and a curse. It would make sleeping rough easier, but it also made the journey much harder work. Adaira's cheeks glowed like two hot coals.

"No time for that." Lachlann cast a glance over his shoulder. "Yer father will be hunting us now."

Adaira frowned. She knew that—she didn't need reminding of it.

"I know ye are tired," he continued, turning his attention away from her once more. "And as soon as we find a place to hide, we can rest. It's safer traveling at night anyway."

That made sense. They'd been fortunate so far and hadn't seen any other travelers, hunters, or farmers. Yet, as they approached the east coast, that would change.

Adaira plowed on behind him. Her wet boots started to chafe her feet. Lachlann had relieved her of her cumbersome mantle and now carried both that and her satchel. All she had to do was follow—yet she could feel herself flagging.

I'm slowing him down, she thought dully. *If we get caught, it'll be all my fault.*

The realization sent a jolt of panic through her. She couldn't let that happen. Capture was unthinkable. She couldn't let Budge get his hands on her.

And so she struggled on, closing her mind off to the exhaustion that pulled down at her with each step.

How far were they from the coast now? She'd long since lost any sense of direction. Lachlann had assured her they were journeying east, toward the port village of Kiltaraglen.

The village lay directly across the water from the Isle of Raasay. Once they found a boat, they would have to travel south, around the island, before turning east to the mainland.

Kiltaraglen was also the closest port to Dunvegan. Nervousness fluttered under Adaira's ribcage. She hoped Kiltaraglen was a wise choice. Perhaps she should have gone to Duntulm instead—to Caitrin.

Adaira's throat constricted. How she wished to see Caitrin. But such wishes were foolish. Malcolm MacLeod would search for her at Duntulm.

No, Adaira wouldn't involve her sister. She'd already risked Rhona and Taran's necks. Best to stick with the original plan: go to her kin on the mainland. Her mother had spoken often of Gylen Castle, where she'd grown up. It sounded like a welcoming place.

They would take her in; they would protect her.

On and on they trudged as the sun rose high into the sky. And, just when Adaira's step was beginning to falter, when she was considering calling out to Lachlann and begging for him to stop awhile, he did just that.

Breathing hard, Lachlann drew up. Standing at the bottom of a rocky gully, he turned to Adaira. His cheeks were flushed with exertion, and his handsome face was haggard and tired. However, his eyes were sharp.

"I've found a hiding place," he announced, pointing above them. Pines loomed high overhead, and the sides of the ravine rose nearly perpendicular. A few yards above them, upon the eastern side, Adaira spotted a gap. It was wide, although barely high enough for a person to squeeze into, even on their belly.

"We're going to hide in there?" she asked, horrified.

"Aye." Lachlann adjusted the satchel, slinging it and the cloak across his back. Then he began to climb. "Come on, Aingeal. Yer bower awaits."

Peering up at the gap above, Adaira frowned. She wasn't sure she had the strength in her arms to climb, but she'd try. Reluctantly, she followed him up the rocky incline. There were plenty of holds for her fingers and toes. Even so, she'd only gone a couple of yards when she started to falter.

Halting, clinging to the rock like a spider, she glanced up. Lachlann had already reached their destination. He threw the satchel and cloak inside before pulling himself under the ledge on his belly.

"Just a few more feet," he called. He reached down, his hand stretching toward her. "Ye can manage it."

Gritting her teeth, she forced her uncooperative limbs to move. Her legs trembled under her, and the muscles in her upper arms and shoulders burned. Not only that, but her skirts were hampering her movement.

"Grab my hand."

Adaira pushed herself up another foot before lunging toward Lachlann. His hand clasped hers, and her breath gusted out of her. A heartbeat later, he yanked her up the cliff-face and under the ledge where he sprawled.

Adaira found herself face-to-face with him, their bodies pressed close. His heat and nearness overwhelmed her. It was dark in the gap, but she could see the gleam of his eyes.

A moment later, the ripe smell of his unwashed body assaulted her.

"God's bones," she muttered, edging away from him. "Ye stink."

Lachlann gave a soft laugh. "So would ye, if ye had spent a week in yer father's dungeon."

Adaira gritted her teeth. She didn't want to be uncharitable, but the thought of being jammed in this crevice next to a man who was in dire need of a bath revolted her. She wouldn't be able to sleep.

"Worry not," he continued, a sardonic edge to his voice. "As soon as we reach the coast I shall scrub myself with lye and rid myself of these rags."

Silence fell for a few moments before Adaira broke it. "I'm sorry," she murmured, chastised. "It must have been terrible being locked up in the dark, not being able to use a privy or bathe."

Lachlann's mouth quirked. "It wasn't so bad."

"But didn't ye despair?"

"I was too busy trying to think of a way to escape."

Adaira's eyes widened. "Really?"

"Aye," he replied without hesitation. "Two of the guards, in particular, liked to bait me ... I was going to use it to my advantage."

Adaira watched him, impressed. "Ye are resourceful."

"I've always had to be."

"Why's that?"

"I've got three younger brothers chafing at the bit to advance themselves," he said with a wry smile. "Plus, I'm Captain of Talasgair Guard ... and in charge of patrolling the Fraser borders. I always have to think one step ahead."

Adaira propped herself up on one elbow, trying to get comfortable on the hard stone ledge. "Ye will be anxious to return home."

Lachlann didn't reply, and she searched his face, noting that his smile had faded. She wondered if he worried about his father's fate. She'd heard her own father bragging about how no mortal man could recover from the injury he'd dealt Morgan Fraser.

"I'm grateful to ye, Lachlann," she said softly. "I couldn't make it to Argyle without yer help."

He inclined his head. "It was a brave decision," he noted, "to free me and flee from Dunvegan. Most lasses, even faced with the prospect of wedding Aonghous Budge, wouldn't do it."

Adaira loosed a long breath. "As ye saw ... I didn't do it alone." She hesitated, wondering whether to confide in him. What did it matter? They were far from Dunvegan now. He could know the truth. "The man who helped me is named Taran. He's wed to my sister, Rhona. They planned my escape."

Lachlann's dark-auburn eyebrows raised. "That's quite a risk they took."

"I know ... my father can never learn of it."

Lachlann rolled away from her, stretching out onto his back and cupping his hands behind his head. "Well ... no one will hear a word of it from me, Aingeal."

Chapter Seven

Decisions

THEY REACHED THE coast and the village of
Kiltaraglen in the middle of the night.

Moonlight frosted the outlines of great mountains
and lit their way. Adaira's belly growled as she walked, so
loudly that Lachlann eventually turned to her.

"Here." He dug the last bun out of the satchel and
held it to her. "Eat this."

Adaira stopped, her gaze dropping to the bun. "Don't
ye want it?"

"Aye, but if yer belly growls any louder, it'll alert half
the village to our presence."

Adaira favored him with a soft snort. Her stomach
wasn't that loud. Even so, she took the bun, sighing with
pleasure as her teeth sank into it. Her appetite had
returned with a vengeance now. Maybe it was because
she'd managed to rest. She hadn't thought she'd sleep
during the day, squeezed into that crevice with
Lachlann—but she had. She'd fallen into a deep,
dreamless sleep, and had only awoken after dark when
he'd gently shaken her.

They'd left the creek behind shortly after starting this
stretch of the journey, traveling across bare hills. The

open landscape made Adaira nervous. Her ears kept straining for the thunder of hoofbeats in the distance. Her father would no doubt send men in this direction, for Kiltaraglen was the nearest port to Dunvegan.

They would need to leave first thing in the morning to stay ahead of him.

Boots crunching on the gravel-strewn road, they crested the brow of a hill, woodland rising up either side. Below them stretched the tiny port of Kiltaraglen.

The village, a collection of thatched roofs lining the edge of the water, slumbered. It was a still, mild night. The water glistened, reflecting the glow of the moon. If Adaira hadn't been so nervous, she'd have found the sight a lovely one.

She'd been to Kiltaraglen once years earlier, for there had been a special market here, and her father had allowed her, Rhona, and Caitrin to visit it. She remembered the village with fondness: the tightly-packed white-washed homes and the long waterfront, where a collection of rickety wooden boats bobbed in the tide.

Adaira swallowed her last mouthful of bun. "There's an inn on the waterfront," she said. "Hopefully it's not too late, and they'll open their doors to us."

Lachlann didn't respond immediately. Instead, his gaze remained on the village below them. He studied it intently. "I don't think it's wise to linger here," he said finally. "We should move on ... tonight."

Adaira tensed. "But surely it's safe to stay here till dawn?"

Lachlann shook his head. "It isn't. The fewer folk who see us the better. Yer father's men will likely arrive here tomorrow, and the inn will be the first place they'll look. The innkeeper will tell them that a couple matching our description lodged there, and then it won't take much digging for them to discover we left by water." Lachlann cast her a fierce, determined look. "It's best we leave no sign of our passing. We should go now."

Adaira drew a shaky breath. This wasn't the news she wanted. Despite that the bun had taken the edge off her hunger, she longed for a decent meal and a bed for the night. She also longed to bathe. At Dunvegan, she'd have added a few drops of lavender oil to the water, for the scent calmed her. She ached for a short reprieve before they set out on the next leg of their journey. Yet she had to admit, his words made sense. She would have to wait till the mainland for a decent meal and a soft mattress.

"But how can we find a boatman to give us passage?" she asked. "No one will be awake at this hour."

A pause followed. Lachlann slowed his pace before drawing to a halt and turning to face her. "We don't have time for that ... we'll have to steal a boat."

Adaira stifled a gasp. "But we're not thieves."

Lachlann's mouth curved into a slow smile, and despite her shock at his pronouncement, Adaira's belly fluttered. Lachlann Fraser's smile was as alluring as it was dangerous. Like the touch of his hand when he'd helped her out of the tunnel, it turned her mind to porridge.

"Now isn't the time for scruples, Aingeal," he replied softly. "Just how desperate are ye to escape Aonghus Budge?"

I can't believe I agreed to this.

Adaira padded along behind Lachlann as they made their way down to the waterfront, hugging the shadows as they went. It seemed an unnecessary precaution, for there appeared to be no one about, but Adaira was glad her protector was being careful. Someone might be lurking nearby. Perhaps the dock was watched at night—or maybe her father's men were here already, looking for her.

Adaira swallowed hard—she hoped not.

They walked down to where a row of small wooden boats bobbed in the water. Unfortunately, the craft were moored right before the inn. The white-washed building, which rose high above all the others in the village, lay in darkness. No light peeked out from behind the closed shutters. Perhaps it was later than Adaira realized. Even the inn-keeper would be abed.

She followed Lachlann down the grassy slope to the water. There, he went to the first boat in the line and hunkered down before the wharf. Working by feel, for the shadows were long here, he started to untie the oiled rope that moored the boat.

"Climb in," he whispered.

Heart hammering, Adaira complied. She lifted her skirts and stepped into the boat. It rocked under her, and she stifled a gasp, lowering herself to the deck. She then shuffled forward and perched upon a plank of wood. Lachlann passed her the satchel and cloak—and then he pushed the boat out into the water.

Adaira clung on to the sides. Her eyes strained in the darkness for any sign of movement around them. Lachlann moved slowly, but even so, every splash, every ripple, seemed obscenely loud.

As he crept out of the shadow of the docks, Adaira caught sight of Lachlann's face illuminated in the moonlight. It was set in grim, determined lines. It seemed Rhona had made the right choice in making him her protector; Morgan Fraser's firstborn was practical, a survivor.

When the water had reached thigh height, Lachlann climbed in and sat himself down opposite Adaira. He picked up the oars and maneuvered the boat around so that he was facing shore. Then he started to row.

The pair of them did not speak. Adaira hardly dared breathe. She kept glancing back over her shoulder at Kiltaraglen, expecting to hear shouts echo out across the water as someone spied them.

Guilt assailed her then. At dawn, a fisherman would wander down to the water to find his boat gone. They were stealing a man's livelihood. How would he feed his family without his boat?

Adaira shoved the thought away. It was too late now to torture herself. She had to put her trust in Lachlann. She realized now that it was too risky to wait till daylight, yet resorting to thievery upset her.

She turned from the village, her gaze traveling east. In daylight, the isle of Raasay rose out of the sound, but tonight she saw only darkness. However, the island would still be there, and they would need to turn south soon.

"Lie down and rest awhile, Adaira." Lachlann broke the silence between them, his voice terse.

Adaira stared back at him, studying the lines of his face. Her heart had settled to its usual rhythm, and now that they were out of danger, she felt weak, wrung out. She was bone-weary.

Still, she resisted. "What about ye?"

He huffed. "Someone's got to row. There is nothing to be gained by both of us having a sleepless night. When dawn breaks, I'll bring the boat ashore so I can rest."

Adaira nodded, stifling a yawn. Despite that she'd slept the day before, she was desperately weary now. Using her cloak as a pillow, she stretched out, curling her torso around the satchel. It wasn't the most comfortable bed she'd ever slept in, but it was wonderful just to lie flat—not to be on her aching feet.

I'll only close my eyes for a short while, she promised herself. *I'll just take a nap*. But the gentle splash of the oars and the subtle roll of the boat had a lulling effect on her. Before she knew it, sleep caught her up in its embrace and carried her away.

Lachlann Fraser stopped rowing and studied the young woman before him. Adaira was curled into a ball, her hands clasped under her cheek. He'd taken to calling her an 'angel', but now she truly looked like one. Her face appeared pale and very young in the hoary light of the moon.

Is she asleep?

It was a breathlessly still night, and even the slightest sound carried. Without the splash of the oars, he heard the steady rise and fall of her breathing.

Yes, she is.

Lachlann's fingers flexed around the oars, and yet he hesitated.

He'd made a pledge to take her to Argyle, but tonight he'd decided that he wouldn't. Gylen Castle was at least three days' travel from here in this tiny rowboat; it would be many days before he saw his home again. In the meantime, Lucas might use Lachlann's absence as an excuse to take his place as chieftain of the Frasers of Talasgair.

Lachlann didn't trust his brother one bit—and he couldn't let him get his hands on the Fraser lands. He had to return home. He didn't have time for this detour.

Once again, his grip on the oars tightened, but he still didn't move.

His conscience was needling him.

Lady Adaira captivated him. She was sheltered—although that was usual with most high-born ladies—and had a beguiling innocence about her. She was also trusting and gentle-hearted.

She'd be upset that he'd broken his promise.

Lachlann loosed a long breath. Adaira would get over it in time. He wouldn't send her back to Dunvegan. He'd arrange for a boat to take her to the mainland from Talasgair, or she could make a new life for herself at the Fraser stronghold if she wished. Either way, her father would never know she remained upon the Isle of Skye.

Adaira would still get what she wanted, to be free of her union with Chieftain Budge.

But right now he needed to think of himself, his own future.

Lachlann turned the boat north and started to row.

Chapter Eight
By Water

ADAIRA AWOKE TO the warmth of the sun bathing her face.

For a moment, she couldn't remember where she was, or why there was a hard plank digging into her back—but then a familiar male voice intruded, and it all came back.

"The aingeal awakes."

Lachlann Fraser.

Adaira pushed herself upright in the boat, rubbed her eyes, and looked around her. They were no longer on the water. The boat sat upon a pebbly beach, beneath sculpted cliffs and a wild sky, where seabirds wheeled overhead. Lachlann was sitting nearby, long legs stretched before him and crossed at the ankle.

"Where are we?" she asked.

"I'm not quite sure. I brought the boat ashore a short while ago."

Adaira massaged a stiff muscle in her shoulder. Her body ached, and her belly was hollow with hunger. She wished now she'd brought more provisions with her. What she would do for a plate of fresh bannocks, slathered with freshly churned butter and heather honey.

Adaira cast Lachlann a shy glance. "So ... how long will we stay here?"

"Long enough for me to bathe and get some rest."

"Bathe?" Adaira tensed. "But ye don't have any soap or a fresh change of clothes."

Lachlann cast her a roguish grin and rose to his feet. As she watched, he pulled off his boots and started to unlace his braies. "Then I'll have to wash both my body and clothing with fresh seawater. It will be bracing, but at least ye won't have to suffer my stench." He finished unlacing his braies and paused. "Ye had best turn around, lest I offend yer innocent eyes."

Adaira sucked in a shocked breath but hurriedly did as bid, shifting around so that her back was to him. Heat suffused her, and she was glad Lachlann couldn't see her burning face. She felt out of her depth, flustered.

Behind her, she heard the sounds of him undressing, then a splash as he entered the water.

A muffled curse followed.

Despite her embarrassment, a smile curved Adaira's mouth. "Is it cold?"

"Freezing," came his choked reply.

Adaira coughed, masking a laugh.

More splashing ensued, and she assumed he was washing his léine and braies. Washed in the saltwater of the loch, the clothing would be stiff and uncomfortable when it dried and would likely chafe his skin. Still, at least he would smell fresher.

While Lachlann bathed, Adaira distracted herself by taking in her surroundings. She wondered where they were exactly. She hadn't realized that the Isle of Raasay or the shores of the mainland had cliffs like these. It reminded her of home.

After a while, Adaira grew bored of staring at the cliffs and the green headland beyond. Eventually, she grew impatient. If Lachlann wanted to rest, he needed to get out of the water and dry his clothing. They'd never get to Argyle at this rate.

When the splashing finally subsided, Adaira let out a long sigh. *Good. Surely he's done now.*

She cast a furtive glance over her shoulder—and froze.

Lachlann was approaching the shore, just a few yards behind her, thigh-deep in water and completely naked. Sensing movement, he stopped, and their gazes met.

Adaira stared, her lips parting in shock.

His body glistened in the morning sun, highlighting each plane of muscle across his chest, shoulders, belly, and thighs. His body was lean and hard. His red hair was much darker when wet, and slicked back from his face.

Without realizing what she was doing, Adaira let her gaze slide from his face, down his chest and flat belly, to the thatch of dark auburn hair at his groin. Heat pooled in her lower belly as she did so.

"There's no point in looking there," he said with a teasing smile. "The freezing water's done its work. I suggest ye take another look later when I've warmed up."

His voice tore Adaira from her reverie. With a choked sound, she whipped her head away from him.

Mother Mary, what was I doing?

"Get dressed," she rasped, mortified.

"I can't yet." The amusement in his voice made Adaira wish a chasm would open up and suck her into it. "My clothing needs to dry first. Hand me yer cloak, will ye?"

Sucking in a deep breath, Adaira did as bid, careful to keep her face averted.

A moment later, he spoke again. "It's safe now ... ye can turn around."

Reluctantly, Adaira twisted, her gaze settling upon him once more. Her cloak was too small, and too short to cover Lachlann properly, but it protected his modesty nonetheless. He'd wrung out his léine and braies and spread them out over two sun-warmed rocks.

Lachlann met her eye, his own gaze gleaming.

Adaira struggled to keep her composure. She was sure her face now glowed red like a lump of burning peat. Clearing her throat, she glanced away. "Shouldn't ye try and get some sleep?"

"Aye ... will ye keep a lookout while I do?"

"Of course," Adaira replied briskly, still refusing to look at him. Instead, she pulled her knees up under her chin and kept her gaze fixed upon the watery horizon.

"Thank ye, Aingeal." The smile in his voice made her embarrassment burn even hotter. "Wake me if anyone approaches."

Adaira gazed up at the castle perched upon the clifftop. "How strange," she mused aloud. "It looks just like Duntulm."

"There are many cliff-top fortresses on this coast," Lachlann replied.

"Really?" Adaira tore her gaze from the high stone walls and the emerald-green hills that surrounded it. "I expected the mainland to look different to our isle. Ma always said it was softer, less dramatic."

"Parts are."

Adaira's attention shifted to Lachlann then. He rowed in long, confident strokes. She took in the way his shoulder muscles bunched and flexed under his still-damp léine. Heat rose within Adaira as remembered what he'd looked like naked.

Shoving the memory aside, she forced herself to focus on the present. "Can't we take the boat ashore at the nearest settlement?" she asked. "I'm faint with hunger."

He gave a curt nod. "Aye ... once we round this headland."

"Ye must be exhausted. Why don't ye let me row for a while?"

Lachlann snorted, meeting her eye. "It'll take us two weeks to reach Gylen Castle if we share the rowing."

Adaira's spine stiffened. "I'm not useless."

"I didn't say ye were. It's just that we'll get there quicker if I row."

Adaira huffed. "Why don't we leave the boat and get horses at the next village?"

"Gylen Castle sits upon an isle just off the coast. If we travel south, and traverse the Sound of Mull, we'll reach it faster."

Adaira frowned. She hadn't realized that.

"How many silver pennies do ye have in yer purse?" Lachlann asked with a smile.

"Three."

"Well, that's enough to keep us fed during the journey. It's just as well we are traveling by boat, because three pennies won't by ye a donkey, let alone two horses."

Adaira fell silent. Lachlann's words reminded her how frivolous she'd been over the years. She wished she'd managed to save more than three silver pennies. Rhona had often teased her about her love for fine fabric, and perfumed oils and soaps. She never missed the monthly market at Dunvegan village, and what coins her father had given her at each Yuletide were spent there.

Frankly, she was surprised she'd managed to save anything at all.

Her fickle ways embarrassed her. She wondered how she must appear to Lachlann Fraser. A silly goose of a girl, with a head full of nonsense.

"Stay with the boat. I'll be back soon."

Lachlann watched disappointment shadow Lady Adaira MacLeod's hazel eyes. "Can't I come with ye?"

Lachlann shook his head. That was the last thing he wanted. They'd landed just below the village of Geary, a small crofting hamlet that sat on the northwestern coast of the isle.

And within MacLeod lands.

Fortunately, Adaira had no idea of their real location.

Traveling this way put Lachlann on edge. Sailing around the coast of MacLeod territory made him nervous. They were close to Dunvegan now, far too close for his liking.

He couldn't risk having Adaira recognized by one of the village folk at Geary. If she spoke to any of them, the game would be up too, for she'd know instantly that they were still upon the Isle of Skye.

"Someone needs to look after the boat," he pointed out. "It's faster if I go alone." He carried one of the silver pennies from Adaira's purse; it would be enough to buy them a decent meal for tonight and enough food for tomorrow morning. He estimated that, at their current speed, they'd reach Talasgair by noon the following day.

Not waiting for her to voice another objection, Lachlann turned and made his way up the shore, toward the narrow path that climbed the hill. He needed to make this journey quickly and draw as little attention to himself as possible. The sooner they were back on the water and rowing away from MacLeod lands, the better.

Adaira was starting to ask too many questions. Although sheltered, the lass was highly perceptive and missed little.

Geary was tiny, little more than a handful of crofters' huts huddled together upon a bleak, windswept hillside. Lachlann knocked on the door of the first hut he encountered, and a woman with two bairns hanging off her skirts answered.

"I don't have much," she said, beckoning him in, "but for a penny, I can fix ye a meal."

Lachlann flashed her a charming smile. "A weary traveler thanks ye."

The woman smiled back, her gaze coy. Lachlann wondered where her husband was; he hoped the man wasn't due back anytime soon. He didn't want any questions.

"I'm a widow," the woman told him as she went to a bench and retrieved a loaf of coarse bread.

Relief suffused Lachlann, although wariness swiftly followed. She had the look of a woman in search of a new husband.

"I'm sorry to hear it," he replied.

"Drowned," she continued, cutting the loaf in half. She then reached for a wheel of cheese. "Left me with these two to raise on my own."

Two grubby faces peered up at Lachlann in the dim light inside the hut.

Lachlann didn't reply. He didn't want to encourage the woman. Instead, he watched as she filled a cloth bag with the bread, cheese, and four boiled eggs. His mouth filled with saliva at the thought of the coming meal. He hadn't eaten anything since those three buns on the morning after their escape from Dunvegan. His belly now burned with hunger.

A penny would have bought him far more in town, but this woman was poor.

He pressed the coin into her palm with a smile and took the cloth bag from her. He then held up the empty water bladder Adaira had given him. "I don't suppose ye have some boiled water I could fill this with?"

"Aye," the woman replied, holding his gaze. She was blonde and curvaceous with a bold stare. "But I've something better than that." She motioned to the barrel behind her. "Apple wine."

Lachlann's smile stretched into a grin. "That'll do nicely."

A short while later, he left the hut, a sack of food and drink in hand.

The woman followed him to the door, her two children still clinging to her like limpets. She batted at them, irritated, but they wouldn't let go. "There's no need to rush off," she called after him. "Dusk will be upon us shortly. Why don't ye stay the night?"

"I thank ye for the kind offer." Lachlann cast her another careless smile, although he didn't slow his stride. "But the tide waits for no man."

Chapter Nine

A Stolen Kiss

"HEAVENS ... THIS IS strong wine." Adaira lowered the bladder, eyes smarting, and handed it to Lachlann. "It has a kick like a pony."

Lachlann raised the bladder to his mouth and took a long draft. "I know ... it's delicious."

The pair of them sat upon a pebbly beach, in an isolated cove a half hour's journey from where Lachlann had bought supplies. He'd not been away long and had been eager to depart the moment he returned. Adaira had wanted to eat first, but he'd been insistent. He'd pushed the boat into the water, leaped in, and rowed away as if the devil was on his tail.

Adaira didn't understand why they couldn't have found lodgings for the night in the village. Surely it was more comfortable than sleeping out under the stars?

"What was the name of the village ... did they tell ye?" Adaira asked. Her words slurred slightly as she spoke. She'd eaten a good supper of bread, cheese, and boiled eggs, but the wine had gone straight to her head.

"I didn't ask."

Adaira studied him. Dusk was settling, and the golden light kissed the proud lines of his face. "Is this yer first trip to the mainland?" she asked.

He shook his head. "Two years ago I visited kin in Inbhir Nis."

Adaira's eyes widened. She longed to visit the large towns on the mainland, including the capital, Dùn Èideann. "What's Inbhir Nis like?"

He met her eye, his mouth quirking in a way that made her pulse quicken. "The town sits on the banks of a great river that leads east out to sea," he replied. "It's a busy port full of fishermen and shipbuilders." He paused here. "There was once a great stone keep overlooking the town, but it's in ruins now … after Robert the Bruce leveled it."

Adaira loosed a sigh. "There are so many places I long to see. Don't ye wonder about the world beyond our borders?"

"Sometimes," Lachlann admitted. She saw the gleam in his eyes and knew that her comment had amused him. Adaira didn't mind though. The wine had relaxed her, and she felt in an expansive, dreamy mood.

"Where would ye visit, if ye could?" she asked.

He shrugged. "I don't know … France maybe. The Frasers are said to hail from Anjou."

Adaira's gaze widened. "Really?"

"Aye, that's why our motto is in French: 'Je suis prest' … *I'm ready.*"

Adaira inclined her head, smiling. "Ours is 'Hold Fast'."

Lachlann snorted. "I know … I heard yer father bellow it as he charged us in battle."

"Da says the MacLeods are of Viking stock," Adaira continued, deliberately steering him away from that subject. "Our ancestor was a man called Leod. Da says he was a son of Olaf the Black … a Norse king who raided this isle."

"That doesn't surprise me," Lachlann replied. "I could well imagine yer father leading a boatload of Norsemen, burning and pillaging as he went."

Adaira didn't reply. She couldn't really contradict him, for she knew first-hand that Malcolm MacLoed was a man to be reckoned with: feared by his enemies and respected by his allies.

They fell silent for a spell. Lachlann offered the bladder of wine to her once more, but Adaira shook her head. She felt light-headed and strange, as if her limbs were floating. The wine had sharpened her senses too. She was keenly aware of the soft evening air caressing her face, and of the attractive man seated just two feet from her.

Not that she needed the wine to be aware of Lachlann Fraser. His nearness was a constant distraction. She could literally feel the heat of his body warming the air between them.

Blinking, Adaira tried to focus on something else. "I wonder where we are." She sank back on her elbows and turned her face up to the sea breeze. "It reminds me so much of home."

"Aye, it's a pretty stretch of coast," he murmured.

Something in his voice made Adaira glance his way. Lachlann sat, propped up on an elbow, watching her. It was a searching look, one that made Adaira's pulse quicken.

Adaira swallowed, her mouth suddenly dry. "Why are ye looking at me like that?"

Lachlann gazed at the young woman before him. The wine had caused the stress of the day to slough away. He'd even forgotten his aching back, shoulders, and arms—from all the rowing he'd done.

"Because ye are bonny," he murmured.

He watched Adaira wet her lips nervously. Yet she continued to hold his gaze.

Innocent, and yet with a certain boldness.

It wasn't a lie; he did find her beautiful. Not in the obvious way some women were—no, Adaira MacLeod's attractiveness lay in something earthier. Her long walnut-colored hair lay in heavy waves around an elfin face. Frank hazel eyes, flecked with green, watched him with guileless interest.

Now that she no longer wore her heavy cloak, he'd noticed that her figure, although girlish, had a delicious lushness at her hips and bust. Her dark-green kirtle was laced over the swell of full, high breasts.

And yet it was her mouth that fascinated him the most: delicate, yet full. Her lips parted slightly as their stare drew out. He saw her bosom rise sharply as she sought to control her breathing.

Lachlann's pulse quickened in response.

"Ye shouldn't say such things," she whispered.

He gave a soft laugh. "Why not?" He shifted closer to her, his hand lifting to where a heavy curl lay across her throat. "I'm merely stating the obvious. Ye are lovely, and I long to kiss ye."

Her breathing hitched then, and before she could protest, Lachlann leaned in and kissed her softly on the mouth. It was a light touch, the merest brushing of the lips, and yet it sent a jolt through his groin that made him catch his breath.

Reaching up, he caressed her cheek with the back of his hand. She trembled, and he leaned in for another kiss. This time he lingered, and when she sighed, her soft lips parting slightly, he slid the tip of his tongue between them and deepened the kiss.

Adaira moaned.

The sound unleashed something within Lachlann, a hunger that he had trouble controlling. She was a maid; this was likely to be the first time she'd ever been kissed. He didn't want to frighten her.

But he couldn't stop. His tongue explored her mouth as they melted into each other.

Lord, she's delicious.

Maybe it was the wine, but he'd never enjoyed a kiss like this. His hands ached to reach down and explore her lithe body, caress those lush breasts. He'd never wanted anything so much. He was grateful that the loose folds of his braies hid his arousal; he didn't want her to panic.

Then his hand grazed the tip of her left breast, and she gasped against his mouth.

Heat surged through Lachlann. He'd only leaned in to steal a kiss, yet the sounds she made nearly made him forget himself.

With a great effort, he pulled back from her.

Breathing hard, they both stared at each other. The sight of her parted lips, her eyes hooded with desire, made him stifle a groan of his own. Suddenly, he ached for Adaira MacLeod—and yet he knew to take things any further would ruin her. He wasn't a man with many scruples, and yet even he couldn't do that.

"Apologies," he rasped. "I forgot myself."

Adaira drew in a shuddering breath. Her heart thumped painfully against her ribs, and her body pulsed with need.

What just happened?

One moment she'd been sitting there, enjoying the warmth of the wine in her belly, a languorousness in her limbs, and the next Lachlann Fraser was kissing her.

And to her shock, she'd hadn't wanted him to stop.

Despite the embarrassing scene earlier that day, Adaira had enjoyed Lachlann's company during the journey. He'd been caring and considerate of her. She'd found it easy to talk to him and had appreciated the way he'd taken charge.

She felt safe with him.

But underlying it all, there had been a growing tension between them, an awareness that made every interaction feel charged—like the air right before a storm.

Lachlann's kiss had been consuming, intoxicating.

But Lachlann Fraser was an outlaw, the son of her father's arch-enemy. They shouldn't be kissing at all.

And yet she couldn't stop watching him. He observed her too, those moss-green eyes deepening to jade. She noted the sharp rise and fall of his chest, the slight flush across his high cheekbones. He dragged a hand through his shaggy dark-red mane—hair that Adaira longed to run her own fingers through.

Mother Mary, what's wrong with me?

Perhaps she should go straight to a nunnery the moment she reached Argyle. If a man's kiss unraveled her so quickly, she'd be easy prey in future.

Adaira swallowed, reached for her cloak, and wrapped it about her. The evening, which had seemed mild earlier, now felt chill. Since leaving Dunvegan, she'd often felt overwhelmed by Lachlann's presence, but now she felt completely lost.

If he hadn't pulled back, she'd have let him ravish her.

Lachlann cleared his throat and moved back so that around two yards of pebbly beach separated them. "It grows late." His voice was more subdued than usual and still carried a hoarse edge to it. "We should both get some sleep."

Lachlann pushed the boat out into the water and climbed in. Then he glanced Adaira's way and caught her watching him. Her look was veiled, and she hurriedly averted her gaze, but he'd seen enough. He'd avoided a number of entanglements over the past few years and knew when a woman had gone soft on him.

Dolt ... ye shouldn't have kissed her.

He'd not cared at the time, for lust raged through his veins, demanding to be sated. But now, in the cool light of morning, he realized he'd unwittingly created a situation for himself.

Suppressing a curse, Lachlann settled himself upon the plank and picked up the oars. However, before he did so, his gaze fell once more upon the young woman seated a couple of feet away. She was deliberately avoiding his eye now. This situation would only get more awkward if he didn't address it.

"Adaira," he said softly. "Look at me a moment."

She turned her face, her gaze meeting his.

"About last night," he began, "let's forget it ever happened." Adaira's hazel eyes widened. For an instant, Lachlann could have sworn he saw hurt flare in their depths. However, he pressed on. "I overstepped the boundaries of our agreement ... I won't touch ye again."

"Very well," she replied softly, although the edge to her voice warned Lachlann that he'd just offended her.

Lachlann loosed a sigh. *Great.* He'd only succeeded in making things more uncomfortable than before. The easy rapport they'd developed during the journey had evaporated. It was just as well they wouldn't be traveling companions for longer than today.

Wisely, he decided to end the conversation there.

Lachlann maneuvered the boat out into deeper water and began to row. His shoulder muscles protested, as did his back, but he clenched his jaw and rowed on. The first thing he'd do upon his return to Talasgair would be to have the servants prepare a hot bath for him. Then he'd soak in it with a tankard of ale at his elbow.

Glancing once more at Adaira, he saw that she was looking away again, her attention focused upon the green headland they were circuiting.

What will happen to her?

The thought was fleeting, yet it irritated Lachlann. Adaira MacLeod's future wasn't his concern. He had more pressing things to worry about—like ensuring Lucas wasn't taking up their father's chair in the Great Hall.

Looking away from her, he concentrated on steering the rowboat past a cluster of rocks and along the last stretch of coast that would lead him home.

"Why are we landing here?"

Adaira's gaze swept the wide bay they'd just entered and shifted to the foaming line of surf rolling into the shingle beach before them. To her right rose a rocky headland. The landscape was distinctive; centuries of wind and rain had carved it into great stone terraces, and behind it reared a huge tawny mountain.

It's so similar to Skye, she mused. *How strange.*

Her attention shifted to the sloping hillside to her left. A hamlet of stone cottages with sod roofs sat at its base, while a fortress perched upon a crag above.

"Lachlann ... where are we?" Adaira glanced back at her escort, however, he wasn't looking her way. After his stinging words earlier that morning, the rest of the journey had passed in silence. Hurt by his obvious regret at kissing her, Adaira had felt foolish. She now resolved to keep him at arm's length, although he seemed to have made the same decision, for he wouldn't meet her eye.

Lachlann jumped out of the boat into the waist-deep surf and began to haul the boat into shore. "We've arrived at our destination," he announced.

Adaira's heart leaped in her chest. She glanced back up at the grim-looking fortress that loomed over the bay. Surely this wasn't Gylen Castle? Her mother had described it as a great stone tower perched on the edge of a rocky coast, surrounded by emerald-green. This place looked too stark to fit such a description. "Are ye sure?"

"Aye." He pulled the boat through the last of the waves and dragged it up onto the beach.

Adaira continued to stare at the broch above her. She could see that part of it lay in ruin. It looked like one of those round towers that the ancient folk of Skye had inhabited, long before the Norsemen arrived upon the shores of her isle. There was one such ruined tower not far from Dunvegan that she and her sisters had once explored.

"It's not what I imagined," she murmured. "I expected Gylen Castle would be ... grander."

Lachlann huffed out a laugh, although there wasn't any humor in it. His mood had suddenly turned strange. "It's grand enough ... although this isn't Gylen Castle or Argyle."

Adaira stiffened. She dragged her gaze from the fortress and focused on Lachlann.

"Where have ye brought me?" Her voice cut through the rumble of the surf and the whine of the wind that whipped her hair in her eyes. "Answer me, Lachlann."

He looked at her then, and the hard look in his eyes made a chill seep into her bones. It was like observing a stranger, and she realized with a sinking sensation in the pit of her belly that, despite spending the last couple of days with him, she didn't know Lachlann Fraser at all.

"This is Talasgair," he said finally. "My father's stronghold."

Chapter Ten

Till My Last Breath

ADAIRA STARED at Lachlann.

For a moment, his words didn't sink in, but when they did, she inhaled sharply, as if someone had just punched her in the belly.

No wonder this coastline looked familiar. While she'd slept during their departure from Kiltaraglen, he'd rowed north.

That had indeed been Duntulm she'd spied on the clifftop.

That was why he'd left her on the shore when he went for supplies. The crofters' village would have been on her father's land; no wonder he'd been on edge and keen to move on quickly.

Betrayal slammed into Adaira with such force that she gasped.

"Ye deceived me!" The words were hoarse; she could barely get them out. "Ye made me a promise, and ye broke it."

Lachlann shrugged. "Deceived is a strong word ... let's not get overwrought."

"Overwrought?" The word came out in an outraged whisper.

Adaira wasn't quick to temper like Rhona or her father. All those who loved her described her nature as sweet and carefree. Few things got under her skin. Yet rage coiled in her now as she stared at the man she'd trusted, the man she'd set free.

The man she'd kissed so eagerly.

Her heart thundered in her chest, beating so loudly she was sure he could hear it.

"I'll not stay here," she ground out finally.

With that, she jumped out of the boat and into the surf. The cold water bit at her legs, the waves pulling at her heavy skirts, yet she ignored the discomfort.

Adaira started to push the rowboat back into the bay. "I'll row myself to Argyle."

"Slow down." The thinly-veiled amusement in Lachlann's voice made a red haze settle over Adaira's vision. He'd betrayed her, and now he was laughing at her. "Ye aren't going anywhere, Aingeal."

He placed a hand upon her shoulder then.

Rage exploded within Adaira, a deep, feral thing that lashed out from a place she didn't even know existed.

She whipped around and struck out at him. Her palm hit his face with a loud 'crack'.

"Don't touch me," she snarled, "and don't call me that ever again. I'm not yer 'Aingeal', ye cheating, lying bastard!"

The shock on his face was almost comical.

Adaira flung herself away from him and shoved her weight against the boat, angling it into the surf.

She'd gone two paces when strong arms fastened about her waist and hauled her backward.

"Sorry about this," Lachlann grunted in her ear, "but I meant it. Ye are staying here for the moment. It would be easier to let ye go yer own way, but ye wouldn't be safe on yer own. I owe ye that much."

Adaira spat out a curse, one she'd heard her father make once when his horse stood on his foot, and drove her elbow into Lachlann's chest.

However, he didn't let go of her. He yanked her against him, trapping her under one arm, while with the other he grabbed hold of the boat.

Then he turned and dragged them both to shore.

Adaira was hysterical by the time they reached it. Fury pulsed through her, and she forgot fear, forgot anything except the fact that she'd given this man his freedom, and he'd tricked her, used her.

She clawed at him, kicked and wriggled in his grip like an eel. If he was going to take her prisoner, she'd not make it easy for him.

"Adaira ... stop it!" Lachlann's voice held no amusement now. "Ye will only do yerself harm."

His words didn't calm her; they only enraged her further. She shouted curses at him, wielding them like sharp boning knives.

They stumbled onto the shingle beach, their boots sinking into the fine grey pebbles. The hull of the rowboat crunched onto the shore as Lachlann let go of it. He needed two hands to manage Adaira now as she became frenzied.

Fear snaked through her then, penetrating the rage.

What was he planning to do with her? Would he send her back to Dunvegan—back to Aonghus Budge?

How Adaira wished she'd asked Taran to show her how to defend herself against attackers, as he had with Rhona. How she wished she was a man. And as they tumbled to the ground, and Lachlann held her still, pinning her limbs against the pebbles, she cursed her weak woman's body. Lachlann was much taller and stronger than her.

"Stop it!" Lachlann stared down at her, his green eyes dark with mounting anger. "I mean ye no harm, Adaira. This is only a detour. If ye wish to continue to Argyle, one of my father's men will take ye."

She glared up at him, her teeth bared. She didn't believe him, not after this lie. She never would again.

"I had to return home," he continued. His handsome face was taut and his gaze narrowed. "My father may be dying—or possibly dead already. I can't risk one of my brothers taking my place as chieftain."

Ice washed over Adaira. *Ambition.* He'd broken his promise to her for purely selfish reasons.

Adaira fought the hands that gripped her wrists. However, she couldn't budge them an inch. He was sitting on her thighs. She was trapped.

"Serpent," she hissed. "I trusted ye."

He gave an exasperated snort. "Well, then ye have just learned a harsh life lesson." He stared down at her. "Ye won't trust so easily in future."

The arrogance of his words momentarily rendered Adaira speechless. Her throat constricted, and her chest felt as if it had a boulder sitting upon it. In the past, she might have wept, but she was still too angry. She wished she had her dirk to hand; she'd have stabbed him in the heart with it. Instead, it was in her satchel.

"Come." He let go of her wrists and heaved himself to his feet. He then retrieved her cloak and satchel from the boat. "We're wasting time here."

"No." Adaira rose to her feet and backed away from him. "I'm not going anywhere with ye."

Lachlann's gaze grew hard. "Are ye going to continue to fight me, Adaira?"

"Aye, till my last breath, ye dog!"

He huffed a breath before slinging the satchel across his front and tucking the cloak through it.

"This is yer last chance. Ye either walk up to the fortress with me, or I carry ye up, slung over my shoulder like a sack of oats. Which will it be?"

Adaira spat at him, whirled, and took off down the beach. Seabirds wheeled overhead, their cries sounding like mocking laughter. The soft shingle hampered her gait, slowing her, but she paid it no mind. She had to get away from him. She was in danger here, more so than if she'd stayed at Dunvegan.

She'd gone half a dozen paces when Lachlann caught her.

He grabbed hold of her arm and swung her around. Then, ducking his head to avoid her flailing fists, he picked her up and swung her over his shoulder. "No more chances," he grunted. "If this is how ye wish to arrive at Talasgair, then so be it."

Adaira didn't stop struggling, didn't stop fighting him, the whole way up the hill. Desperation and fear turned her savage. She was aware that they walked past cottages, where cottars and their families worked fields of kale, turnips, and onions. Folk stopped to gawk at them, but Adaira didn't care. Their murmurs and choked-back laughter just served to enrage her further.

It was a long walk, made longer still by her humiliation and mounting panic, and the climb was steep. Lachlann was breathing heavily, and she felt the heat of his body through the thin léine he wore.

On the way up, they passed a number of sheilings, low-slung huts made of stacked stone with turf roofs, where more folk stood and stared at them.

Eventually, even Adaira couldn't withstand exhaustion, and she slumped against his shoulder. Her hands ceased beating his back and hung there, although they were still balled into tight fists. He clasped her legs, an arm clamped over them like an iron band, lest she try and knee him.

He carried her through an archway of a high, yet crumbling, double wall, and into a wide, grassy yard.

There, Lachlann set Adaira down.

Panting, Adaira glanced around. Her body trembled, yet she couldn't fail to note how different Talasgair was to Dunvegan. Her father's keep was a huge, solid fortress with deep curtain walls. Yet this place was a blend of ancient and new. The great round tower that rose before them had been built onto on both sides. Another newer watchtower rose on its southern side. Its battlements etched against the sky, where the Fraser pennant fluttered in the wind.

Men, horses, and servants filled the bailey, all going about the last of their morning chores before the nooning meal was upon them.

"Lachlann!"

A man's voice echoed across the yard. Lachlann took hold of Adaira's arm, his grip firm, and they turned to see a huge warrior with wild red hair and a short beard stride toward them.

One look at the man and Adaira knew he was kin to Lachlann, although he was heavier in stature.

"I thought MacLeod would have ye strung up by yer balls by now," the man boomed before he crushed Lachlann in a bear-hug.

Lachlann was forced to release Adaira then as he staggered back. Adaira watched them. The anger had seeped out of her now, replaced by a dread that made her legs tremble under her.

"It's good to see ye too, Lucas." Lachlann drawled, pulling back. "Worried about me were ye?"

The warrior snorted, although his eyes—the same moss-green as Lachlann's—were wary. "I thought ye were dead."

"No, just left to rot in Dunvegan dungeon. Were any of ye planning to come after me?"

Lucas frowned. "Aye ... we were discussing it this morning."

The man didn't even bother to disguise the insincerity in his voice.

Lachlann's gaze narrowed. "Aye ... were ye?"

Lucas pursed his lips as if he found the topic distasteful. Then he glanced over at Adaira. "And who's this?"

Adaira tensed under the man's scrutiny, her body going rigid when Lachlann caught hold of her arm once more and pulled her close. "This is Lady Adaira MacLeod."

The man's brow furrowed. "Ye brought a MacLeod here?"

Lachlann huffed. "She's the reason I'm free." He met Adaira's eye then, for the first time since he'd thrown her over his shoulder on the beach. There was a warning in his gaze as if he dared her to start raging at him again. "Lady Adaira, meet my younger brother ... Lucas."

Chapter Eleven

What a Mess I've Made

"SO YE DRAW breath still."

"Frasers are hard to kill, Da. I see that MacLeod didn't finish ye off either."

Morgan Fraser, propped up by a mountain of pillows in his sickbed, frowned. "Disappointed?"

Adaira, who stood at Lachlann's side, watched him fold his arms across his chest and favor his father with an arrogant smile. "Of course not ... it's a great relief to see ye are alive."

Morgan Fraser huffed, before wincing.

Adaira had heard of the wound her own father had inflicted upon him. Malcolm MacLeod had bragged that he'd slit the Fraser chieftain open down one side. She couldn't see his wounds, for he wore a loose léine over his bandages, but she knew her father would be disappointed to know his enemy lived.

They stood in the chieftain's bed-chamber, which sat halfway up the fortress's new tower. The window was open, letting in a brisk sea-breeze.

Lachlann's three younger brothers—Lucas, Niall, and Tearlach—stood to the right of their father's bed. Big, red-haired, and intimidating, all three of them resembled their sire. Watching them, Adaira wondered what their mother had looked like. Una had been Morgan's second wife, and she had not borne him any children.

Morgan Fraser's attention shifted from his first-born then, to Adaira. She'd been waiting for this, yet the force of his stare nearly made her wilt. Even pale-faced and in pain, the Fraser chief's gaze was frightening.

"Lady Adaira MacLeod," he said her name softly. "What an unexpected delight."

He didn't smile as he spoke, so the word 'delight' sounded more of a threat than a welcome. Adaira glanced at Lachlann. She didn't know why she looked his way, for the sight of him made her feel ill, yet he was the only one in this chamber who knew how much she wanted to flee Skye. As much as it galled her, he was the closest thing she had to an ally here.

But Lachlann didn't look her way. He merely watched his father, his expression impassive.

Adaira swallowed and glanced back at the chieftain. Morgan Fraser was still observing her, a speculative look in his green eyes. He was around her father's age, yet whereas her father was corpulent and gouty, Morgan was lean and craggy. She could see that he'd been very handsome in his youth, but something—bitterness perhaps—had given his features a hard edge.

Out of all four sons, Lachlann resembled him physically the most. He had his father's lean ranginess, his watchfulness.

"I'd say I was grateful to ye for saving my son's life," Morgan Fraser continued, his tone still soft, "yet I hear ye didn't do it out of love for the Frasers, but rather a desire to escape yer betrothed."

"Aye, Aonghus Budge," Lucas spoke up, his mouth curving. "Can't say I blame her either."

Morgan ignored his son, instead continuing to observe Adaira.

Swallowing, Adaira dropped her gaze to the floor. His stare was making her sweat; she didn't like the calculating look in his eyes.

"Ye are a bonny wee thing," Morgan continued, "although I've heard yer sisters are true beauties: one as hot as flame, the other as cold as ice." He paused here. "I wonder what that makes ye, Lady Adaira?"

She went still, wishing she was anywhere but here. This man made her feel like she was a cornered deer.

"The earth." Lachlann's answer made Adaira glance up in surprise. "Natural ... and honest."

Morgan grunted in response. "Sounds like ye are half in love with the lass."

Lachlann's brothers sniggered.

"No ... just observant," Lachlann answered coldly.

A smile stretched Morgan Fraser's mouth, but no warmth reached his eyes.

Adaira cleared her throat. This conversation was giving her belly cramps. She longed to be far from all five of these men but needed their help to get away. "Chieftain Fraser," she began softly. "Will ye provide passage for me to travel to the mainland? I still wish to reach my kin in Argyle as planned."

Morgan Fraser's mouth compressed. "Why would I help a MacLeod?"

Adaira glanced at Lachlann, panic rising within her. "But ye said I could—"

"I rule here, lass," Morgan Fraser cut her off. "I don't care what my son told ye."

Adaira went ice-cold at these words. "Please," she whispered. "I have to leave this isle ... I must—"

"Quiet, girl," Morgan snapped, his gaze pinning her to the spot. "Spare me yer pitiful bleating."

Adaira stared back at him, heat rising to her cheeks. Anger, although not the wild fury of earlier, rose within her. She decided then that she hated Morgan Fraser even more than she did his son.

"What does it matter?" Lachlann spoke up, his voice a drawl. "Surely, if ye help the lass escape, ye are hurting MacLeod."

"Perhaps so," Morgan mused. He reached for a cup that sat upon a low table beside the bed and took a sip.

Lowering it, he leaned back against the pillows. "But by keeping her here I'd hurt him more."

"No !" Adaira stepped forward, hands clenching by her sides. She turned to Lachlann, meeting his gaze squarely. "Ye swore ye would take care of me. Is this another promise ye are going to break?"

Her comment brought snorts of laughter from his brothers.

"She's got some fire in her belly after all," the one named Niall chortled. "I can see why ye have gone soft on her, brother."

Lachlann ignored the jibe and held her gaze. His expression was hard, although his eyes were shadowed, his jaw tight. His lips parted as he readied himself to respond to her, but his father interrupted. "Never explain yerself to a woman, Lachlann." He snapped his fingers then, the sound cracking like a whip across the bed-chamber. "Look at me, lass."

Reluctantly, Adaira did as bid. However, her heart was now galloping, and her belly roiled. She felt close to being sick. Bile bit the back of her throat when she saw the cold smile on Chieftain Fraser's face.

"I've got many bones to pick with MacLeod," he continued, each word biting. "The bastard stole my wife, nearly gutted me, and would have let my first-born rot in his dungeon. One hundred years wouldn't be long enough for me to take my vengeance upon him." He paused here, letting each bitter word sink in. "But Lachlann has brought me a prize. Ye are now my prisoner, as he was once yer father's."

"Da—" Lachlann interrupted, his gaze narrowed now, but Morgan cut him off with a gesture.

"Our dungeon is a foul pit, no place for a lady, even a *MacLeod*," the chieftain continued, his gaze pinning Adaira to the spot, "so ye will be confined to the top room of this tower until I decide yer fate." Morgan shifted his gaze to Lachlann, who now stood silent and stone-faced next to Adaira. "Take her up and lock her inside."

Lachlann followed Adaira up the tower stairs. Her slender back was ramrod straight, her shoulders rounded. Her hands were hidden from view as she had lifted her skirts to climb the steps.

Neither of them spoke.

Keeping his gaze on her, lest she turn and attack him halfway up the stairs, Lachlann silently cursed.

This wasn't how he'd envisaged his return to Talasgair.

The old bastard was supposed to be either dead or on death's door, not well enough to continue his blood feud against MacLeod.

He hadn't wanted Adaira to be drawn into his father's wrath either. She'd asked him to help her, and he'd gotten her imprisoned.

They entered the tower room. Lachlann hadn't been up here in a while. The room had once been where he and his brothers had taken their lessons with Brother Took, a monk who'd visited from a nearby monastery to teach the Fraser sons their letters.

It was an austere space furnished only with a narrow sleeping pallet, a long table, and four hard wooden chairs. Cold stone pavers covered the floor. There was a tiny hearth in one corner, but it was unlit this afternoon. A narrow window stared out at where the bulk of Preshal More, the tawny mountain to the south, jutted against the sky.

Adaira walked to the center of the room and turned to face him.

He'd expected to see tears in her eyes, yet there were none. She was too angry for that. Just like during their scuffle on the beach, he was struck by how lovely she was when riled. When they'd first met, he'd thought her comely, but when she was angry, Adaira MacLeod was like no other woman. She was magnificent.

Adaira glared at him now as if she'd like to blacken his eye. In fact, her right fist was clenched at her side.

Lachlann stopped before her and dragged in a deep breath. "I shouldn't have brought ye here," he said, his tone terser than he'd intended. It was the closest he could manage to an apology. "I didn't stop to think how Da would react."

"Liar," she hissed out the words between clenched teeth. "Ye have given him exactly what he wanted."

Lachlann frowned. "I'll speak to him. He might soften toward ye in time."

"Aye, and the sun might set in the east. If ye believe ye can change his mind, ye are worse than arrogant—ye are a fool!"

Lachlann's frown deepened. He was getting tired of her insults. Some of the things she'd screamed at him down on the beach would have made a whore blush. Yet underneath it all, she was scared; he could see it in her eyes.

Her small body trembled. He realized then that she was barely clinging to her courage.

Lachlann loosed a sharp breath. "I've made a mess of things," he admitted roughly, "but I promise ye I will try to mend this. Ye will reach Argyle as ye had planned."

Her throat bobbed, and two spots of high color appeared on her pale face. Then she stepped toward him, her hazel eyes glittering. "A promise from Lachlann Fraser is a vain, empty thing." Her voice shook as she forced out the words. "The only person ye care about in this world is yerself."

Chapter Twelve

A Warm Welcome

LACHLANN STRODE INTO the Great Hall to thunderous applause.

His confrontation with Adaira had left a sour taste in his mouth, but the strain of the past few hours dissolved when his father's men slapped him heartily on the back and their wives and children beamed at him.

"It's good to see ye back, lad." Morgan Fraser's right-hand, a grizzled warrior named Thormod, boomed, pushing a tankard of ale into his hands. "Yer brother was getting too comfortable in yer seat!"

"Aye, I'll wager he's been polishing it with his arse morning, noon, and night," Lachlann replied, his gaze swiveling to the long table upon the dais at the far end of the hall. He was pleased to see that Lucas didn't sit in his elder brother's place, to the right of the chieftain's carven chair, but in his usual seat.

He noted too, that Lucas wore a sour look on his face.

Lachlann grinned at him, raising his tankard. He then turned his attention to the crowd of excited retainers that jostled around him. "Open a fresh barrel of ale," he shouted, his voice carrying across the hall. "My return calls for a celebration."

"Aye, and ye brought yer father back a worthy prize too!" Thormod's wife, a rawboned woman named Forbia, cried out. "A MacLeod daughter!"

A roar went up, although this time Lachlann didn't join in the laughter.

The less said about that the better.

Making his way to the chieftain's table, he stepped up onto the dais.

"Generous of ye, brother," Lucas grumbled as Lachlann approached. "To make free with Da's ale."

"He won't mind," Lachlann replied with a grin, enjoying his brother's irritation. "Make sure ye have a tankard for him."

Then, instead of taking his place next to Lucas, Lachlann deliberately lowered himself into the chieftain's carven chair.

Lucas let out a hiss of outrage, while around them, heads swiveled to stare. "What are ye doing?"

Lachlann stretched back in the chair, placing his arms on the ornate armrests. "Just trying it out ... not as comfortable as I imagined though."

"Ye had better move," Tearlach, the youngest of the four brothers warned him. Unlike Lucas, he wasn't glaring at Lachlann though. Instead, he was grinning and had a wicked gleam in his eye. "Da will have ye flogged for sitting in his chair."

Lachlann cast Tearlach a rueful look. "No, he won't. He's too pleased to have his first-born safely home."

This drew snorts from his brothers. All of them knew the truth of it: Morgan Fraser wasn't a sentimental man. He had four sons and if one died there was always another to take his place. Besides, Lachlann and his father had always butted heads.

Lachlann leaned back in the chair and took a deep draft of ale, sighing at the sweet, sharp taste: the taste of home.

On the floor beneath him, the folk of Talasgair were now taking their seats at the long tables while servants circled with pots of steaming stew. A group of them approached the dais.

Lachlann's belly grumbled in anticipation, reminding him that he'd last eaten at dawn.

"How did ye get out of Dunvegan Castle?" Lucas spoke up, drawing his attention. "It's been puzzling me."

Lachlann studied his brother's face for a moment. Lucas wore an inscrutable expression, although his eyes were hard, suspicious.

"We crept out in the middle of the night," he replied. "Lady Adaira drugged the guards with a sleeping draft."

Lucas inclined his head. "That wee lass ... she freed ye without any help?"

"There was a man who helped her escape. He was big and blond with a scarred face ... one of her father's warriors, I'd wager."

Lucas scratched his short beard as he considered this. "Still ... it's a wonder ye managed to get through the gates unseen ... even at night. Dunvegan's said to be impenetrable."

"Well, we did." Lachlann took another draft of ale, his attention shifting to the huge bowl of venison stew that now sat before him. He reached forward, ripped a chunk off a loaf of bread, and dipped it into the rich stew. He started to eat, aware that his brother's gaze still bored into him.

Lucas didn't believe him, but he had no way of proving him a liar.

Taking another mouthful of stew, Lachlann wondered why he'd withheld the truth of how they'd escaped. Back in Dunvegan dungeon, he'd sworn to Adaira that he'd tell no one about the secret passage—and yet since he hadn't upheld his promise to get her to Argyle, this one shouldn't matter either.

But his knowledge of the hidden passage into the keep was power, and as such was worth keeping to himself.

Adaira managed to hold the tears in until she was alone.

After that, there was no stemming them.

As soon as Lachlann left her, and she heard the grate of a heavy key in the lock, her vision blurred. His footsteps receded down the stairwell before fading into silence.

Adaira sank to the flagstone floor and clapped a hand over her mouth as a sob rose.

She should be on the mainland now, and on her way to her mother's kin. Lachlann's betrayal was a raw, bleeding wound. Did a promise mean so little to him? Anger rose hot and churning within her.

Selfish, lying dog.

But just beneath the anger lay a burning mortification. She'd liked Lachlann Fraser—been drawn in by his good looks, easy manner, and self-confidence. When he'd kissed her, she'd melted in his arms. Despite the awkwardness afterward, that kiss had succeeded in intensifying her growing feelings for him. During the last step of the journey to Talasgair, she'd found her gaze returning to him, an ache of need growing within her.

And all the while he'd been betraying her.

Adaira covered her face with her hands and let out a muffled cry. This was what Rhona had warned her about—predatory men who cared nothing for the wellbeing of foolish lasses. She remembered the worry in her elder sister's eyes as she'd told Adaira to be more careful around men, but Adaira had brushed away her concerns. Even the arranged marriage to Aonghus Budge hadn't made her cautious. From the first moment she'd locked eyes with Lachlann in Dunvegan dungeon, she'd been slowly falling under his spell.

How she must have amused him.

Her father had said never to trust a Fraser, but she'd always believed that was just his bitterness speaking. She now realized MacLeod had spoken true.

Tears burned down Adaira's cheeks, and she pulled herself up off the floor and crawled over to the narrow sleeping pallet. There, she curled up into a ball and wept until her throat was sore, until her eyes burned and her ribcage ached.

At some point servants arrived, two young men. One bore a tray of food, while the other stood in the doorway, eyeing her warily as if he expected her to attack him like a rabid dog.

Lachlann had probably warned them of her terrible temper.

Adaira watched them from the sleeping pallet. She didn't move, didn't speak, just eyed the young man as he placed the tray upon the table, cast her a cool look, turned, and left the room.

Alone once more, Adaira didn't rise from her bed.

The thought of eating made her gorge rise despite that she hadn't eaten properly in days. She was too upset to touch a crumb of it.

What will become of me?

Morgan Fraser terrified her. She'd looked into the chieftain's eyes earlier and felt dread claw its way up her throat.

That man was out for vengeance. She was going nowhere.

Such was his hate for her father he was capable of anything. Would he have her tortured? Would he behead her himself in front of a crowd of his baying kin?

The thoughts made her bowels cramp with terror. She'd been deathly afraid of wedding Aonghus Budge, but she realized now that she hadn't been truly scared, not like now. The thought of what terrible fate might await her made the walls of the chamber close in on her. She shivered as if caught in a fever.

Her father would still be hunting for her. Would he think to look for her at Talasgair? She doubted he would. Suddenly, she missed her father with a force that made her chest ache. He'd be furious with her for running away, yet he'd never let Fraser hold her prisoner. He'd break down the walls of this broch with his bare hands to get her out.

Only, Malcolm MacLeod didn't know she was here—and likely never would.

Lachlann sank into the hot water and released a long sigh.

Finally, he almost felt back to his old self.

He sat in the deep iron tub in his bed-chamber, a medium-sized room with a narrow window looking east over the hills behind Talasgair. Outside, daylight was fading, and the sky was ablaze with red and gold.

It felt good to be back here. It was a drafty, damp space, and cold in winter despite the hearth that burned against one wall—yet this afternoon it felt as spacious and warm as his father's solar.

The servant had added a drop of lavender oil to the water, and the scent wafted through the damp air. Lachlann closed his eyes and inhaled deeply. The smell reminded him of summer, of the courtyard garden on the southern edge of the keep.

Never again would he take the sweet scent of freedom for granted.

Home. His return was bitter-sweet. He was pleased to be here, but circumstances had made things awkward.

On one level he was relieved his father still lived—just because they'd never gotten on didn't mean he wished the old man dead—but on another it complicated life. With Morgan Fraser in charge, he would resume his role as captain of Talasgair Guard, which often took him away from the broch for days at a time. That didn't please Lachlann, for he'd have preferred to stay close to Talasgair. He wanted to keep an eye on his scheming younger brother. Even before Lachlann's capture, Lucas had been forever trying to ingratiate himself with their father.

And then there was Adaira. Lachlann couldn't help her at present, and that frustrated him. He hated having his hands tied like this.

Lachlann let out a long sigh, sinking deeper into the hot water.

The crash of the door flying open and slamming against the wall yanked Lachlann from his reverie. His gaze snapped up to see Lucas striding into his bed-chamber. "What are ye doing in here?" his brother boomed. "The men are still celebrating yer return downstairs. They want stories and boasts of yer escape from Dunvegan."

"They'll have to wait," Lachlann drawled back. He pushed himself up, retrieved a cake of lye soap, and began to scrub under his arms. Despite his sea-water bath, his skin itched with filth. "I'm busy."

Lucas pulled up a stool and lowered his heavily muscled bulk onto it. Lachlann eyed his brother. Lucas seemed to get bigger by the year. Folk here had nicknamed him 'The Giant of Talasgair', such was his height and breadth. He was formidable in a fight although Lachlann was quicker. He'd always been the fastest of the four of them—but that hadn't helped him during the battle against the MacLeods.

"I've just been to see Da," Lucas said after a pause. "If ye take his chair again, he'll have ye flogged."

Lachlann threw back his head and gave a belly laugh. "Bootlicking worm ... I should have known ye would go straight to him."

Lucas's mouth twisted, but he didn't reply to the insult. "Da wants to know if ye have had yer way with the MacLeod lass."

Lachlann stopped soaping himself and favored Lucas with a slow, dark look. However, he didn't answer.

"Well, have ye?"

"What is it to him?"

His brother gave an off-hand shrug. "Who knows ... maybe he's worried she's carrying yer brat. He might have to kill her for that."

A chill feathered across Lachlann's naked skin despite the heat of the bathwater. He thought back to the kiss he'd shared with Adaira and of how he'd wanted to take it further. It was just as well he hadn't.

"I never touched her," he lied. A kiss was a touch. "As far as I know, she's still a maid." That was the truth at least.

Silence fell between them then. Lachlann resumed soaping himself, although the pleasure he'd found in his bath had gone. He wished his brother would take himself off and leave him in peace. Lucas's toadying toward their father irritated him. He'd only been back at Talasgair a few hours and already his brother, the one who'd stood to inherit if Lachlann had never returned home, was seeking to undermine him.

Ye won't get my lands, ye bastard, he thought grimly. *Over my dead body.*

Lucas heaved himself off the stool and rose to his feet, towering over Lachlann. "I'll leave ye to it," he said. His gaze was shuttered.

Lachlann watched his brother leave the chamber, slamming the door behind him with his usual finesse.

Heaving a sigh, Lachlann sank down under the water. The heat enveloped him like a soothing blanket. Resurfacing, he reached for the cake of lye soap once more and started to soap his wet hair.

A frown furrowed his forehead as he did so.

No doubt Lucas would go straight to their father.

Chapter Thirteen

The Happy News

"YE WANTED TO see me?"

Lachlann stepped inside his father's bed-chamber to find the healer tending to Morgan Fraser's wounds.

"Aye," his father rasped. "Come in, and shut the door."

The healer, Domhnall, smeared salve over an ugly scab that stretched down the chieftain's naked flank. Domhnall was a portly man of middling years; his kindly face was tense in concentration as he worked.

One glance at that wound told Lachlann that his father was indeed lucky to still be alive. Though healing, the gash looked angry and sore.

"Had a good look at my war-wound, eh?" His father's voice was sharp. "I can assure ye it looked far worse a few days ago."

"Aye, it did," Domhnall agreed with a grimace. "But it's healing well now ... ye shall make a full recovery, milord."

"Good to hear," Lachlann replied, his mouth quirking. He swore his father was indestructible. He'd be well into middle age himself before Morgan Fraser went to his cairn.

"Wrap the wound now, Domhnall," Morgan grunted. He was frowning. Even a moment or two in his presence and Lachlann was already wearing upon him. "I want to speak to my son alone."

"Aye, milord." The healer gave a brisk nod before reaching for a clean linen bandage. "This shouldn't take long."

The healer worked deftly, wrapping the chieftain's torso with practiced ease. While the healer finished tending to his patient, Lachlann took up a place next to the window. It was a grey, windy morning outdoors. Leaden clouds moved sluggishly across the sky, promising stormy weather to come. Despite the chill in the air, his father had insisted Domhnall left the window open.

A short while later, the healer collected his basket of healing powders, tinctures, unguents, and bandages, and hurried from the chamber. After Domhnall had departed, Lachlann remained silent. He watched his father with a hooded gaze, arms folded across his chest. Two days had passed since he'd returned to Talasgair; he'd been awaiting another summons.

"Have ye seen the MacLeod lass since ye locked her up?" Morgan asked finally.

Lachlann shook his head. "No ... why?"

His father's mouth thinned. He didn't appreciate Lachlann answering with another question. "The girl is refusing to eat."

Lachlann nodded. This wasn't news to him. He'd already heard the same. The cook had ranted that they should let the MacLeod scold starve rather than allow good food go to waste. Half the time, Adaira hurled the food back in the faces of the servants. She'd broken over half a dozen clay bowls and cups in the past two days. Nonetheless, the cook dutifully sent up trays at each mealtime as instructed.

"She's unhappy," Lachlann pointed out, "and angry."

"With ye, no doubt."

Lachlann shrugged. "With the world."

"Do ye think MacLeod will come after his daughter?"

Lachlann shook his head. "Only if he knows she's here. Once he exhausts his search on Skye ... he'll think we've crossed to the mainland."

He was aware that his father was observing him keenly then, with a cunning glint in his eye that Lachlann knew well.

"It suits me that Adaira MacLeod doesn't waste away to skin and bone," Morgan said softly. "She must live."

Lachlann's gaze narrowed. He didn't like his father's tone. It made the fine hair on the back of his neck prickle. "Ye have decided what to do with her then?"

Morgan Fraser leaned back against the pillows, wincing as he did so. "Domhnall says I'll be well enough to resume my old duties by Samhuinn. I plan to wed Adaira MacLeod on that date."

For a heartbeat Lachlann merely stared at his father. Had he misheard? "Ye will wed her?"

The Fraser chief's mouth curved into a rare smile. "Aye."

Lachlann didn't move from his position against the window sill. "Why?"

"MacLeod robbed me of a wife," Morgan growled. "And I will rob him of a daughter."

Lachlann drew in a slow, steadying breath. "Malcolm MacLeod will be rabid when he hears ye have wed Adaira," he pointed out. "Do ye want to reignite feuding between ye?"

His father's face tightened into a hard line. "The feud still lives," he spat out the words. "And so does my enemy. This will hurt him in a way no blade could. He'll bleed where no one can see."

Vindictiveness dripped from Morgan's voice. The hatred he bore MacLeod was no natural thing; it had soured into an illness of late.

Morgan Fraser spoke little of Lachlann's mother—the woman who'd borne him four strapping sons—but all at Talasgair knew how he'd loved Una. He'd sworn never to remarry, not while she still lived. But he would break that promise now if it was for vengeance.

Silence fell in the chamber. Lachlann digested this news before realizing that it sat ill with him. His father wore a gloating expression. Adaira was nothing more than a weapon in his hands.

"Can I go now?" Lachlann asked finally. He'd had enough of his father's scheming.

"Not yet," Morgan replied. He'd been observing Lachlann with a hard, predatory gaze, watching his reaction to the news. "I have a task for ye, son."

Lachlann pushed himself off the sill. "Aye, what is it?"

"I want ye to be the one to inform Lady Adaira of the happy news. Go up and tell her now."

Lachlann climbed the stairwell to the tower room, his jaw clenched with anger.

Vicious bastard.

This was punishment, although for what Lachlann wasn't sure. Sometimes when Lachlann looked into his father's eyes, he thought he saw dislike there. Father and son often clashed. Lucas had once told Lachlann it was because they were too alike—but Lachlann hadn't liked that.

I'm nothing like that bitter old curmudgeon.

Reaching the landing before the door, Lachlann halted. He wasn't going to enjoy this, yet it was best to get it over with quickly.

He unlocked the door, pushed it open, and stepped inside.

"Get out!"

A tray flew at his head. Lachlann ducked, and the missile clattered against the pitted stone wall.

He closed the door and backed up against it, ducking again as half a loaf of bread flew at him. He wasn't fast enough this time, and the bread bounced off his temple.

Lachlann reeled back. The bread was stale and had a hard crust.

Cursing, Lachlann rubbed his forehead, his gaze settling on the fury who faced him. "Was that necessary?" he growled.

"Aye," she spat. "Leave! I have no wish to see or speak to ye."

Lachlann's gaze traveled over her bedraggled form. Her brown hair was wild and dirty. She'd lost weight, even in the two days she'd been in here. He could see it in the delicate lines of her face. The green kirtle and cream léine she wore were both soiled and in need of laundering. She clenched her fists at her sides, the remnants of her last untouched meal scattered over the floor.

However, it was not her appearance that took Lachlann aback, but her eyes. They were desolate, lost.

Adaira MacLeod was suffering.

Lachlann opened his mouth to speak before hesitating. He knew he could lack charm—but then it didn't matter how he phrased this news, she wasn't going to like it.

"Adaira," he began, gentling his voice as if talking to a nervous horse. "My father has decided yer fate." Their gazes met and held. "Ye will wed him ... at Samhuinn."

His voice died away, leaving a deep silence in its wake.

For a long moment, Adaira merely stared at him. Then he watched as her face drained of color and her eyes rolled back in her head. Lachlann stepped forward to catch Adaira as she collapsed upon the floor.

Chapter Fourteen

Despair

WHEN ADAIRA CAME to, she felt someone stroking her cheek. The touch was soft, although the skin was slightly rough: a man's hand.

Adaira's eyes flickered open, and she looked up into Lachlann Fraser's face.

Like a breaking wave, the memory of his news crashed over her.

I am to be Morgan Fraser's wife.

Tears leaked from Adaira's eyes, trickling down her face.

Lachlann stared down at her. A shadow moved in his eyes. His face was serious, and a nerve flickered in his cheek. He drew his hand back from her face. "Are ye well?"

Hysteria bubbled up within Adaira. "No," she rasped.

She pushed herself up into a sitting position and closed her eyes for a moment. Her head still spun, although she supposed lack of food was partially to blame for her faint. Adaira covered her face with her hands. "Leave me, Lachlann ... please," she whispered.

When he didn't move, she tried to stand up. However, her knees buckled under her. Lachlann was there in an instant, supporting her.

"Sit down on the bed, Adaira." He guided her over to the pallet and lowered her down onto it. Then he hunkered down so that their gazes were level. There was concern on his face now. "I'm going to bring ye up another tray of bread and stew," he said, his voice low and firm, "and ye are going to eat it. Ye will make yerself sick if ye continue to refuse food."

Adaira's mouth twisted, even as despair pressed down upon her. "Good."

Lachlann huffed a frustrated breath. "Ye don't mean that."

"I do."

Lachlann frowned. "If ye don't eat, Da will have servants force ye." He gave her a long, steady look. "Ye won't escape him by starving yerself, Adaira. Da's a powerful man. He nearly always gets what he wants."

She stared at him, anger welling like a springtide within her. Adaira welcomed the sensation, for it quelled the urge to start weeping uncontrollably. "This is all yer fault," she rasped the words. "I hate ye, Lachlann Fraser."

His mouth compressed. "And ye are welcome to … but it changes nothing."

Adaira's right hand balled into a fist. She longed to strike him. He was so hard, so arrogant. The man didn't have an ounce of pity in him.

But Adaira didn't hit him. Instead, she pressed her fist into the straw-stuffed mattress. Her short spell at Talasgair had taught her that the Frasers were ruthless. Morgan Fraser had treated her harshly, and his sons were cut of the same cloth. Lachlann hadn't raised a hand to her when she'd fought him on the shore below the fortress, but he might now.

No wonder Una fled this place.

For the first time, Adaira felt some sympathy for her stepmother. She'd never liked Una much but now realized why she'd left Morgan Fraser. No woman could abide such an arrogant man.

Thinking about Una reminded Adaira of her father, her sisters, and everything she'd left behind at Dunvegan. Fresh tears rolled down her cheeks. She wished now that she'd never run away.

Lachlann rose to his feet before her. Adaira's gaze didn't follow him. She merely stared down at her bare feet and wished him gone.

"Ye need to eat," he said gruffly. "I'll return shortly with something from the kitchen."

"Why the grim face?"

Lachlann glanced up from his half-eaten trencher of stew to find Lucas watching him. They sat at the chieftain's table in the Great Hall with Niall and Tearlach. The high-backed carven chair where the chieftain usually sat was still empty—Lachlann had heeded his father's warning. It would be a few more days yet before Morgan Fraser would be well enough to join his kin and retainers at mealtimes.

"I spoke to Da," Lachlann replied, reaching for a cup of ale.

Understanding lit in his brother's eyes. "So, the lass knows?"

Lachlann nodded. He took a deep draft of wine, draining his cup. It was plum—sour and strong. It suited his mood. He reached for a ewer and refilled the cup to the brim.

"What's wrong?" There was a goading tone to Lucas's voice. "Wanted her for yerself, did ye?"

Lachlann favored him with a dark look and took another gulp of wine. He wouldn't respond to that question, although if Lucas continued to goad him, he'd answer with his fist instead.

Lachlann took another gulp of wine. *Do I want her for myself?* The question arose, unbidden.

He hadn't liked seeing Adaira MacLeod in that state, and he knew he was responsible for it—but that didn't mean he was jealous of his father claiming her. Even so, his mood had been black ever since he'd departed from her chamber. He'd brought a fresh tray of food up to her and stood over her while she slowly ate it. Neither of them had spoken a word.

"It'll seem strange to have Lady Adaira as a stepmother," Niall spoke up, helping himself to another bowl of boar stew. "She's younger than any of us."

"I can't believe he's wedding her," Tearlach grumbled. "She's a MacLeod for God's sake."

"I can see the appeal," Lucas replied, favoring his brothers with a wolfish grin. "MacLeod or not, the lass is a bonny wee thing." He cast Lachlann a look, his grin widening. "The old dog will live forever now."

Niall and Tearlach laughed at that, but Lachlann said nothing. He'd had enough of this topic. He took another gulp of wine, his gaze traveling around the hall. Most of the retainers had finished their nooning meal and were getting up to return to their chores. Some, however, lingered over a cup of wine. Without their chieftain's strict eye upon them, they relaxed more than usual. Since returning, Lachlann had noticed there were a number of faces missing among the men here.

"How many warriors did we lose in the end ... against the MacLeods?" Lachlann asked finally, deliberately changing the subject.

His brothers' expressions sobered.

"Thirty-two," replied Tearlach.

Lachlann tensed. It would take the Frasers of Skye years to recover from such a loss.

"Many of our men are on the mainland still, aiding King David's cause," Lucas added, his face grim, as if reading his elder brother's thoughts. "Warriors are thin on the ground at Talasgair."

Of course. With everything that had happened of late, Lachlann had almost forgotten. The Scottish king was planning a raid across the border. There was currently a truce between the English and the Scottish, but David planned to break it, to push south while the English king's focus was on France.

Lachlann would have joined them if his father hadn't been plotting against the MacLeods. Morgan Fraser had wanted all his sons by his side when he faced his enemy.

"I'll take the Guard out to patrol our borders then," Lachlann replied, his gaze sweeping over his brothers' faces. "MacLeod will know we've been weakened. We don't want the bastard getting any ideas."

Adaira leaned against the stone window ledge and looked out at where the last of the sun's light gilded the huge mountain to the south. Preshal More—that was its name. She'd seen it once from afar when she'd joined her kin on a trip to visit the MacDonalds of Sleat on the southern edge of the isle.

She stared at the bald, rocky outline of the mountain. Its bulk was strangely comforting, a reminder that despite all that had befallen her of late, some things remained constant.

Three days had passed since Lachlann had told her she would wed his father, and in that time an odd calm had descended upon her.

She'd been through such extremes of emotion in the past few days that she now felt drained.

This evening Adaira couldn't summon much feeling at all, save a dull dread that had lodged in the pit of her belly.

On the table a few feet away sat the remains of her supper. Remembering Lachlann's warning, she'd eaten most of it, although every bite had stuck in her throat. Still, her body felt stronger since she'd resumed eating, and her head no longer spun.

A cold breeze fluttered in through the open window. The nights had a bite to them now, and although the servants had lit the hearth in this room, Adaira found herself huddled deep inside a nest of blankets upon her sleeping pallet every morning. The stone she leaned against was as cold as a lump of frozen snow.

Adaira continued to stare out the window, her gaze turning inward now. She thought back to her days at Dunvegan. She'd never fully appreciated how blessed they were, but she did now. Her father's servants loved her, and she'd taken their warmth for granted. Here, the woman who brought up her food and cleared away her chamber pot was stone-faced and cold-eyed.

At Dunvegan, she'd had her own horse and often gone riding with her sisters or her father's men. Her father had even let her keep Dùnglas, her wolf-hound pup, although she wasn't sure Aonghus Budge would have ever let the dog accompany them to Islay.

Adaira swallowed hard, remembering how she used to flit about the keep, carefree and more than a little silly. She'd spent her days learning the pursuits befitting a lady. She could play the harp well enough and was a neat embroiderer.

She'd lived a privileged life, and even seeing her sisters' own struggles—Caitrin's unhappy marriage and Rhona's forced one—hadn't truly touched her. She'd always lived a little apart from it, always believed she'd remain happy.

She didn't believe that now. Her old life seemed as if it had belonged to a princess, and she wasn't that girl anymore. She felt as if she'd aged years in just a few days. That laughing, carefree lass was dead.

The sound of the key grating in the lock drew Adaira from her thoughts. Turning, she watched the door open and Lachlann Fraser step inside.

Adaira went rigid. It was the first time she'd seen him since he'd delivered the news she would wed his father.

Despite that the sight of him made her belly churn, she would have been blind not to notice how attractive he was. His slightly disheveled appearance today only highlighted his arrogant good looks, his swaggering self-confidence.

Lachlann was clad in dusty leathers, a travel-stained cloak hanging from his broad shoulders. His hair was sweaty and plastered against his scalp as if he'd just removed a helmet. He looked as if he'd returned from a patrol.

Shutting the door behind him, Lachlann leaned up against it, surveying her.

Adaira hissed out a breath. "What do ye want?"

His mouth curved. "I've been away … checking our northern border. Now I'm back I thought I'd check on ye." Lachlann's gaze shifted to the empty tray a few feet away. "I see ye are eating."

Adaira clenched her jaw. "The servants could have told ye that."

"Aye, but I'd prefer to check on ye in person."

Adaira folded her arms across her breasts. The sight of this man was a painful reminder of her own gullibility. Still, the knowledge that he'd been patrolling the border with the MacLeods rattled her.

"There was no sign of yer father or his men," Lachlann said quietly as if sensing the direction of her thoughts. "I'd wager he doesn't suspect ye are here."

Bleak disappointment flooded through Adaira. "Ye can go now," she rasped.

Lachlann pushed himself off the door and crossed to her. Adaira took a rapid step back, cowering against the window frame.

He stopped a few feet short of her, his dark-auburn brows knitting together. "There's no need to shrink from me like I'm Satan himself," he murmured.

Adaira glared at him although underneath her despair she felt a frisson of satisfaction. Finally, a chink in his armor of unshakable self-confidence. He wasn't used to having women revile him. "Ye *are* Satan," she countered. "Ye are arrogant, deceitful, and without a heart."

Chapter Fifteen

Reckless

THE WIND WHISTLED across the hills, bringing with it the scent of autumn. Lachlann urged his horse up to the brow of the hill and reined it in next to his father's. The hawk's claws gripped his left wrist through its leather sleeve, its hooded head moving toward him. Saighead—Arrow—sensed he was about to let her off her leash.

Lachlann cast a glance in his father's direction. This was the first time Morgan Fraser had been out on his horse since the battle. He sat a little stiffly in the saddle, his face tense with discomfort. Yet his gaze was determined as he surveyed the sky. His father's hawk, Stoirm—Storm—shifted upon the chieftain's arm. He too was ready to hunt.

"Shall we let them off?" Lachlann asked. Behind him, he could hear the thunder of hooves as his brothers approached.

"Aye," his father grunted. "I've just spotted a pair of pigeons. They'll do for a start."

The two men removed the hoods from their hawks and unleashed them. Lachlann raised his left hand, letting Saighead launch herself into the sky, her powerful wings causing a draft behind her.

Lachlann watched, momentarily enraptured. There were few things more beautiful to watch than a bird of prey taking flight. Saighead stretched her wings wide and soared high, joining Stoirm as they began their hunt.

Aware that someone was watching him, Lachlann tore his gaze from the sky and met his father's eye.

"Is the MacLeod lass behaving herself?" Morgan asked.

His father rarely referred to Adaira by her given name these days. The chieftain hadn't seen her since her incarceration nearly two months earlier. But with Samhuinn looming, the fire festival that marked the end of the harvest season and the beginning of winter, that soon would change. The nights had started to become long and cold, and the handfasting drew near.

"Aye, well enough," Lachlann replied tersely.

"Is she eating? I've no wish to wed a scarecrow."

"I check on her most days ... and see to it she finishes her meals."

Morgan nodded. "Good."

Lachlann drew in a deep breath then, glancing over his shoulder at where his brothers drew near. He had just a few moments alone with his father. He would have to speak now, or they'd have an audience.

"Are ye really going through with this?" he asked, his voice low.

Morgan huffed. "Aye." He inclined his head, studying Lachlann with a hard, searching look. "Why wouldn't I?"

"Because Adaira doesn't deserve it." The words surprised Lachlann as they left his mouth, yet he didn't stop. This impulse had been growing within him for weeks now. "Da, don't punish her for MacLeod's crimes against ye."

Whenever Lachlann climbed the steps to the tower chamber, he steeled himself to look upon Adaira's pale face, her haunted eyes. Occasionally they exchanged a few awkward words, but for the most part, they remained silent. The first few times he'd visited her, Adaira had raged at him, but after a while, she'd run out of insults and ignored him instead. And with each visit,

Lachlann had felt something grow inside him—
something that had led to this.

His father stared back at him for a long, drawn-out
moment. "MacLeod loves his daughters," he replied
softly. "Aye, he's a bully, but there's nothing he wouldn't
do for them ... I want him to know what it feels like to
lose something he loves."

Lachlann held his gaze. His brothers had reached
them and were now reining in their horses.

"God's bones," Lucas panted, his voice rough with
irritation. "Ye two ride as if all the demons of hell were
behind ye."

Lachlann ignored his brother. His attention remained
upon his father. "It won't bring Una back to ye," he said
coldly. "Nothing will do that."

Morgan Fraser's gaze narrowed, something
dangerous moving in the depths of his eyes. None of his
sons ever spoke of Una. She was a forbidden topic at
Talasgair. Lachlann had just stepped over an invisible
line, but he didn't care. Today, he felt reckless.

"No, it won't," his father replied, his voice developing
a lethal edge. "But it'll cut MacLeod deep. That lass will
suffer at my hands, and her father will know of it. A man
doesn't cross me and get away with it. This is a grudge
I'll take to my grave."

Lachlann stared back at him, but in place of his father
all he saw was a man—a vengeful and bitter one.
Lachlann's younger brothers had always ribbed him over
how much he was like his father—how they were
destined to forever lock horns, for they knew just how to
provoke each other.

If it were true then Lachlann faced a bleak and
unhappy future. Was this what he would become?

Adaira watched with suspicion as Lachlann entered the chamber. He carried a large hessian bag, which he set down on the table.

"Good afternoon," he greeted her.

Adaira didn't reply. She noted that he hadn't called her 'aingeal' since their struggle on the beach. There was an odd formality in him these days—very different to the brash individual who'd fled Dunvegan with her. Sometimes he almost seemed subdued in her presence, although today he appeared a little more cheerful.

"What's in the bag?" she asked, deliberately rude. Spending day after day in this tiny chamber was slowly chipping away at her, eroding her naturally optimistic spirit. Apart from Lachlann, the only face she saw was that of the sour-faced maid who delivered her meals, emptied her chamber-pot, and brought her clean clothes.

"A diversion," he replied with a half-smile.

He withdrew a large clay bottle stoppered with a cork and two clay cups. Then he produced a wooden board marked with squares and a small cloth pouch.

"Have ye ever played Ard-ri?"

Adaira frowned. She was a clan-chief's daughter, of course she had. Reluctantly, she nodded.

"Good," he replied. "I'm not the world's most patient teacher." He pulled out two chairs and took a seat on one. "Come on … let's play a game."

"I'm not playing Ard-ri with ye, Fraser."

He raised an eyebrow. "Why not? Ye must be growing witless with boredom." He reached for the clay bottle and unstoppered it. "I've brought plum wine to make the experience more bearable for ye."

"I don't care. Take yer wine and yer game and leave me be."

Ignoring her, Lachlann poured two cups of wine, before he emptied the cloth pouch and started placing small brown and white counters upon the board before him. One of the counters was twice as high as the others and marked with a crown on top: the king stone.

"Playing Ard-ri with a Fraser doesn't mean ye have to stop hating me," he said as he worked. "I'm not asking for friendship. Just a game."

"I don't understand why ye keep visiting me," Adaira replied. "Haven't I made it clear ye aren't welcome?"

"Ye have, but we Frasers are thick-headed as well as stubborn. I'm the reason ye are here so I like to check ye are well."

Adaira went still. That was the first time he'd even hinted that he felt guilty for what he'd done, and even then the comment was spoken with the flippant edge she'd come to expect from him.

Lachlann fixed her with a level look. "Just one game, Adaira. That's all I ask."

Silence fell between them and then, reluctantly, Adaira rose from the bed, where she'd been perched, and walked to the table. She sat down, pushing her chair back in an attempt to put as much space between them as possible.

Before them, the Ard-ri board sat ready. Ard-ri—or High King—was an old game, and one her father loved. The game simulated a Viking raid: four attacking Viking drakkars were pitted against the Scottish king and his defenders.

Adaira wasn't a strong player; both Rhona and Caitrin had always beaten her at it. She imagined this game would be over with merciful swiftness.

"Do ye want to be the attacker or the defender?" Lachlann asked.

Adaira picked up her cup of wine and took a sip. It was delicious, deep and rich, not like the sour wine that accompanied her meals. "I'll attack," she replied.

Lachlann flashed her a wolfish smile. "Then it's up to me to put up a strong defense." He motioned to the board. "Ye take the first move."

Adaira stared back at him but made no attempt to reach for a counter. "I liked ye once, Lachlann," she said after a pause. "When we fled Dunvegan together, I was in awe of yer courage. I thought ye were a good man, an honorable one."

Lachlann's smile faded. "I'm no saint, Adaira," he replied softly, "but nor am I the worst man ye will ever meet."

"Is that so?"

"Aye … now go on, make yer move."

Adaira cast Lachlann a look of simmering hate before she dropped her gaze to the board. She focused on it, her lips compressing as she remembered her father's advice on how to play Ard-ri well. He'd told her to attack aggressively, and so she did, moving a counter diagonally across the board so that it sat up against the defending pieces.

Lachlann inclined his head, eyes gleaming. "Interesting move."

Adaira gave him a cool look in reply before she took another sip of wine. "Yer turn."

Hours, and four games of Ard-ri later, Adaira held up her hands in defeat.

"That's it. I'm not playing with ye anymore."

Lachlann leaned back in his chair and crossed one long leg over his knee at the ankle. "Why not?"

"Because I'm tired of losing," Adaira said ungraciously. "Ye crow like a rooster every time ye beat me."

He cast her a look of mock-hurt. "No, I don't."

The clay bottle of wine had long been emptied, and although she felt the most relaxed she had in a long while, she also felt drowsy and hungry. Outside, the light had faded. The maid would arrive with supper shortly.

Realizing their games had indeed ended, Lachlann shrugged and began to put away the counters. Adaira watched him, lazily admiring his profile, before she caught herself.

This afternoon had been a distraction, but he was still the man who'd broken his promise to her. She wouldn't let attraction pull her in, drown her good sense, as it had on the journey here.

"How many days till Samhuinn?" she asked, breaking the silence between them.

Lachlann looked up, his gaze meeting hers. "Five."

Adaira's belly clenched at this news. *So soon*. It felt an eternity since she'd been locked up in here, and yet at the same time, it wasn't long enough. Time marched on. She'd known autumn was slipping toward winter, for the days grew short and the breeze that wafted in through her window had a bite to it in the mornings and evenings. Only, she'd told herself that Samhuinn must be still some way off.

"I tried to talk to Da ... to get him to change his mind," Lachlann said. His face was stern now, his gaze hooded. "But it's impossible. His need for vengeance consumes him—and I'm the last person he'd take counsel from. He'll not be swayed."

Adaira's pulse accelerated. She'd tried not to think of the future, about what it would be like to be Morgan Fraser's wife. Suddenly, Aonghus Budge almost seemed an appealing alternative. He was a boor and a bully, but at least the chieftain of the Budges of Islay wasn't driven by blind hate.

Swallowing hard, Adaira wished she had some more wine to calm her nerves. "What will become of me?" she asked, a tremble in her voice.

Lachlann held her gaze, his jaw tightening. "I don't know."

Adaira leaned forward and grabbed his arm, squeezing tight. "Help me, Lachlann," she gasped. "Ye can't let me wed him."

Lachlann blinked. It was as if a portcullis had just slammed down between them. He took hold of her hand and gently pried her fingers free, then he pushed back his chair, rising to his feet. His face was like hewn stone when he answered her, "I can't."

Chapter Sixteen

A Feast for the Betrothed

"YE WILL JOIN the chieftain and his kin for supper this evening," the maid informed Adaira coldly, setting down the tray of bannocks, butter, honey, and fresh milk.

Despite that she'd been expecting a summons from Fraser, Adaira tensed. Samhuinn was just a day away now. The waiting was finally over.

The maid, a tall, slender young woman with dark-blond hair pulled back in a severe braid, ran a disparaging look over Adaira. "Ye look like a peasant. I will bring ye up a fresh léine and kirtle to wear."

Adaira no longer wore the soiled clothing she'd been captured in. Instead, she was clad in a coarse ankle-length tunic with a tattered plaid shawl around her shoulders. It wasn't what Morgan Fraser would wish to see her in.

The maid's face screwed up then, and she sniffed. "Ye also reek. I'll have a bath prepared."

Adaira sat there numbly, not bothering to answer. Over the past weeks, she'd spoken so seldom she was beginning to wonder if she would lose the use of her tongue. That afternoon a few days earlier playing Ard-ri

with Lachlann had contained the longest conversation
she'd had with anyone in a long while.

She hadn't seen him since.

Her plea for help had failed, but Adaira wasn't sorry
she'd asked him, only that he'd denied her. She knew
she'd been trying for the impossible, but she'd had to do
it. She'd hoped Lachlann had been nursing a guilty
conscience, yet if he had, it wasn't enough to help her.

Seeing that her comments weren't going to be
responded to, the maid muttered a curse under her
breath and headed toward the door. "Dull wit."

Two burly male servants brought in an iron tub and
then filled it with hot water. The maid added scented oils
to the bath and left a cake of lye soap, drying cloths, and
fresh clothing. Then all of them departed.

Alone in the chamber, Adaira stripped off her
scratchy tunic and stepped into the tub. She loosed a
deep sigh as she sank into the hot water. Despite the
dread that dogged every waking thought, she couldn't
deny the bath was a thing of delight.

The scent of rose, a perfume that reminded her of
Rhona, wafted up, and she inhaled deeply. She closed
her eyes, and for a moment, she was back in Dunvegan
in her bower being fussed over by her hand-maid, Liosa.

Adaira's eyes snapped open.

That happy existence belonged to someone else.

Even so, the heat of the water seeped into her chilled
bones, and the scent of rose relaxed her. She'd opened
the shutters, although she could see little beyond a
helmet of grey skies.

In Dunvegan, the locals would be getting ready for
Samhuinn, in a yearly ritual that never changed. Groups
of men would build bonfires on the hills around the
keep. Adaira loved the festival, even if it heralded the
arrival of winter. She'd always taken her turn at apple
bobbing, although she'd never been good at it. Unlike
Rhona, who nearly drowned herself while grabbing hold
of the apple with her teeth, Adaira hated getting water up

her nose. The taste of roasted hazelnuts and salty oaten bannock were Samhuinn to her.

Although from this year, the festival would take on a different reminder.

Adaira loosed another deep sigh and tried to push thoughts of her impending handfasting from her mind. She glanced down at her nakedness. Her skin had turned pink from the hot water. Her breasts bobbed on the surface, their nipples pebbled from the cold air inside the chamber; the lump of peat burning in the hearth barely took the chill off. She'd regained the weight she'd lost during her first days here.

In a day's time, Morgan Fraser would see her naked, would put his hands on her. Would he hurt her?

Adaira squeezed her eyes shut. She must not think of it. She had to remain strong.

She stayed in the tub until the water cooled, making sure to wash her hair and rinse it thoroughly. Then she climbed out, dried herself off, and dressed. The maid had left her a soft cream-colored léine and a deep blue kirtle. Adaira fingered the fine material before lacing up the front of the kirtle. She wondered if these clothes had once belonged to Una before she ran away. She and Una were of similar stature and build so it was possible.

When the maid re-entered the chamber, flinging open the door without knocking and striding in, she found Adaira seated on her sleeping pallet, combing out her wet hair.

The girl's mouth thinned, and she halted, her gaze sweeping over Adaira from head to foot. Then her lip curled.

Something in that gaze made Adaira's temper flare. She welcomed the heat in her belly, for it consumed the dread. How dare this woman look at her as if she was some lowly wretch.

"Do I pass yer inspection?" she asked coldly

The maid's gaze widened. For a moment, she stared at Adaira, before her cheeks flushed. Adaira's gaze didn't waver. She stared back until the maid looked away. "At least ye are presentable now," the girl muttered.

Lachlann was lowering himself onto the bench at the chieftain's table when an explosion of voices in the hall made him glance up.

His father's retainers, who were also taking their places at the long tables below the dais, were talking excitedly. Their gazes followed the slight figure who entered the hall, flanked by two male servants.

Dressed in flowing blue, her long brown hair curling in heavy waves over her shoulders, Adaira walked proudly into the Great Hall.

Like the lady she was.

Lachlann's gaze devoured her, taking in the slight sway of her hips and the way the kirtle hugged her supple body.

She held her head high, looking straight ahead. Only the tension in her neck, in her unsmiling face, gave her away. Her stoic behavior was impressive, especially after the raw desperation he'd witnessed in her eyes the last time he'd seen her.

Lachlann had deliberately avoided returning to the tower chamber since that day, and yet the look on her face still haunted him, as did her words.

I thought ye were a good man, an honorable one.

He shouldn't have spent so long in her company. The wine and the companionship over games of Ard-ri had lowered both their defenses. Still, her plea for help, which he had so harshly denied, had shadowed him ever since. Seeing her now made his chest ache.

Lachlann tore his gaze from Adaira, to where his father sat next to him. Morgan Fraser also watched his betrothed approach.

With each passing day, the chieftain grew stronger. He still couldn't wield a sword, and the healer warned him that he might never be able to, but outwardly at least he appeared as if he would regain his former strength.

His father tracked Adaira across the floor as if she was a lamb and he was a wolf. It was a cold, predatory look that made Lachlann's hackles rise.

Careful, he cautioned himself. *What do ye care how he looks at her?*

But the truth was he did.

The look on his father's face made Lachlann want to grab him by the neck and slam his face into the table.

Morgan Fraser would ruin Adaira. He would destroy her.

Adaira walked toward the dais, running the gauntlet of hard male stares, and paused before the table. Despite that he sat to his father's right, her gaze never strayed to Lachlann, not once. He was invisible to her. She bowed her head and made a curtsy. It was a brisk, neat gesture.

"Lady Adaira," Morgan Fraser greeted her. "How graceful ye look this eve."

Adaira raised her chin and met his eye briefly before dropping her gaze. She gave the merest nod in response but did not speak.

"What's the matter with her, Da?" Niall spoke up. Lachlann glanced at his brother to see him smirking at Adaira. "Did ye cut out her tongue?"

Morgan cut his son a humorless smile. "Her time in the tower has taught the lass the virtue of silence it seems."

His comment caused laughter to ripple down the table. Lachlann didn't join in.

"Lady Adaira." Morgan Fraser picked up a goblet of wine and turned his attention back to his betrothed. "Come sit next to me. We shall break bread together and speak a little."

Lachlann's mouth thinned. Only his father could make a request sound like a threat.

Adaira tensed but obliged. She walked to the edge of the dais, stepped up, and made her way to the chieftain's side. There she sank gracefully down onto the smaller chair to the chieftain's left.

Around them, the Great Hall was still silent. Every gaze was riveted upon the dais, upon Morgan Fraser and his young wife-to-be. This was the first time many of them had laid eyes upon Adaira. News of her had circulated the fortress for weeks now.

With a click of his fingers, the chieftain motioned to the line of servants that stood, backs ramrod straight, against the wall next to the entrance to the kitchen. "Serve the meal now," he commanded.

Conversation resumed once more: a low rumble, like surf breaking upon a shingle shore. The noise filled the hall, rising up to the blackened rafters above.

This was a special supper indeed, Lachlann noted. The servants brought out swan roasted in butter and herbs, a rich venison stew, tureens of braised leek and kale, wheels of aged cheese, and loaves of fresh bread studded with hazelnuts.

Under other circumstances, Lachlann's mouth would have watered at the sight. But tonight the feast that was set before him didn't appeal. His stomach felt as if a boulder had lodged in the pit of it.

None of his three brothers shared his sentiments though. With grins and laughter, they fell upon the meal as if they hadn't been fed in a week. Wine flowed, and they teased and ribbed each other.

In their midst, Lachlann remained quiet.

Next to him, his father was serving up some swan to his betrothed.

It was a rare thing to see Morgan Fraser wait upon a woman. Even with Una, he hadn't done so. But this was an occasion for ceremony. He was putting on a show for the folk of Talasgair. Tomorrow there would be a handfasting, and they wanted something to celebrate.

Chapter Seventeen

Ill-Tidings

ADAIRA CHOKED DOWN a mouthful of swan.

The meat was rich and smothered in butter. She'd had it once before, at her father and Una's handfasting feast. She'd enjoyed it then, but the taste sickened her now.

Morgan Fraser was not a garrulous man. He said very little as the meal stretched out, yet his silence made the tension within her grow. He watched her with a vulturine look that made her heart race, her palms grow clammy. The last time she'd seen him, he'd been on his sickbed, recovering from a terrible wound. He'd been frightening then, yet the full force of his personality had been checked.

This evening he appeared completely healed. Clad in plaid and leather, his grey streaked red hair pulled back at the nape, he watched her with hard eyes.

"Malcolm MacLeod took a jewel from me," he said after a long while.

The comment was unexpected, and Adaira tensed. She glanced at him, and he snared her gaze, holding it fast. Adaira swallowed. She wanted to look away but found she couldn't.

"My first wife was sweet-tempered but plain-faced," the Fraser chieftain said, his voice barely above a whisper so that none but Adaira could hear him. "She bore me four sons, but I found her company irksome. I was relieved when she died."

Adaira drew in a sharp breath. She didn't want to know all this. She wished he'd cease this tale, but he did not.

"But then Una came into my life. She was Una Campbell then: small, dark-haired, and wild." He paused, his eyes turning a murderous shade of green. "We had barely a year together before yer father stole her from me."

Adaira's pulse fluttered in the base of her throat. He made Una sound like the passive recipient of her father's affections, when in fact it had been her stepmother who'd taken the initiative and fled.

She wasn't about to point this out to Morgan Fraser though. He'd likely draw that dirk at his side and stab her through the throat with it.

She saw the promise of vengeance, of violence, in his eyes, and a shudder went through her. She knew then with certainty that he'd never treat her gently.

He would make her suffer.

Adaira tore her gaze away, breathing quickly, and stared down at the platter of food before her.

"Ye are afraid," Fraser noted. "Good. I want to see fear in yer eyes every time ye look at me."

Heaven knows what would have happened then, what more he might have said. But at that moment, the sound of a commotion from the far end of the hall drew the chieftain's eye.

A tall man clad in leather armor, a travel-stained cloak billowing behind him, strode down the aisle between tables. He wore a weary, hard expression. His dark eyes were riveted upon Morgan Fraser.

"Marcas," Morgan greeted him. Adaira forgotten, he rose to his feet. "What news from the mainland."

The man, who had dark-auburn hair and a chiseled jaw that reminded Adaira of Lachlann's, pursed his lips, his eyes glittering. "Ill-tidings."

A hush settled over the Great Hall.

"Tell it then," Morgan Fraser commanded.

"The battle," the newcomer spoke once more, his gaze never leaving the chieftain's face. "The English crushed us."

The silence grew chill. Adaira glanced across at her betrothed's profile and saw that his face had turned hawkish. "What happened?" he demanded, his voice cracking like a bull-whip across the hall.

"Twelve thousand of us crossed the border," Marcas replied. "We marched south to Durham and faced them there." He broke off, a nerve flickering in his cheek, before pressing on. "And though their army numbered only half the size of ours, they bested us."

The news, humiliating for their people, echoed across the silent hall. However, Marcas wasn't finished.

"We had no choice but to retreat." His face turned stony. Adaira could see that he was a proud man, and each word cost him. "Scotland has lost many men, including a number of clan-chiefs and chieftains. Yer brother Seumas was among them."

Morgan Fraser's face showed no emotion, no reaction to the news. After a heartbeat he leaned forward, his fingers clenching around the handle of a bone-handled knife before him. "And the king?"

The warrior held his gaze. "David was injured in the fighting. He and a few others were taken prisoner. I know not if any of them still live."

Adaira stood within the tower chamber that had been her prison for over the past two moons, and stared at the kirtle the maid had just hung on the wall.

It was exquisite, made of a shimmering lilac material. It glowed in the light of the lantern that burned on the table.

"The handfasting will take place mid-morning tomorrow," the maid told her. She'd brought up jeweled slippers and a gauzy shawl that Adaira would wear for the ceremony.

Adaira tore her gaze from the kirtle, focusing upon the scowling girl.

The maid boldly looked Adaira up and down, her eyes cold. "I will come up shortly after dawn to get ye ready. It's not enough time to make a MacLeod slut presentable though."

"Get out," Adaira said softly.

The maid huffed. "When I'm ready."

Adaira swung around, grabbed a pitcher of water off the table, and threw it at the maid.

The girl squealed and ducked, but it was too late. The earthen jug shattered against the wall, drenching her.

"Get out!" Adaira shouted. "And when I see ye tomorrow, I want to see that sneer wiped off yer face."

The maid backed up, eyes brimming with tears. Adaira advanced toward her, hands balling into fists. The girl gave a squeal of terror, turned, and fled from the room.

Breathing fast, Adaira listened to the key turning in the lock.

It felt a cowardly thing to do, to take the rage she felt toward Morgan Fraser and unleash it upon a servant, yet the maid's rudeness toward her seemed to grow with each passing day.

Her situation here was bad enough without the servants turning on her. She had to start as she meant to go on, or they would think her weak and torment her.

Morgan would bully her, but they wouldn't.

Adaira ran a hand over her face, relieved to finally be alone once more. Ever since Marcas Fraser had delivered the news of Scotland's bitter defeat against the English, the mood at Talasgair had turned grim. The cursing that had followed the initial shock shook the rafters.

Men had leaped to their feet roaring with rage. Morgan Fraser's sons were the loudest of them. All except Lachlann.

He alone had remained silent, hunched over his goblet of wine. His face had been stone-hewn, his gaze shuttered.

Although Adaira had pretended to ignore him throughout the feast, she'd been painfully aware of Lachlann's presence, just a few feet away.

Had he heard the things his father had said to her?

Crossing to her sleeping pallet, Adaira lowered herself down. Her hands were shaking, so she clasped them together and rested them upon her knees.

"Courage, Adaira," she whispered. "What would Rhona do?"

A wry smile twisted her face then. Her sister would have slapped that girl's face weeks ago.

Adaira inhaled a ragged breath as Morgan Fraser's softly spoken threats returned to her. He'd said them to scare her. He wanted her to be a trembling wreck by tomorrow night. He wanted her to weep and cringe before he took her maidenhead.

He's mad, twisted by hate.

Her belly cramped with fear. She just hoped she was strong enough to endure him.

Adaira couldn't sleep that night.

She lay awake in the darkness, staring up at the rafters and listening to the silence. It was quiet up in the tower; the noise in the rest of the fortress didn't reach here.

Adaira's thoughts circled, fear pressing down upon her chest. The wedding loomed like a hangman's noose before her. She didn't want to think of it, yet she couldn't stop herself.

Time stretched out, and she continued to stare into the darkness. It was strange, but she didn't even feel remotely drowsy.

She was still wide awake when she heard the light scrape of footfalls on the stone outside her door—and then a heartbeat later, the clunk of an iron key in the lock.

Adaira sat up, heart pounding.

Who would come to her chamber at this hour? Had Morgan Fraser come to rape her before the handfasting?

Terror exploded in her chest. He'd been angry enough tonight to do it. His rage upon hearing of Scotland's defeat had been a terrible thing to behold. Her own father had a blistering temper when roused, one that could send both his kin and servants running for cover. But she was less afraid of MacLeod than she was of Morgan Fraser. The Fraser chieftain's temper was a cold, vicious thing.

The door opened, and Adaira clutched the blanket to her. "Go away," she hissed, terror pulsing through her. "Or I'll scream these walls down."

Chapter Eighteen

By Moonlight

"QUIET," CAME A harsh male whisper. "Noise travels in this place."

Adaira froze. She recognized Lachlann Fraser's voice instantly.

Fresh panic seized her.

What does he want with me?

Wordlessly, he entered the chamber, crossed to the window, and threw it open. Moonlight filtered in, illuminating his tall form. Adaira's gaze swept over him. He wore a heavy cloak and boots and carried a bundle under his arm.

Lachlann hunkered down so that their gazes were level. His eyes gleamed in the moonlight. "Do ye still want my help?"

Adaira stared at him before silently nodding.

"Good. We're leaving Talasgair ... now."

Adaira stifled a gasp. "Ye will take me to Argyle?" she whispered.

He nodded. "Aye ... if that's where ye wish to go."

Adaira's breathing hitched. She didn't want to hope; this could be some cruel trick. Lachlann could be toying with her.

But before she could question him further, he pushed the bundle he carried into her arms. "Get dressed and put on this cloak and boots," he ordered softly. "We need to go."

He rose to his feet and stepped back, giving her space.

After a moment's hesitation, Adaira pushed aside the blanket and got to her feet. She still wore the fine cream léine of that evening. She pulled on the blue kirtle she'd worn for the feast over the top, her fingers fumbling with the laces. Then she reached down and hauled on the fur-lined boots. Finally, she slung the heavy woolen cloak about her shoulders, fastening it about the throat.

All the while, Lachlann watched and waited. She'd never seen his face so serious. "Ready?"

Adaira nodded once more.

"Follow close behind me ... and don't speak. My father's a light sleeper."

They left the tower chamber, padding softly down the worn stone stairs.

Adaira held her breath as they inched their way across the wide landing, past the door to the chieftain's bed-chamber. Adaira imagined Morgan Fraser slept with one eye open. He didn't seem the kind of man to let his guard down—ever.

It was a long, tense trip to the bottom. At the foot of the stairwell, a single torch burned upon a bracket against the wall. It threw a soft light across a guard, who sat, slumped on the floor.

Adaira drew up sharply, her gaze searching the man's face. For a moment, she thought he was dead, but then she saw the gentle rise and fall of his chest.

Loosing a breath, she cut a glance to Lachlann. Their gazes met and held for a heartbeat.

With a jolt, she realized he really was helping her escape.

Adaira's mind whirled. This didn't make sense. After everything that had happened, she couldn't understand why Lachlann Fraser would help her. What had changed?

There was no time to ask him about it now though; her questions would have to wait.

Lachlann led the way out of the tower, toward the oldest part of the fortress: the ancient stone round tower. Adaira wondered how he planned for them to escape this place. There would be guards everywhere.

But there didn't seem to be, or at least not in the passageways Lachlann was taking. They entered the round tower, where the Great Hall sat in the midst of the old broch, but Lachlann didn't take her into the hall itself. Instead, they skirted a passageway around it.

Halfway along the passage, the scuff of boots against stone alerted them to someone's presence.

Lachlann ducked into the shadows, pulling Adaira with him. Crushed against the long hard length of his body, her heart thundering so loudly she was sure the whole fortress could hear it, Adaira listened to the approaching footsteps.

It was a heavy, unsteady tread. A shadow passed by, a drunken man on his way to the privy.

They waited until all sign of him had passed before Lachlann released Adaira and the pair of them emerged from the shadows. The near-miss had put her on edge; her heart still pounded. However, Lachlann's face, lit by a guttering torch on the wall, was hard and focused.

He then leaned in close to Adaira, his breath tickling her ear. "We're taking the back way out," he whispered. "Keep a few paces behind me until the path is clear. The East Gate will be guarded. Whatever happens, stay silent. Prepare yerself ... things may get bloody."

Adaira nodded, although her belly now pitched and roiled with nerves. She suddenly needed to pee, but there was no time to find a privy.

Lachlann led the way to the back of the broch. As instructed, Adaira followed in his wake, keeping to the shadows a few feet behind him. They passed under a wide stone arch, and Adaira felt crisp air fan her face. The doorway was before them. Lachlann moved out into a moonlit yard and broke into a light-footed sprint. A high stone wall reared up before them, and a narrow wooden gate lay straight ahead.

Silhouetted by burning torches on the walls, Adaira spied two dark outlines of guards on either side of the gate. Adaira covered her mouth with a hand and slowed her pace. Lachlann was running straight for them.

Steel flashed as Lachlann drew his dirk.

A flurry of movement, grunts, thumps, and the scuff of booted feet on dirt followed.

Heart pounding, Adaira crept across the yard. Two prone figures lay on the ground. Lachlann had his back to her as he unbolted the gate.

Adaira stepped over the guards, her legs trembling now. "What did ye do to them?" She'd only whispered the question, but it seemed to echo across the yard.

Lachlann whipped around, gaze narrowed, and grabbed her by the arm, hauling her against him.

"I told ye to keep silent," he hissed in her ear.

"I know, but the guards ... are they—"

"Dead? Aye. Now hold yer tongue. We're not out of danger yet."

Lachlann shoved his shoulder against the gate and, with a creak, it opened. Once again, the noise seemed to reverberate in the night's stillness. There wasn't even the moan of the wind to disguise it.

Tension thrummed through Adaira. Her senses were stretched so taut that she imagined every soul in Talasgair must have heard. She drew in a sharp breath, bracing herself for shouts and the tattoo of running feet.

But no sounds came.

Lachlann took Adaira by the hand and led her through the gate. The land rose steeply on Talasgair's eastern side, and the pair were forced to scramble their way up a rocky slope before they crested the hill.

They'd only traveled a couple of furlongs from the walls when Adaira's lungs started to protest. Her legs felt weak and clumsy under her. After two moons locked away in the tower, her body wasn't used to this sudden exertion. She was relieved that Lachlann held her hand, towing her behind him as he broke into a run.

A short while later, they approached the ruins of another broch, entering it through the remains of an ancient archway. Stacked stone walls, crumbling with age, rose around them. A star-strewn night sky arched above, for the broch's roof had fallen into ruin long ago.

"Where are we?" Adaira gasped, struggling to regain her breath.

"This is Dun Sleadale, an old Pict fort," Lachlann replied. "Come on ... we can't linger here either."

He led her to the far side of the ruins, where a horse awaited them. Relief kicked within Adaira at the sight of it. She watched Lachlann untether the horse and run a hand down the beast's neck.

"Ye planned this?" she breathed.

"Aye," he replied, busying himself with tightening the horse's girth. "We wouldn't get far on foot."

"Why are ye helping me?"

Lachlann stilled before casting a look over his shoulder. "It doesn't matter. Ye asked me to, didn't ye?"

"Aye ... and ye refused."

His expression shuttered, and he turned away. "I ... changed my mind."

Lachlann swung up onto the back of the horse. He then stretched his hand down to her. "Climb up."

Adaira grasped his hand, slipped her foot into the stirrup, and sprang up, settling herself down behind him. She tried to sit back as far as possible, but the shape of the saddle meant that she slid down toward him, her breasts pressed up against his back. Tensing, Adaira loosely wrapped her arms about his waist.

They moved off, leaving the ruin of Dun Sleadale behind. The horse picked its way down the pebble-strewn hillside. The hoary light of the moon lit the path before them.

Adaira tried to guess the time. It was very late, or early depending on how ye looked at it. They would have to ride hard to be far from here by dawn.

The maid would raise the alarm shortly after sunrise if someone didn't discover the dead guards at the East Gate first.

The chill night air stung Adaira's cheeks. It was cold enough tonight for a frost to settle. It didn't take long for her fingers and toes to grow numb.

At the bottom of the hill, they reached an unpaved highway.

"Where does this road lead?" Adaira asked.

"This is the main highway southeast," Lachlann replied, drawing the horse to a halt. "If ye want to take the fastest route to Argyle, this is it."

Adaira caught the edge in his voice and tensed. "What's wrong?"

"My father will be after us at dawn," he said flatly. "He knows yer kin reside at Gylen Castle and that's where we were heading last time. Neither of us will find refuge there."

Anxiety fluttered up under Adaira's ribcage. In their escape from Talasgair, she hadn't even considered that. "So, ye think we *shouldn't* go to Argyle?"

A brief silence stretched out between them. "It would be wiser to find somewhere to wait him out before we cross to the mainland," he replied. "But ye may never be able to go to Gylen Castle as ye had planned ... not now."

Adaira drew in a deep breath. His words were unwelcome, yet she realized he spoke the truth. Once they were far from Talasgair, she'd have to make new plans, but for now, they had other priorities. "Where can we hide in the meantime?"

"My brothers told me that Baltair MacDonald fell in battle. Yer sister is now chatelaine of Duntulm, is she not?"

Adaira went still, caught off-guard by the question. "Aye."

Lachlann turned his profile to her. He was frowning. "Would she shelter us?"

"She would," Adaira replied without hesitation. She trusted Caitrin with her life. "But ye do realize we'll have to ride through my father's lands to reach MacDonald territory?"

"Aye," he growled. "It hadn't escaped me."

"But ye would take the risk?"

Lachlann muttered a curse and raked a hand through his hair. "If Baltair MacDonald was still chieftain of Duntulm, I wouldn't go within ten leagues of the place. The man was loyal to yer father. But if ye think yer sister can be trusted, we can stay with her till the dust settles."

Adaira considered his words. Her first impulse was to insist they rode like the wind south for Kyleakin before taking a boat across the water. She hated the thought of delaying. Every day that she remained on Skye put her at risk of being caught by either Malcolm MacLeod or Morgan Fraser.

And yet, without a destination in mind, they'd be fleeing blind.

She was also wary of Lachlann. He'd risked his neck to free her, but she didn't trust him. The man never did anything unless he stood to gain from it; she'd learned that the hard way.

However, he did have a valid point. His father would follow them to Gylen Castle if he didn't catch them first.

Lachlann's idea to seek refuge at Duntulm was only marginally less dangerous. They risked capture by her father's men, and there was no guarantee Morgan Fraser wouldn't follow them.

"Will yer father hunt us if we cross into MacLeod lands?" she asked, giving her fears voice.

A pause followed, and when Lachlann answered, his voice was bleak. "Aye ... our only advantage is that if we travel northeast, he won't know where we're headed."

Chapter Nineteen

I Did It For Ye

LACHLANN'S GAZE FIXED ahead.

It was fortunate there was a full moon tonight, on the eve of Samhuinn. Without it, they couldn't have traveled in the dark. Even so, Lachlann's attention swept the bare hillsides around them, on the lookout for trouble.

He and Adaira now rode cross country. They'd left the highway behind, and instead of traveling southeast as he'd initially planned, they were riding northeast. Their path would take them through the mountainous heart of the isle, through narrow passes and uninhabited land. He could see the bulk of those mountains in the distance now, their sculpted silhouettes frosted silver.

Adaira pressed up against his back. She'd wrapped her hands around his waist. Despite the layers of clothing they both wore, he could feel the length of her body pressed up against him, and the softness of her breasts, jolting against him with every stride.

The sensation was distracting, although his thoughts were focused on what lay ahead—and on what he'd left behind.

There were some bridges that could only be crossed once—some steps that could never be retraced.

With an ache in his chest, he knew he'd never see the walls of Talasgair again, never catch sight of the Fraser pennants snapping in the wind or hear the wail of a highland pipe calling him home.

The ache increased till it hurt to breathe.

What have I done?

Lachlann's own behavior stunned him. He'd struggled ever since refusing to help Adaira, but when he'd watched his father with her at the feast, something inside him—a cord that had long been fraying—snapped.

The arrival of his cousin Marcas Fraser had thrown the whole evening into an uproar. For a short while, everyone inside the hall had forgotten that there would be a wedding the following day. Instead, they had been outraged to discover Scotland's defeat against the English.

Lachlann too had reeled from the devastating news—but all he'd been able to think about as he sat at the table, listening to Lucas bellow in rage next to him, was getting Adaira out of Talasgair.

It had been the perfect evening to arrange an escape. Everyone was distracted, including his father, who finished the feast early and took Marcas away with him to his solar to discuss the grim details of the battle at length.

Lachlann had taken his horse out for an evening ride and tethered it inside the ruins of Dun Sleadale nearby, before making his way back to the broch on foot. He'd made some excuse to the guards at the West Gate about how the beast had thrown him and galloped off into the gloaming. He'd told them he would go looking for it in the morning.

After that, he'd waited in his bed-chamber, listening as the broch slowly went to sleep. And when the moon had risen high into the sky, he finally made his move.

"I can hear ye thinking," Adaira spoke up, shattering the silence between them. Her voice was soft, yet wary.

"Why? Are ye a sorceress?" he replied. He'd meant to use a teasing tone, but instead, his voice sounded brittle.

Adaira huffed. "I don't need to be a witch to hear the chatter of yer thoughts. Ye are as tense as a board."

Lachlann didn't answer. For once, he had no idea what to say.

Silence fell between them before Adaira eventually broke it. "It was a brave thing ye did ... and I thank ye for it."

Lachlann snorted. He wasn't sure whether it was brave or the act of an idiot.

"I still don't understand why ye did it," Adaira continued.

"Ye don't need to," he replied. "Ye are free, aren't ye?"

"Aye, but—"

"Enough, Adaira," he said, his voice weary. "I'd prefer we traveled in silence."

The rosy blush of dawn stained the eastern sky. Adaira glanced up before bowing her head and splashing water on her face. The water's chill made her suck in a breath.

They had halted in the bottom of a rocky valley. The bulk of huge mountains reared high above them, and a clear burn trickled through the vale. The water was icy and fresh. Filling her cupped hands with it, Adaira drank deep before refilling their water skin. Around her, a glittering frost carpeted the ground.

She glanced behind her, at where Lachlann was in the midst of a long stretch. She heard the muscles and bones in his back and shoulders creak. It'd been a long, tiring night, but they couldn't rest yet.

Adaira's gaze settled upon Lachlann's face. His expression was tense, his features strained. She'd felt the tension growing in him with each furlong they traveled from Talasgair. His mood put her on edge and worried her.

Was he planning something? Would he betray her again?

Adaira drew in a slow, steadying breath. The time had come for them to have a frank conversation. She'd been avoiding this moment, for he'd been evasive every time she'd tried to speak to him—yet a resolve now filled her.

"What's wrong, Lachlann?" Adaira asked, breaking the silence.

Lachlann glanced toward her, his gaze narrowing. "Nothing."

Adaira inhaled sharply. "Ye are lying. Something *is* bothering ye … and I wish to know what it is."

His brow furrowed. "Adaira." His voice lowered in warning. "Don't—"

"Enough," she cut him off. "Talk to me!"

Lachlann muttered a curse. "What do ye want to know, woman?"

"I want to know why ye helped me … have ye finally grown a conscience?"

He snorted.

"Do ye regret helping me … is that it?"

She watched him tense. "Of course not."

"It seems that way to me."

Lachlann stepped back and ran a hand over his face. "Satan's cods," he muttered, frustrated. "I crossed a line last night. I can never go back home."

"It's more than that though, isn't it?" Adaira folded her arms across her chest. "Ye are disappointed because ye wanted to rule."

"I did," he admitted roughly.

Adaira's mouth thinned. "How it must have chafed to see Morgan Fraser still alive when ye returned home."

A muscle ticked in Lachlann's jaw. "I didn't wish him dead."

"Didn't ye?" She noted a faint color now tinged his high cheekbones. She'd succeeded in angering him, but Adaira didn't care. Recklessly, she pressed on. "Ye were so desperate to get home and seize power that ye didn't care about anyone else. Ye didn't care what happened to me."

"I saved ye, didn't I," he growled back. "Ye could show some gratitude."

"It was the least ye could do!" Adaira spat. His arrogance riled her. "All of this mess is yer fault!"

Drawing her cloak around her, Adaira stalked past him.

Lachlann raised an eyebrow as she went. "Where do ye think ye are going?"

"To Duntulm—alone."

"Ye won't get far on foot."

Adaira came to an abrupt halt and spun on her heel, glaring at him. Lachlann had turned and was watching her with a patronizing look that made her want to kick him in the cods. "The Devil take ye, Lachlann Fraser. I couldn't care less where I go, only that I never have to set eyes on ye ever again."

Giving him her back, Adaira strode away, up the rocky incline toward the northeastern edge of the valley.

"Adaira," he called after her. "Come back here."

Adaira ignored him. She was so angry that she felt like picking up stones and pelting him with them.

To think she'd actually thanked him for saving her.

"Adaira!"

He sounded angry now. Good. She hoped he choked on it.

Moments later, she heard footfalls behind her. He was coming after her.

Adaira broke into a run. Her legs were still weak after her incarceration, but she pushed herself on nonetheless. Rage gave her feet wings.

She'd nearly reached the top of the hill when he caught up with her, grabbing her by the arm and pulling her up short.

Adaira swung around, her right fist balling, and punched him in the neck. However, the blow just seemed to glance off him.

"Let me go!" she shouted.

But Lachlann didn't. He held her firm, fending off the blows and kicks she now aimed at his chest and shins.

"Stop it, Adaira," he commanded, his voice tight. She ignored him, writhing in his grip like a landed pike.

"Filthy whoreson," she shrieked. "Get yer hands off me!"

But he didn't.

Instead, Lachlann pulled her roughly against him. His mouth slanted over hers, and he kissed her.

Adaira was so shocked that she momentarily went limp in his arms. She gasped, her lips parting. His tongue slid into her mouth. His kiss was savage, devouring, and hot. It turned the frosty morning into a steam bath. Adaira was helpless under the onslaught.

She'd almost forgotten what Lachlann Fraser's kiss could do to her, that it could literally scatter her wits to the four winds and drain every ounce of will from her body.

The rage drained from her, replaced by a different kind of madness.

His kiss demanded, took, and gave all at the same time. And as it deepened, Adaira melted against him, her fingers splaying across his leather vest. She felt the hammer of his heart against her palm, and a thrill went through her.

When Lachlann ended the kiss and pulled back, he was breathing fast. His skin was pulled tight across his cheekbones. His gaze burned into her. Adaira stared up at him, the spell he'd cast over her slowly drawing back. She started to tremble.

Lord ... no.

"Ye asked me why I did it, and I'll tell ye," he rasped. "I did it for *ye*, Aingeal."

Chapter Twenty

Everything In My Power

LACHLANN CLOSED HIS eyes. He couldn't believe he'd just said that. He wasn't even sure where the words had come from.

He opened his eyes and saw that Adaira was still staring up at him. She'd looked shocked at first, but now her face softened. His chest constricted. The lass had such a pure, good heart. She put him to shame.

"I don't understand," she whispered.

Lachlann drew in a slow, steadying breath. Suddenly, he found it impossible to speak. He released his hold on her shoulder and, reaching up, stroked her face. To his surprise, he noted his hand trembled slightly.

God's bones, what's wrong with me?

Lachlann's fingers trailed down Adaira's cheek, and he felt her quiver under his touch. He watched her lips part, her pupils dilate. He'd wanted her before, on that evening during their journey to Talasgair, but the sensation paled in comparison to how he ached for her now.

He wanted to pull her to the ground, tear off her clothes, and lose himself in her soft, sweet body. The need was so strong it felt like a kind of insanity. But the heavy frost that sparkled around them, and the surety his father would have discovered both their disappearances by now, kept him in check. They couldn't linger here.

Wanting her like this was selfish. She deserved better than the likes of him. Self-loathing welled within Lachlann then, filling his mouth with a bitter taste.

"I couldn't stand by and watch ye wed my father," he finally managed. "I couldn't let him destroy ye."

She gazed up at him, her hazel eyes as wide as moons. "Really?"

Lachlann managed a smile. "Aye," he murmured. "I'm a selfish cur, but not completely without a heart." He paused a moment before he reluctantly released Adaira and stepped back. Frosty morning air filled the gulf between them. "I can't let ye travel alone. It's not safe. Will ye let me escort ye to yer sister's as planned?"

Adaira swallowed before she nodded.

Adaira craned her neck, peering up at the mountains that rose either side. They had become the heavens, with only a thin strip of blue sky between them. The morning sun gilded the peaks, turning some tawny and others red as if they were aflame. Their craggy, carven bulk made Adaira feel small and insignificant—even so, she loved to look upon them.

She would leave these shores soon, but this isle with its great mountains and wild landscape would always have a piece of her heart.

Adaira must have fallen asleep for a while, for she found herself jolted awake against Lachlann's back as the horse stumbled. The stallion had slowed its gait on the uneven footing. However, they had crested the highest point of the pass and were now making their way down the long slope northeast.

As they rode, Adaira found herself reliving their confrontation at dawn and the heated kiss that had followed. It was impossible not to think about it.

I should still be wary of him, she cautioned herself. He'd seemed sincere as he'd gazed into her eyes—but the past two months had taught her that trust had to be earned.

She wasn't sure what to think, what to say, or how to react. Instead, she took refuge in silence.

Even so, Adaira was keenly aware of the heat of his strong back pressed against her breasts, the texture of his fiery hair that kept tickling her nose, and the male musk of his skin that made her breathing quicken.

Desire. He'd given her a heady taste of it.

Adaira closed her eyes and breathed Lachlann in. She shouldn't want him, yet she did.

That afternoon, when they lay deep within MacLeod lands, Lachlann drew the stallion up for a proper rest.

Leaning forward, he patted the horse's slick neck. It had done well, but now the beast needed a breather. They'd stopped on the edge of a stand of pines, where a shallow creek bubbled over grey rocks. The landscape had changed during the day's journey, gradually growing less barren and arid, and more wooded—a sign that they were approaching the northeastern coast. Despite that the sun had shone on them all day, the air was cool.

Lachlann unsaddled his horse, while Adaira sat down on the ground upon a bed of pine needles a few feet away.

"Lachlann," Adaira spoke up, breaking the long silence between them. He could hear the nervousness in her voice. "About what ye said earlier ..."

Lachlann tensed. Removing the saddle, he cast a glance over his shoulder. She was sitting, watching him, her brow furrowed.

"Do ye actually care what happens to me?" Her cheeks pinkened as she said these words. It embarrassed her to bring this up, but he could see she was determined.

Lachlann set the saddle down on its pommel and turned back to the stallion, rubbing it down with a twist of grass. "Ye speak as if such a thing is impossible," he replied. "Do ye think it strange that a man would want to protect ye?"

"No … but it shocks me that *ye* would."

Lachlann huffed. "Ye must think me a cold bastard."

Her answering silence made him grimace. Pausing in his work, he turned to Adaira. Around them, the wind sighed through the pines, yet Lachlann paid it no mind. He couldn't take his gaze off the young woman seated upon a bed of pine needles. She looked like a woodland fairy maid, caught resting in a glade by an unsuspecting traveler.

Lachlann grew still, his gaze feasting upon her.

He could see the signs of fatigue upon Adaira: her face was paler than usual, and there were dark smudges under her eyes. But even so, she was still lovely; her long brown hair spilling over the shoulders of her cloak.

"Have ye ever been completely ignorant of something … and then wondered how ye could have missed what was right before ye?" he asked softly.

Her head inclined. "No … I don't think that's ever happened to me."

Lachlann dragged a hand through his hair. "I wasn't brought up to be sentimental," he admitted with a wince. "It took me too long to realize that I'd made a terrible mistake."

To his surprise, Adaira's mouth curved into a faint smile. "Is that the beginnings of an apology I hear?"

Lachlann snorted. "Aye … Frasers aren't just known for our stubbornness. We also have difficulty admitting to our mistakes."

He broke off there, realizing that he felt on edge, nervous. Pushing the sensation aside, he went to Adaira then and knelt before her, reaching for her hand. Adaira's gaze widened, and he felt her stiffen under his touch—yet she didn't pull away.

"I did ye a great wrong Adaira MacLeod," he said, his voice low and firm, "and I'm truly sorry for it. Now, I will do everything in my power to put things right."

It seemed strange to see Kiltaraglen again.

So much had befallen Adaira since she was last here. She felt like a different person, as if years not months had passed.

Dusk was settling, the last of the sun gilding the world with a beauty that only autumn sun seemed to possess. The loch glittered, and the wind that had chased them north all day died away.

As they rode in, Adaira spied the mounds of unlit bonfires on the hills to the south and north of the village. After dark, those fires would be lit, and the folk of Kiltaraglen would venture outdoors to celebrate Samhuinn.

The road brought them into the port village, in-between twin hills where two more piles of twigs and branches rose against the darkening sky. Men were rolling up barrels for the apple-bobbing.

Adaira gave a wistful smile as she thought of Dunvegan. Would Rhona and Taran be getting ready to enjoy tonight's festivities? She imagined them wandering amongst the crowd, arms linked. They made a striking couple, for, despite their different looks, they were both tall and proud.

Adaira's throat constricted. She missed Rhona. How she wished to see her. Soon though, she'd see Caitrin again. Warmth flowed through Adaira's breast at the thought.

"We'll need to be careful in Kiltaraglen," Lachlann warned her as they rode in. His gaze scanned their surroundings with a warrior's sharpness. "Yer father might have left men here to keep an eye out for us."

Adaira tensed. She hadn't thought of that. She imagined her father might have sent warriors to Argyle, to seek her and Lachlann there, but she hadn't thought he might still be patrolling his lands for them. The thought made a chill prickle her skin.

"We can't stay in the village," Lachlann continued. "News of us will spread fast if we make ourselves visible."

Adaira digested this before sighing. She'd secretly been hoping they'd have a comfortable night in the inn this time at least. "Where do ye suggest we sleep then?"

"We'll make camp in the woods north of the village," Lachlann replied. He then glanced over his shoulder, casting her a smile. "Ye should be able to see the Samhuinn fires from there too."

Chapter Twenty-one

Keeping Warm

THE RHYTHMIC THUD of drums echoed through the night, like the steady beat of a heart.

Adaira sat, back pressed up to the rough bark of a birch, nibbling at a slab of bread and cheese, as she watched the fires of Samhuinn burn.

They lit up the darkness like glowing embers, beacons to call the spirits home.

"A roast hazelnut, milady?"

She started as a tall figure stepped out from the shadow of the trees and knelt next to her.

The aroma of warm roasted nuts wafted over her, and Adaira's mouth watered.

"Lachlann!" She peered down at the tiny basket of nuts he held. "Where did ye get those?"

His face, kissed by the glow of the distant fires, was so handsome it made her belly flutter. His nearness made it difficult to breathe calmly.

"Ye can't have Samhuinn without hazelnuts."

"But ... I thought it wasn't safe for us to wander amongst folk?"

"Together, aye. But a man alone buying a wee basket of nuts doesn't intrigue folk much." He held the basket out to her. "Go on ... I bought them for ye."

Adaira took the basket and helped herself to a handful. They were fresh off the brazier, still hot. Their aroma brought back so many memories that, for a moment, her throat constricted. Then, she popped the nuts into her mouth and sighed. She offered him the basket. "Here ... have some too."

Lachlann took a handful and sat down next to her, stretching his long legs out in front of him. Although they weren't touching, Adaira could feel his nearness. The fine hair on the back of her arms prickled in response.

On the hillside below, laughter rang out. Torches moved, glowing like fireflies in the darkness, traveling up and down from the village.

For a while Adaira and Lachlann merely watched, silence stretching between them. It wasn't a companionable silence but a weighty one. Much had passed between them that day. Adaira felt odd, as if her skin were too tight, too sensitive. She was jittery around Lachlann. To distract herself, she focused on the bonfires in the distance and the showers of red sparks that erupted high into the sky

Finishing off the nuts, Adaira brushed the skins off her hands and met Lachlann's eye briefly. "Thank ye for the hazelnuts. They were delicious."

He smiled back but said nothing.

After a moment Adaira glanced away, her gaze fixing upon the bonfires once more. The tension between them was becoming unbearable. She was so aware of him that, although she was tired from traveling, her body felt restless.

Did it bother him as much as it did her?

It dawned on her then that she ached for him to kiss her again. On a practical level, she was wary of him, but her body told a different story. It obliterated all good sense and filled her with a heady carelessness.

Adaira looked up, to find Lachlann watching her. His face was serious, although his intense gaze ensnared her.

Heart racing, Adaira found herself leaning toward him.

"Adaira." He said her name softly, a hoarse edge to his voice.

Wetting her lips, she swallowed, aware that his attention had shifted to her mouth. Heat rose within her, spreading out from her core.

Lachlann shifted closer to her and reached up, cupping her head with his hands. His fingers tangled in her hair, and then his lips brushed over hers. This kiss wasn't like the one earlier in the day—that embrace had been a claiming. This one was gentler.

Adaira's eyes fluttered closed. Without thinking upon her actions, she parted her lips and allowed her tongue to timidly slide into his mouth.

Lachlann's answering groan emboldened her. She gently bit his lower lip, gasping when he hauled her against him. His kiss changed now, his mouth searing hers. Adaira's head spun, and she clung to him, answering Lachlann's passion with her own. Her tongue explored his mouth, tongue, and lips. His taste made molten heat pool in the cradle of her belly.

A moment later, Lachlann ended the kiss and drew back, breathing hard. Disappointed, Adaira reached for him, but he held her at arm's length. His face was strained, his gaze pleading.

"The Devil roast me alive ... we need to stop ... or I'll forget myself."

Adaira gazed at him, longing for him to do just that. She didn't know what had come over her. The desire he'd sparked that morning had been kindling all day, and now it had burst into flame. She ached for his kiss and felt bereft that he'd deny her.

"Please, Aingeal," he rasped. "Stop looking at me like that."

Confused, Adaira drew back. "Don't ye want to kiss me?" she whispered, hurt.

Lachlann muttered a curse and leaned back against the tree. "Ye have no idea how much."

"Then why won't ye?"

He cast her a look of pure frustration. "Because once I start, I won't want to stop. Ye are a maid ... I don't want to ruin ye."

Adaira tensed. In her haze of lust, she'd forgotten about that. A high-born lass's maidenhead was a valuable thing. It seemed Lachlann understood that better than her.

A wave of recklessness swept over Adaira then. She'd be no chieftain's wife. She had no virtue to cling to. She wanted Lachlann to kiss her again, to discover the magic he'd shown her a glimpse of. A strange thing had happened to them both since leaving Talasgair; it was as if they'd stepped through a door into another world—one she was eager to know more of.

Adaira craved the oblivion of his touch.

Still, wanting Lachlann to pull her into his arms for another fierce kiss was one thing, actually demanding he do it was another.

Shyness overrode recklessness, and Adaira shifted away from him. She now felt embarrassed and a little foolish.

How can ye want someone ye don't even trust? Her conscience needled her then, reminding her just how fragile the bond was between them. It was just as well that Lachlann had pulled away—but all the same, she still ached for his touch.

They sat in silence for a while, and when Lachlann spoke, his voice was subdued. "There's something ye should know, Adaira."

Tensing, Adaira looked over at Lachlann to find him watching her, his gaze shuttered.

"What?" The question came out as a croak. Her nerves were getting the better of her.

His mouth curved. "One promise I did keep. I never told my father or brothers how we escaped from Dunvegan. None of them know of the hidden passage into the dungeon."

Adaira drew in a sharp breath. His admission surprised her, distracting her from her heated, tormented thoughts and disappointment that he'd withdrawn his touch. "Why not?"

He held her gaze. "Some secrets are best kept."

The Samhuinn fires burned, and the laughter and revelry of the folk of Kiltaraglen echoed long into the night.

Adaira and Lachlann eventually turned their backs on the fires and moved away from the edge of the woodland. Moonlight shone through the trees as Lachlann led his horse deep into the woods. Adaira followed. A cold veil settled over the world now, and another night of clear skies promised a frost in the morning. Shivering, Adaira pulled her cloak close.

They made camp for the night in a tiny glade surrounded by ash and oaks. The trees were losing their leaves, and Adaira's feet rustled through them. She stopped, waiting while Lachlann tethered the stallion.

"It's so cold," she breathed. "Can we not light a fire?"

He glanced over at her, his face all sculpted planes in the moonlight. "Not this close to Kiltaraglen ... there will be folk up for a while yet."

Adaira drew her cloak closer. "But we'll freeze."

He cast her another look, one so heated that it made her belly flutter.

Adaira went still. After Lachlann had ended their last kiss abruptly, she'd thought he would avoid looking at her like that. Suddenly, it didn't seem so cold in the glade. Adaira was acutely aware of Lachlann's nearness. Her heart started to hammer. They stared at each other for a long moment. She saw the hunger in his eyes, the way his chest now rose and fell sharply, but he didn't reach for her.

She realized then that he wouldn't.

Lachlann wanted her to make the decision. This needed to be her choice.

Breathing shallowly, Adaira stepped toward him. "Will ye keep me warm?"

She couldn't believe she'd asked him such a thing. Part of her was terrified, and yet another part—one she'd only just discovered—was thrilled by her boldness.

Lachlann wet his lips. "I shouldn't."

Adaira took another tentative step toward him. "What do ye want, Lachlann?"

"Don't make me answer that," he said huskily. "It'll scare ye off."

Adaira held his gaze, her heart hammering so loud she was sure he must have heard it. "I'm not scared," she lied. "And I know what *I* want ... *ye.*"

Silence fell between them. Adaira saw a nerve flicker in his cheek and knew he was struggling.

"Come here, Aingeal." The raw edge to his voice made her stomach dive.

Without stopping to think, for she would surely lose her nerve, Adaira stepped forward into the circle of his arms.

Lachlann reached out and cupped her face. The feel of his touch made her stifle a gasp. It had a magical effect, both steadying and exciting her.

Heart pounding, Adaira leaned toward him. Her gaze was on his mouth now. She ached for another taste of him.

With a growl, Lachlann captured her mouth with his.

Adaira couldn't help it; a low groan escaped her. The feel of his lips moving over hers, the glide of his tongue, and the heat of his mouth, unleashed something primal within her. She linked her arms about his neck, pressing herself against him, while she responded to his kiss hungrily.

He was delicious. She could happily drown in the feel of his mouth ravaging hers.

Adaira's hands traveled down, over his broad shoulders to his chest, exploring, before they slid over the hard muscles of his upper arms. Even through the layers of clothing separating them, she could feel his strength, his contained power.

Lachlann gently bit her lower lip, before his mouth trailed down to her neck.

Adaira sighed and sank against him. Her cloak fell away, and his hands explored the curve of her back. Then he cupped her bottom and pulled her hard against him.

Even through the loose material of his braies, Adaira felt Lachlann's arousal—his rigid, hot shaft—pressed up against her belly. A pulse began between her thighs, a deep throbbing ache that made her writhe against him.

Lachlann muttered a curse, grabbed hold of Adaira, and steered her backward.

Two paces brought the pair of them up against the trunk of an oak, a mattress of fallen leaves around their ankles. Pressed against the rough bark, Adaira wound her arms around Lachlann's neck once more, her mouth seeking his.

Their kisses turned wild, wet. Her body pulsed with need, the sensation intensifying when he slid his leg between her thighs. His hands gripped the hem of her léine and kirtle, drawing them up around her hips. The cold night air kissed Adaira's naked skin, but when she shivered, it wasn't from the chill.

Lachlann took hold of her right thigh, lifting it so that she could wrap her leg around his hips. An instant later her core was pressed against the rigid length of his shaft.

Instinctively, Adaira arched up, moving her hips sinuously against him.

Lachlann groaned loudly. He almost sounded as if he was in pain. He clasped his hands around her naked buttocks and ground her against him.

An aching pleasure spread through Adaira's loins. She writhed against him, searching for something nameless, something that teased her, tormented her. Something just out of reach.

Lachlann leaned back from Adaira a moment, tearing his mouth from hers. His chest was heaving, and in the glow of the moonlight, she saw the strain on his face. His eyes were dark and luminous. A light sheen of sweat now covered his skin.

"Ye have no idea," he ground out, his voice ragged, "how much I want ye, Adaira. I could lose control. If ye wish me to stop, it has to be now."

Wild need reared up within her. "Don't stop," she whispered.

He drew in a sharp breath. "I don't want to hurt or scare ye."

"Ye won't." She reached for him, dug her fingers in his hair, and pulled him roughly to her for a bruising kiss.

Lachlann's tongue tangled with hers, all hesitation gone. Then with one hand, he reached down and unlaced his braies.

Breathing hard, Lachlann freed his shaft. Adaira reached down to touch him. Her trembling fingertips traced him. His rod quivered and pulsed under her touch, its tip slick with his need.

Excitement ignited deep in Adaira's belly. She'd never known what sensuality was till that moment, what it meant to want someone with every part of one's body.

Her breathing came in short gasps as he grasped her hips and spread her thighs wide. The slick heat of their bodies connecting caused a whimper to escape her. He held her, pressed at the entrance to her core.

Nervousness fluttered up under her ribcage. This was really happening. Once they did this, there was no going back.

Slowly, taking his time, Lachlann slid into her. The sensation of him filling her, stretching her, made her moan. A deep aching pleasure spread through her lower belly before a sharp pain made her catch her breath.

Lachlann stilled, letting the moment pass and waiting for her to relax against him once more. Then he slid the rest of the way in one smooth movement so that he was buried deep inside her.

Adaira raised her chin and met his gaze. It was almost too much to look at him, too intense, too raw. The pain

had been fleeting, and the feeling of exquisite fullness
that replaced it made her quiver.

Holding her hips tight, Lachlann began to move
inside her in slow, deep thrusts.

Adaira sucked in a breath, and the trembling in her
body increased. How good it felt. Her body sang with
pleasure.

"Lachlann," she gasped. "I don't ... I can't..." She
wasn't even sure what she was trying to articulate. It was
just that she could feel a tension building within her, like
a rising tide behind a seawall. It scared her just a little.

"Let go, Aingeal," he whispered. "Give yerself up to
it."

And she did. Her head fell back as tension rose to its
peak within her, and a great wave of pleasure crested the
seawall and slammed into her.

Lachlann's body went taut. He threw his head back
and gave a deep, raw groan. Then, they collapsed against
the oak together, limbs tangled, bodies spent.

Chapter Twenty-two

What will ye do now?

SHIVERING, ADAIRA PRESSED her back up against Lachlann. Once the glow of their lovemaking had faded, the cold started to gnaw into her bones. Yet Lachlann's body burned like a furnace compared to hers, and when he wrapped his heavy mantle about them, a sigh of pleasure gusted out of her.

Adaira felt a rumble in his chest as he laughed. "Better?"

"Aye," she murmured. "Much."

They fell silent then. A sense of well-being, unlike any other Adaira had experienced, settled over her. His warmth cocooned her. She listened to the rhythmic whisper of his breathing, the steady beat of his heart. The scent of leather and warm male skin enveloped her.

She felt Lachlann place a gentle kiss upon the crown of her head. "Are ye comfortable?"

"I think so," Adaira mumbled sleepily. Truthfully, her body had never felt so alive. The dull ache between her legs reminded her of what they'd just shared, of the pleasure he'd given her.

She wanted to ask him if what they'd shared was usual. She had no prior experience, but he would know.

Yet she suddenly felt shy in his presence. Her cheeks flushed when she remembered how bold she'd been with him, how lustily she'd responded to his touch.

She'd done it—she'd coupled with Lachlann. There was no undoing it.

She wondered what he thought of her now.

Tomorrow, in the cold light of day, she might end up regretting tonight's abandon, but right at that moment, wrapped in her lover's arms, Adaira could not.

Gradually, fatigue pulled her down into its embrace. Then she felt her eyelids droop and knew she was lost.

Lachlann held Adaira in his arms and listened to her breathing change. It grew deeper, and her body fully relaxed against his.

The feel of her pressed up against him, the tickle of her soft, heather-scented hair against his face, was both a balm *and* a torture.

Despite that exhaustion now dug its claws into him, he still ached for her. He'd wanted to take her again, this time on the leaf-strewn ground, but Adaira looked ready to collapse. He had to show the poor lass some mercy.

Lachlann loosed a deep breath and let his head fall back against the rough bark of the trunk.

This time tomorrow they'd be in Duntulm—and when they reached the fortress, things would change.

Adaira wasn't his wife, or even his betrothed. Indeed, she was promised to *two* other men: Aonghus Budge and his own father. Lachlann had no claim on her.

Once she was safe with her sister, Adaira might change her attitude toward him. She might remember all the reasons she distrusted him—that she'd once hated him.

Lady Caitrin would hear the tale of how he'd made Adaira a promise and then broken it. Adaira's sister wasn't likely to want him to remain at Duntulm once she knew the truth.

Lachlann gently stroked Adaira's hair. She gave a soft sigh and snuggled deeper into his chest.

Swallowing hard, Lachlann stared up at the night sky through the spreading branches of the sheltering oak. There wasn't much he was sure of these days. His decision to help Adaira flee Talasgair had thrown his world into chaos. All the things he'd once set so much store in no longer mattered.

One thing he knew though was that he wanted to protect Adaira, to keep her safe.

He had to find a way to ensure he stayed at her side.

Adaira gazed up at the giant thumb of dark rock, silhouetted against the morning sky. The land rose steeply to the north, and the familiar jagged outline of rocky pinnacles reared overhead. One, in particular, stood out.

She smiled before tapping Lachlann on the shoulder and pointing up to it. "Look ... Bodach an Stòrr."

The Old Man of Storr was one of the isle's most distinctive landmarks, although it had been a few years since Adaira had seen it last.

"Aye, it does indeed look like a giant's thumb buried in the earth," Lachlann replied. "We're headed in the right direction at least."

They had left the woodland north of Kiltaraglen as the first glow of dawn lit the eastern sky, and pushed onward. It was a day's journey north along the coast to Duntulm.

The morning was tranquil, the loch's waters as still as a polished iron disc. However, it was cold enough that their breaths steamed. The frosty morning air bit into Adaira's face, and she found herself huddling against Lachlann's back for warmth.

Despite that they'd slept sitting up on the hard, root-strewn ground, Adaira had rested better than she had in a long while.

She'd slept the whole night through and only woke up when Lachlann stirred.

"Time to go, Aingeal," he'd murmured in her ear.

She'd awoken to find his arms around her, to find her face pressed up against the hard wall of his chest.

Their gazes had met, and he'd given her a lopsided smile that made her breathing catch. "Did ye sleep well?"

"Aye ... thank ye."

He'd bent his head and kissed her then, a soft, lingering touch that still made fire curl in the pit of Adaira's belly. She'd reached up, her fingertips tracing the line of his stubbled jaw.

Last night had seemed like a dream, but this kiss told her it wasn't so.

However, disappointingly, Lachlann had ended the kiss and risen to his feet. Reaching down, he'd helped Adaira up and brushed leaves out of her hair. "We'd better make a start if ye want to reach Duntulm by nightfall."

He'd turned away then, and crossed to the stallion, readying it to ride out. As soon as his back was turned, Adaira had hurriedly smoothed out her kirtle and brushed more oak leaves from her cloak. She'd suddenly felt self-conscious about her appearance and knew she must look disheveled after sleeping rough.

Lachlann, on the other hand, had never looked more attractive to her. She'd longed to step forward and press herself up against him, to tangle her fingers in his hair as she had the night before.

Now, perched behind Lachlann, she was acutely aware of the strength of his back, the breadth of his shoulders, and the play and flex of the muscles in his thighs.

They rode along the narrow road that hugged Skye's northeastern coast. They left MacLeod lands, riding through the smaller territories belonging to the MacNichols and the MacQueens, before entering MacDonald territory. It was a wild, bare coastline battered by prevailing winds. They passed coastal hamlets, where locals fished the cold waters of the Sound of Raasay, and long stretches of stony beaches where puffins nested. And all the while, a chill wind whipped in from the north, bringing with it the promise of winter.

Adaira was glad of the warmth of Lachlann's body against hers, and of the fact that he sheltered her from the wind. The air bit at her exposed flesh this morning.

They stopped at noon, resting the horse and taking a meal of bread and cheese upon the rocks—supplies Lachlann had picked up in Kiltaraglen.

Lachlann's cheeks were flushed with exertion and cold as he handed Adaira her food. "That's the last of it," he announced. "We'll both be hungry by the time we reach Duntulm."

Adaira smiled. She tried to catch his eye, but he looked away. Was she imagining it or did he seem tense, distracted?

"Caitrin will make sure we eat well, don't worry," she assured him.

Lachlann sat down on the sun-warmed rock beside her. "Ye are very close to yer sisters, aren't ye?"

Adaira nodded. "We are friends as much as siblings ... I miss them both."

A shadow passed across his face, and Adaira grew still. "What is it?"

He shrugged. "Ye are fortunate. Ye have seen how things are in my family."

"Aye ... why don't ye get on with yer brothers?"

Lachlann snorted. "Ye have met them. Lucas is a scheming bastard and the other two aren't much better."

Adaira huffed. "Lucas will inherit now."

"Aye," he growled, frowning. "Don't remind me."

Adaira watched him, her own brow furrowing. She knew how ambitious he'd been. It was difficult to let go of such things.

"What will ye do now?" she asked softly. "Now that ye have given all that up." Her pulse raced as she waited for his response. Last night had changed everything between them; suddenly she had to know what his plans were.

Their gazes fused and held, tension rising between them. Adaira's heart started to thunder against her ribs now.

Lachlann tore his gaze away and looked out across the sound. "I don't know," he said roughly. "My focus for the moment is keeping ye safe."

Adaira swallowed. She hadn't taken a bite of her bread and cheese, for her stomach had suddenly closed. "And after that?" she asked, her voice barely above a whisper.

Lachlann's attention swiveled to her once more. "Things will change soon, Adaira ... once we reach Duntulm, we won't be free to act as we please."

Adaira drew in a deep, steadying breath. "What are ye saying?"

He held her eye. "I won't find a warm welcome with yer sister. I'm an outlaw ... she'll want rid of me."

"We won't have to stay with Caitrin long," Adaira countered, her voice rising slightly. "We don't have to wait. We could cross to the mainland immediately."

"And go where? Ye know Gylen Castle isn't a safe choice."

"It doesn't matter. We'll go somewhere else."

Lachlann's mouth thinned. "Ye deserve better than that."

Adaira stared back at him, sickly panic rising within her. "Are ye going to abandon me?"

Lachlann cursed, rising to his feet and scattering the remnants of his bread and cheese. "No, of course I'm not."

"So what are ye saying then?"

He stared down at her, his face suddenly fierce. "I'd bind ye to me, Aingeal," he said, his voice low and firm. "I'd make ye my wife ... but I have nothing to offer ye but myself. No fortune, no lands. Only a price on my head that makes yer life forfeit as well."

Adaira stared up at him, her gaze widening. "Are ye proposing to me?"

His throat bobbed. "Aye ... and I'm making a mess of it."

Adaira's breathing hitched. "No, ye aren't," she whispered. "Ye have just caught me by surprise. This all seems so sudden."

It was. Just two days earlier she'd hated him, and he'd seemed indifferent to her suffering. It felt like a lifetime ago now though.

Lachlann loosed a deep breath, his gaze never leaving hers. "Time runs against us. I promised to look after ye ... but I fear that soon something, or someone, will stop me."

Adaira swallowed. "Lachlann," she said softly, her vision blurring. "Ye don't have to wed me to keep me safe. I'd never let ye do that."

Lachlann shook his head, his expression turning strained. "What if I told ye that I'm in love with ye?" he rasped. "Would that change things?"

Adaira's lips parted in shock.

"I can't give ye a lady's life," he pressed on. "But I will protect ye ... I will love ye."

Adaira drew in a shaky breath. Her mind whirled as she struggled to take his words in. His proposal, and his declaration, had completely thrown her—and yet underneath the confusion, a warmth welled within her.

Lachlann watched her for a long moment, a nerve feathering in his jaw. When he spoke, his voice was husky. "Will ye be my wife, Adaira MacLeod?"

Adaira drew in a shaky breath. Tears escaped then, spilling down her cheeks, but she smiled through them, joy flowering in her breast. "Aye," she whispered back, "gladly."

Chapter Twenty-three
The Lady of Duntulm

ADAIRA CRANED HER neck to view Duntulm's proud outline against the darkening sky. Perched high upon a basalt cliff, the fortress overlooked a stretch of water called 'The Minch' and the isles of Tulm and Lewis in the distance.

It was a bleak evening; a wind whipped in from the sea, and the sky had turned leaden with the promise of bad weather. Yet the sight of the MacDonald stronghold filled Adaira with such relief that her vision swam with tears.

Caitrin. She'd see her again.

They approached the castle over a hump-backed stone bridge spanning a river and then through Duntulm hamlet. The village was small, little more than a scattering of stone cottages around a central dirt square. The peaked roof of a kirk rose to the south. There were few folk about, just one or two women bringing in washing before the foul weather hit. Adaira breathed in the pungent odor of peat from cook fires and the aroma of what smelled like mutton stew.

Her belly growled in response.

They rode up the hill toward the keep. Adaira couldn't think of any fortress as well defended as Duntulm. The steep cliffs provided protection on three sides while on the landward side a deep ditch surrounded the high curtain wall. Even Dunvegan, although bigger, wasn't as secure.

Peering around Lachlann, Adaira spied the outlines of men in the gloaming as they readied themselves to raise the drawbridge for the evening.

"Wait!" Adaira called out. "We're here to see Lady Caitrin!"

That got the guards' attention. They halted at the sound of Adaira's voice, and the sight of the huge horse bearing down upon them, before shifting back to let them pass.

A moment later the stallion thundered over the drawbridge and into the fortress.

Lachlann swung down from his horse before helping Adaira to the ground. He craned his neck then, taking in the huge basalt keep and tower that reared overhead. This was his first visit to Duntulm. Perched on a lonely cliff top and commanding a view for many furlongs distant, the castle was an impressive sight.

His attention shifted to the steps that led up to the entrance to the keep, where a tall man with long pale-blond hair tied back at the nape of his neck descended. Clad in leather and plaid, his expression forbidding, the warrior reached the bailey courtyard and strode across to greet the newcomers.

"Good evening." His voice was as unfriendly as his expression. "Who are ye, and what business brings ye to Duntulm?"

Lachlann opened his mouth to reply, for he was used to taking charge in situations like this. However, this time he hesitated. His name wasn't one he should be speaking loudly on this island, if at all.

"My name is Lady Adaira MacLeod, and this is my escort," Adaira replied confidently, meeting the warrior's gaze. "I'm here to see my sister."

The man's eyes widened. His expression softened a little. "Lady Adaira ... does yer father know ye are here?"

Adaira's mouth thinned. "No ... and no one is to tell him."

The warrior nodded slowly, his gaze shifting to Lachlann. His expression hardened.

Tensing under the scrutiny, Lachlann knew this man guessed at his identity. The flame-red hair of the Frasers of Skye was well-known on the isle. One glance at him and folk could guess his parentage.

"Does yer escort have a name?" the guard asked, still staring at Lachlann.

"Aye, but it's best I keep it to myself right now," Lachlann answered.

Adaira broke the tense silence that followed, stepping in front of Lachlann so that she drew the man's gaze. "What is *yer* name?"

"I'm Darron MacNichol," he said after a pause, dragging his attention back to Adaira. "Captain of Duntulm Guard."

Adaira raised her chin. "Captain MacNichol ... please take us to my sister."

MacNichol nodded, his face turning grim once more. "Follow me."

The captain led the way into the keep. They crossed a wide entrance hall and began to climb a narrow stone stairwell. On the way up, Lachlann noted how different Duntulm was to his father's fortress. Talasgair was a blend of the past and the present—an ancient broch attached to a newer tower—but Duntulm was an imposing rectangular-shaped keep. The main tower rose four floors high. It was a solid fortress, with walls over two feet thick, and built of the same basalt as the cliffs on which it perched.

MacNichol led them to a solar on the third level of the keep. It was a large chamber with two windows: one looking south over green hills, the other facing north across the sea. A fire roared in the hearth, casting the chamber in a warm glow.

"Wait here," the captain ordered. "Lady Caitrin will be with ye shortly."

He left them alone then. Lachlann and Adaira shared a look. He could see the excitement in her eyes; she couldn't wait to see her sister. However, Lachlann didn't share the feeling. He knew this meeting wasn't going to go as smoothly as Adaira hoped it would.

Reaching out, he stroked her cheek. However, he jerked his hand away when he heard footsteps rapidly approaching outside the solar.

"Adaira!"

Lady Caitrin MacDonald flew through the door and launched herself at her youngest sister.

Lachlann backed up, giving the pair of them space.

Caitrin was as he'd heard her described: tall and willowy with hair the color of sea-foam. Dressed in mourning black, she was a striking sight. It reminded Lachlann of looking upon a frosty morning. Beautiful, yet cold.

A large set of iron keys hung from a girdle around Caitrin's waist, revealing her status here as chatelaine of Duntulm. The keys rattled as she pulled back from Adaira. Tears streaked her face.

"God's Bones, Adi," she gasped. "When I heard ye had run away, I thought ye lost forever."

Adaira wiped away her own tears. "As ye can see, I'm not lost."

Lachlann moved back farther, edging toward the hearth. He was intruding here.

Eyes glittering, Caitrin reached out and stroked Adaira's cheek. "Da scoured the isle looking for ye. He even sent men to Gylen Castle," she said softly, "and when they said ye weren't there either, I imagined the worst."

Caitrin broke off there, her gaze shifting to Lachlann for the first time. The tenderness on her face disappeared, and her gaze narrowed. Although Lachlann hadn't introduced himself to Darron MacNichol, the man would know who he was—and he would have informed his mistress. A Fraser: her father's escaped prisoner.

Caitrin looked back at Adaira, her frown deepening. "Where have ye been all this time?"

Adaira heaved in a deep breath. "Do ye want to sit down?"

Her sister shook her head, folding her arms across her breasts. "I'd prefer to stand—go on."

Adaira cast a look over her shoulder at Lachlann. He could see the concern in her eyes, but Lachlann merely nodded. They both knew this wouldn't end well. It couldn't be helped or avoided though.

Turning back to her sister, Adaira began to speak. And as she did so, Lachlann stood in silence, watching Caitrin's face.

The woman didn't give much away. Yet when Adaira revealed that Lachlann had betrayed her, taking her back to Talasgair rather than to the mainland as promised, Caitrin's expression altered. Her blue eyes hardened, and her jaw tensed.

Adaira pressed on, explaining how she was locked in the tower and informed by Morgan Fraser that she was to become his wife. She chronicled her time at Talasgair, finishing with how Lachlann had freed her on the eve of Samhuinn.

"We hope Morgan Fraser won't follow us here," Adaira concluded, with another glance at Lachlann. "For he'll have to cross MacLeod lands to do so."

Caitrin didn't answer. Her face, even when she looked upon her sister, had gone stony.

Adaira stepped forward, and took one of her sister's clenched hands, squeezing it. "We won't impose on ye for long," she continued. "As soon as it's safe, Lachlann and I will travel to the mainland."

"Ye can't go to Gylen Castle," Caitrin replied, her voice clipped. "Da has left instructions with our uncle to send word if ye ever turn up there."

"Then we'll go somewhere else," Adaira countered. "Will ye give us shelter in the meantime? Da must never know though."

A ponderous silence fell in the solar, broken only by the crackling of the hearth.

Caitrin drew in a long measured breath before she eventually replied. "Of course I will give ye shelter, my sister," she murmured. "Da has stopped searching for ye, for now, so ye should be safe here."

Caitrin then swung her gaze to Lachlann, favoring him with a baleful look.

Lachlann tensed. He knew what was coming next.

"I thank ye for bringing my sister here," she said coldly. "But at first light tomorrow ye will leave Duntulm."

Lachlann held her eye. He hadn't opened his mouth once during the sisters' reunion and knew that to do so now would only damn him. Even so, Lady Caitrin's imperious attitude was starting to chafe.

Adaira surprised him then.

He'd thought she'd appeal to her sister, plead with her. But instead, she moved back and stood next to Lachlann, her arm curling around his waist. Instinctively, he looped his arm over her shoulder in response.

"No," Adaira said softly. "Lachlann stays here ... with me."

The Lady of Duntulm stared at Adaira, her face paling. Her gaze shifted from Adaira to Lachlann as realization dawned. "This man's a self-serving liar," she finally managed. "Ye shouldn't have anything more to do with him."

Adaira shook her head, and when she answered, there was steel in her voice. "*This* man will be my husband soon. We will not be parted."

Chapter Twenty-four

One Chance

CAITRIN'S SLENDER JAW tightened. Adaira could see anger flickering in her sister's eyes, yet she didn't care. A thrill had gone through her as she'd stood up to Caitrin. Like Rhona, her eldest sister had a habit of thinking she knew what was best for her.

Not anymore.

Caitrin heaved in a deep breath and smoothed her hands upon her skirts. Then, her attention settled upon Lachlann. "Can ye give me a few moments alone with my sister?"

Lachlann inclined his head before nodding. Adaira tensed and looked up at him, but he merely smiled. "I should see to my horse," he murmured. Reaching down, he gave Adaira's hand a gentle squeeze.

With a nod to Caitrin, he left the solar.

Silence followed him.

Caitrin waited a few moments before she pinned Adaira with a hard look. "Please tell me ye haven't lain with him?"

Adaira held her gaze. Her first instinct was to deny the accusation—what business was it of Caitrin's anyway? But then stubbornness intervened. She'd not lie or pretend she was ashamed of what had passed between her and Lachlann.

However, she didn't need to say anything. Her face told the whole story.

Caitrin groaned and ran a hand over her face. "Satan's Cods, no!" Her sister then crossed to the mantelpiece and poured herself a goblet of wine, which she took a large gulp from before turning on Adaira. "Why?"

"Because I wanted to."

"But he *betrayed* ye." Caitrin shook her head as if she couldn't believe her ears. "He gave ye to his father … a man who would have made ye his whore."

The harshness of her sister's words made Adaira flinch. Caitrin had changed. Time was, she'd never have said such things. "Morgan Fraser never touched me."

Caitrin glared at her. Her face was ashen, with high spots of color upon her cheekbones. "Aye … but his son has."

"And I welcomed his touch."

"Ye are too trusting. Rhona and I always warned ye that some man would take advantage of it … and the worst sort has!"

"Enough!" Adaira's temper finally snapped. Caitrin spoke to her as if she was an empty-headed goose. She'd not tolerate it a moment longer. "Ye think ye know me, but ye don't. I have the wits to know a good man from a bad one."

Caitrin's eyes grew huge, and she drew back as if Adaira had just slapped her. "I'm just trying to protect ye," she replied, a rasp to her voice. "I thought ye were dead. And then ye turn up alive and well, with this awful tale. How do ye expect me to react?"

"I expect ye to listen to me. To trust my word."

"But that man's a Fraser! He's—"

"Going to be my husband. He loves me, Caitrin."

Adaira moved over to the hearth and sank down into a chair. Her legs felt weak. Caitrin muttered an oath and took a seat opposite. Her fingers clenched around the stem of the goblet she clutched. Watching her, Adaira noted the lines of tension that bracketed her sister's mouth. Despite that he'd been dead over three months now, her marriage to Baltair MacDonald had taken its toll. Adaira had little idea of what Caitrin had endured during the two years she'd been wedded, for her eldest sister kept her own counsel, yet the change in Caitrin spoke volumes.

"Love is the easy part," Caitrin murmured, staring into the fire. "But what happens when ye are living rough, eight months gone with a bairn? Will love fill yer belly and keep ye warm when ye are both living on gruel in the midst of winter?"

"Lachlann knows how to survive," Adaira replied tightly, "and I'm not completely useless either."

Caitrin favored her with a condescending look that made Adaira's anger rise once more. Caitrin had often resorted to such expressions when Adaira said or did things she thought immature.

Leaning forward, Adaira held her sister's eye boldly. "I'm not who I was, Caitrin. I'll never be a lady now ... not like ye." Her voice was low and steady, even if her heart raced. "For the first time in my life, I can choose my own path. Ye of all people should understand what that means."

Caitrin stared back at her. The scorn drained from her face, replaced by a fragility Adaira had never seen before. Her eyes glistened, and for a moment, it seemed she would weep. Then, Caitrin inhaled deeply, mastering her reaction. "But are ye sure of him?" she asked finally, a husky edge to her voice. "I also know what it means to make the wrong choice."

"Lachlann understands me, and I know he'll keep me safe." Adaira's mouth curved into a soft smile. "I'm happy to be an outlaw's bride."

Lachlann stared at Caitrin, shock filtering through him. "We have yer blessing?"

Caitrin loosed a sigh before nodding. "Adaira and I have spoken ... at length ... and although I still don't fully understand her choice, I will respect it—for her sake."

The evening was drawing out, and the three of them sat at the table in Caitrin's solar. A simple supper of bread, cheese, salted pork, and apples lay before them. Lachlann had warily taken his seat at the table, expecting another attack from the Lady of Duntulm. But instead, she'd informed him that he could stay on and that she no longer opposed their marriage.

Lachlann cast Adaira a look of disbelief. What magic had she woven here?

In response, Adaira flashed Lachlann a small smile before reaching across and placing her hand over his. Lachlann turned his hand over and laced his fingers through Adaira's. Then he turned his attention back to Caitrin, meeting her eye. "I do love yer sister."

Caitrin pursed her lips. "So she says."

"I *will* make her my wife."

A groove formed between Caitrin's delicately drawn brows. "Aye, on that we are both agreed. The sooner ye wed the better."

Lachlann raised his eyebrows before glancing at Adaira. Seeing her pink cheeks, he realized Caitrin knew what had passed between them. Adaira's sister would be worried he'd planted a bairn in her womb.

The thought had crossed his mind as well.

Lachlann met Caitrin's eye, favoring her with a wry smile. If she wanted them to wed in haste, he wasn't going to discourage her. "Do ye have a date in mind, Lady Caitrin?"

She nodded. "The day after tomorrow. Ye can be wed in Duntulm village kirk. I shall call for the priest."

"That went better than I thought," Lachlann admitted as he escorted Adaira to her chamber later that evening. "I expected Lady Caitrin to have me stoned out of Duntulm."

"I just needed to have a quiet word with her." Adaira glanced up at him, smiling. "Caitrin isn't unreasonable."

Lachlann raised an eyebrow. "She glared at me all through supper. I think she expects I'll abandon ye at the altar."

Adaira huffed. "No, she doesn't … she'll warm to ye eventually."

"Aye, perhaps—but not any day soon."

They reached a wooden door framed by a stone arch, and Adaira halted. She turned to Lachlann, raising her chin so she could meet his eye. He gazed down at her before reaching out and caressing her cheek. His thumb slid along her plump lower lip and desire quickened his breath. Adaira had a lush mouth that was made for kissing.

"Would ye mind if I shared yer bed tonight?" he murmured, his gaze still riveted upon her mouth.

"Best not," Adaira replied, her voice husky. "Caitrin's had a chamber prepared for ye … downstairs."

"What about a goodnight kiss then?"

"Very well," Adaira breathed, "just one."

Lachlann's mouth curved. Leaning down, he brushed his lips over Adaira's—once, twice—and then he parted her lips with his tongue. Her answering gasp inflamed him. He loved how responsive Adaira was. Her soft moans and gasps excited him beyond measure, as did the way she melted under his touch.

God, how he longed to carry her into that chamber and tear her clothes off. Last night he'd been frustrated by the layers of wool, leather, and linen that separated their bodies. It had been too cold to strip, but he ached to see her naked.

Just two more nights, he reminded himself as he tore his mouth from Adaira's, *and then she's mine.*

"Wicked temptress." Lachlann braced himself against the door and pushed back. Adaira stared up at him from within the cage of his arms. Her hazel eyes were luminous, her lips slightly parted. He stifled a groan. When she looked at him like that it was difficult to keep a leash on his self-control. "I should go then."

"Good night, Lachlann." The hoarse edge to her voice made him ache to take her right there up against the door.

The thought sobered him. Lady Caitrin would definitely cast him out of Duntulm for such an act.

"Sleep well, Aingeal," he replied, stepping away from her. "I shall see ye in the morning."

Chapter Twenty-five

Ill-timing

ADAIRA PICKED UP Eoghan from his crib. "How he's grown," she murmured, holding the bairn against her breast as she turned to Caitrin. "What are ye feeding the lad?"

Caitrin huffed. "Just milk for now, but he's a hungry bairn."

Adaira glanced down at Eoghan's thick thatch of dark hair. Not for the first time, she felt a jolt. Even though he was still a babe, Eoghan MacDonald looked so much like his father it was eerie. Baltair MacDonald had been very handsome to look upon, and Adaira could see that one day his son would rival him in looks. A shadow of misgiving fell over her then, as she stared down at the bairn's chubby face. His sea-blue eyes were his mother's. But would he inherit her or his father's character?

Adaira carried Eoghan over to where a large log burned in the hearth. After the drama of the day before, it now felt peaceful inside the solar. Caitrin was seated at the table, bent over a huge leather-bound ledger as she went through Duntulm's accounts. Alban MacLean, the castle's steward, sat at her side, looking over the chatelaine's shoulder as she copied down the sums he read to her from scrappy leaves of parchment.

"No, milady," he corrected her quietly. "It was thirty sacks of oats we bought from MacLeod this year, not forty."

Muttering an oath under her breath, Caitrin dipped her quill into the pot of ink beside her and corrected the ledger.

Oblivious to Caitrin and Alban's discussion, Lachlann perched on a window seat. It was early afternoon, and although the chill wind had died outside, the sky was grey. Even so, Lachlann seemed content to sit there and gaze upon the view to the south, across the hills that stretched over MacDonald lands. His expression was pensive, his gaze veiled.

Adaira could see he was deep in thought so she didn't disturb him. Instead, she allowed herself to study the man who'd soon become her husband.

Dressed in clean braies and a loose léine belted at the waist, his red hair brushed out over his shoulders, Lachlann entranced her. He'd shaved, and she admired now the clean, strong line of his jaw.

Her belly fluttered as she imagined trailing her lips along it.

This time tomorrow she'd be his wife.

Eoghan squirmed in her arms, his tiny chubby hands reaching up and tangling in her hair. Distracted, Adaira gently pried his fingers free before placing a kiss on the top of his head. His hair was downy and sweet-smelling.

Adaira closed her eyes a moment. Happiness flowed through her, its warmth suffusing her like a hot bath on a cold winter's day. One day, she'd hold her and Lachlann's bairn in her arms. One day, they'd have a family together. She could hardly believe this was real, that soon he'd be her husband.

A tremor of misgiving curled in the base of her belly. After the events of the past months, she wasn't used to things working in her favor. She worried that this happiness would somehow be ripped from her grasp.

At the window, Lachlann shifted.

Adaira yanked her thoughts back to the present and saw that he was frowning. "What is it?"

He tore his gaze from the view, to where Duntulm's chatelaine sat, her brow furrowed as she scratched out sums onto the ledger. "Lady Caitrin, ye have visitors."

"Really?" Caitrin placed the quill in its pot and rose gracefully to her feet. "I'm not expecting anyone." She moved toward the window, Alban and Adaira following her.

Adaira stopped by Lachlann's shoulder, her gaze moving past him to the rumpled blanket of green hills beyond. Sure enough, a large company of riders approached. From this distance, they were tiny, appearing like a column of marching ants. As the four of them watched, Adaira made out the outlines of banners.

Her breathing faltered. What if Morgan Fraser had tracked them north after all?

Beside her, Caitrin drew in a sharp breath. "It's Da."

Cold washed over Adaira, while Lachlann tensed. He tore his gaze from the approaching riders and met Caitrin's eye. "Are ye sure?"

Caitrin nodded, her jaw firming. "The standards bear the MacLeod plaid."

Adaira stared out across the hills, her own gaze narrowing. A moment later she too recognized the gold, grey, and black of her family's plaid.

The warmth of wellbeing that had cocooned her since the day before fell away, and a wave of panic rose. "We can't stay here," she choked. "We have to go ... now."

Caitrin shook her head. "It's too late. They'll see." She reached out and took Eoghan from Adaira. The bairn squawked, sensing the shift in mood. "Ye are going to have to hide while he's here." Caitrin turned her attention briefly to Alban. "Warn Darron and the others not to breathe a word."

"Aye, milady," the steward replied, his heavy featured face creasing with consternation.

Caitrin nodded her thanks and moved away from the window. She then motioned to Adaira and Lachlann. "Follow me."

Caitrin smoothed her damp palms upon the skirts of her black kirtle. She hoped her nervousness didn't show on her face, that her father wouldn't see through her brittle smile of welcome.

Malcolm MacLeod was the last person she wished to see right now.

Standing in the bailey, she watched her father's banner-men ride in through the gate, their horses' hooves thundering over the drawbridge. Suddenly, Duntulm's bailey was filled with them. Alban stood at Caitrin's right shoulder, while Darron flanked her left side. Their silent, stoic presence calmed her, reminded her that she was in charge here.

Her father would not intimidate her.

Clan-chief MacLeod was easy to spot: a broad, thick-legged figure with a wild mane of greying auburn hair and a beard to match. He rode a heavy-set destrier, a beast strong enough to carry his weight.

Caitrin's gaze narrowed. It was nearly two moons since she'd seen her father last, and he'd grown even fatter than she remembered. Una rode into the keep behind him, dark and fey-looking, her blue-eyed gaze sharp.

Caitrin's breath caught when she spotted two familiar faces behind them.

A big man with short blond hair and a scarred face rode through the archway, with a fire-haired beauty at his side: Taran and Rhona.

Joy exploded within Caitrin's breast, and she realized how lonely she'd been of late. Her nervousness forgotten, she hurried forward to greet them.

Rhona reached her first. Her sister swung down off her chestnut mare and rushed at Caitrin. They hugged, and when Rhona pulled away, her grey eyes were shining.

"I've missed ye," she greeted her. "With both ye and Adaira gone, the keep feels so empty."

At the mention of their youngest sister, Rhona's joy dimmed. Caitrin hadn't spoken to Rhona since Adaira's disappearance. But since Adaira had explained everything, Caitrin now knew that Rhona and Taran had helped her escape.

Rhona would be wondering why they'd never arrived in Argyle.

"Ye look well, daughter," Malcolm MacLeod boomed as he lumbered over to them. "Although black washes ye out."

Caitrin's mouth thinned. She would have to wear black for a while yet.

"Good day, Da," she greeted him with a kiss. His whiskers tickled her cheek. "What brings ye all to Duntulm? Had I known, I'd have had a feast prepared for this evening."

"Can't a man pay his daughter a surprise visit?" he rumbled.

"We've all missed ye," Rhona spoke up with a smile.

Taran had stepped up next to her, acknowledging Caitrin with a nod. "We thought a visit north was in order," he added. "Before the bitter weather sets in."

"Ye are all welcome," Caitrin replied, keeping a smile plastered on her face. However, inwardly she cursed their ill-timing. Duntulm wasn't as big as Dunvegan; it wouldn't be easy to keep Adaira and Lachlann hidden. She'd found them lodgings next to the kitchens, in two tiny chambers usually occupied by servants.

It was away from the main keep, and somewhere that Malcolm MacLeod was unlikely to go without good reason.

"Good to hear, lass," MacLeod boomed. "Now, enough chatter. Lead the way to the Great Hall, and open a barrel of yer finest ale. I've got a plague of a thirst."

Chapter Twenty-six

Soft-hearted

"STILL NO WORD of Adaira?" Caitrin took a sip of wine and surveyed her father over the rim of her goblet. She was reluctant to bring her sister up but thought her family might get suspicious if she did not.

"No." Malcolm MacLeod was onto his third cup of ale and was showing no sign of slowing. His face turned thunderous. "I've sent men out far and wide," he growled, "but it's as if she was taken by fairies. The only place we haven't searched is Talasgair itself. If I ever find Lachlann Fraser, I'll rip his head off with my bare hands."

Caitrin nodded, schooling her face into a grave expression. Her father's blustering and threats were commonplace whenever he mentioned his escaped prisoner; only, he had no idea that the man he hunted was hiding in this very keep.

Trying not to think of the chaos that would ensue if her father ever found out, Caitrin glanced across at where Rhona sat. Her sister looked so sad that Caitrin's chest constricted. Rhona needed to know Adaira was safe. Somehow, she had to find a way to tell her.

They sat upon the raised dais at the far end of the Great Hall, a spread of food before them. The servants had pulled what they could from the larder, while cook was furiously preparing some apple and bramble tarts to serve later with thick cream.

"Excellent drop this." Her father wiped his mouth with a meaty hand. "The MacDonalds know how to brew a good ale."

Caitrin frowned. Her father had deliberately changed the subject. He wasn't here to talk about Adaira it seemed. Malcolm MacLeod did nothing by chance. She didn't doubt that Rhona had missed her, but there would be something behind her father's visit.

As if sensing her suspicions, MacLeod fixed her with that level iron-grey stare she knew so well.

"We need to speak of yer future, Caitrin."

Her heart sinking, Caitrin held his eye. "Aye, and what of it?" She knew her tone was surly, yet she didn't care. She was getting used to being the chatelaine of Duntulm and didn't wish for things to change.

"Ye are young and fair, daughter. In time, ye must wed again."

Caitrin drew in a long, steadying breath. Next to Caitrin, Rhona cast her a sympathetic look. They both knew what Malcolm MacLeod was like when it came to finding his daughters husbands. An unwed daughter was a millstone around his neck, a burden he had to rid himself of.

"And in time, I might," she replied. It was a lie. As she felt right now, she never wished to be shackled to another man.

"Have ye heard of our defeat against the English?" MacLeod's face screwed up as he asked this, as if the subject was deeply distasteful—but necessary.

"Aye," Caitrin replied. She doubted there was a soul upon the isle who'd not heard. He must think her a hermit.

"Many Scots died in that battle," her father continued, still scowling. "None of the MacLeods who joined King David have returned yet ... few will."

Caitrin frowned. He was leading up to something.

"Baltair's younger brother joined the king, did he not?" Una spoke up. She sat at Malcolm's side, a goblet of wine in hand. She wore a sanguine expression. However, her blue eyes were assessing.

"Alasdair," Caitrin replied. "He joined the army before Baltair and I wed, and hasn't been back to Skye since. I know not where he is."

"I sent word to him after Baltair's death," her father rumbled. He was watching Caitrin with a penetrating look now. "If he lives, he will return to claim his rightful role as chieftain. He will no longer need yer services as chatelaine. Ye will have to return to Dunvegan."

Caitrin swallowed. "And if Alasdair MacDonald never returns? There are no other heirs."

"Then ye remain Lady of Duntulm," Rhona piped up with a grin. She raised her chalice to her sister. "Here's to that, dear sister."

Malcolm MacLeod glowered at them. "No, she won't. One of the MacDonalds of Sleat will step into the breach. Like it or not, Caitrin, ye will still have to wed again."

"Don't worry." Una favored Caitrin with a sweet smile. "We'll begin a search for a suitable husband for ye upon our return to Dunvegan."

Caitrin swallowed a cutting reply. It wouldn't do her any good to start an argument with Una or her father; Malcolm had a fiery temper, and when riled wouldn't let a subject drop. Best to be quietly defiant, as she'd always been.

"Apple and bramble tarts, milady." A servant appeared at Caitrin's elbow, bearing a huge platter of fragrant sweets.

"Thank ye, Galiene," Caitrin responded with a smile. Never had she been so grateful to have a conversation interrupted. "Please, serve them."

Galiene, an older woman who helped Duntulm's cook prepare meals, began to circuit the table, serving Malcolm first.

Seeing her father was distracted, Caitrin leaned toward her sister. "I need to speak to ye," she whispered. "As soon as supper's over, meet me outside the kitchen."

Adaira walked into the kitchen to find Caitrin, Rhona, and Taran waiting. Her step faltered at the sight of them, joy exploding within her.

"Rhona!"

She flew across the kitchen and crushed her elder sister in a fierce hug.

Pulling back from the embrace, Adaira saw that Rhona's eyes glittered with tears. However, her face appeared frozen in surprise. "Adi ... what are ye doing here?" she gasped.

Likewise, Taran appeared floored. His ice-blue gaze searched Adaira's face before it shifted to where Lachlann had stepped up behind her. Taran's expression then hardened.

It was warm in the kitchen, the air fragrant with the aroma of baking. The old cook had stepped outside with her assistants, leaving the party alone. It had been a nervous wait in their chambers. Caitrin had told Adaira and Lachlann she would meet them in the kitchen after supper. They had waited a long while before the cook knocked on the door and whispered that it was safe to come out.

Sensing the shift in mood, the sudden tension in the air, Adaira stepped back so that she and Lachlann stood shoulder to shoulder. She glanced up at him, and their gazes fused for a moment.

Lachlann then swung his attention back to Rhona and Taran. "After Adaira and I left Dunvegan we made our way to Kiltaraglen, where I stole a boat," he began without preamble. "However, instead of taking her to Argyle, I brought her back home with me ... to

Talasgair." Lachlann paused here, drew in a deep breath, and plowed on. "I wanted to get home fast, in case my father died and one of my brothers took his place as chieftain. At the time I didn't spare a thought for Adaira. It was only later—when my father announced he planned to wed Adaira at Samhuinn—that I began to realize what a grave mistake I'd made. On the eve of their wedding, I helped her escape ... and here we are."

Silence followed his words. Eventually, Taran finally broke it, his voice wintry. "Ye swore a promise to see Adaira safely to Gylen Castle ... upon yer life. Don't deny it, for I heard ye speak the words."

"I don't deny it," Lachlann replied, "I swore an oath ... and I broke it."

"I told ye what would happen if ye failed to uphold yer end of the bargain, Fraser."

Lachlann frowned. "Aye, and I warned ye not to threaten me."

"Dog!"

In an instant, Taran was on him. A large hand clamped over Lachlann's throat. Taran slammed him backward, and they crashed onto the large scrubbed oaken table that dominated the heart of the kitchen.

"Taran!" Adaira cried out, lunging toward where the two men now wrestled. "Stop it!"

She never reached him, for Rhona grabbed her and hauled her back. "Leave them," she bit out. "That Fraser bastard deserves it."

"No, he doesn't! He—"

The sound of shattering pottery echoed through the kitchen. Lachlann had just grabbed a jug and broken it over Taran's head.

Taran roared and punched Lachlann in the face. An instant later Lachlann arched up under him and drove his knee into Taran's belly. Fists flew as the two men rolled down the table, sending cups and bowls flying.

In the midst of the chaos, Caitrin approached them and threw a pail of water over the brawlers.

"Enough!" she shouted. "Ye will not destroy my kitchen!"

Dripping wet, Taran pushed himself up off the table and wiped the water out of his eyes. Next to him, Lachlann sat up and massaged his jaw, his expression murderous.

Taran cast Adaira a despairing look. "Ye are far too softhearted, lass. Lachlann Fraser can't be trusted."

Adaira glared back at him. She yanked against Rhona's grip, but her sister held her fast. "Lachlann Fraser and I are to be wed tomorrow."

Rhona let go of her so suddenly that Adaira nearly toppled over. She caught herself on the table edge and turned to face her sister. Rhona's face had gone pale, her features taut. "Have ye lost yer wits?"

Adaira clenched her jaw, refusing to answer. However, she could feel anger rising within her like steam off a boiling cauldron of water.

Rhona's attention snapped to her elder sister. "Did ye know about this?"

"Aye," Caitrin replied, her face pained. "I've organized for the priest to wed them in the village kirk tomorrow morning."

Rhona's gaze narrowed. "Ye have been helping them?"

Caitrin nodded.

Rhona cast Caitrin a look of disgust before she rounded on Adaira. "I don't understand."

"Ye don't need to." Lachlann had climbed off the table and now stepped up next to Adaira. He took her hand, his fingers lacing through hers tenderly; yet his face was hard. "This isn't yer life, or yer choice to make. If Adaira doesn't want to wed me then let that be *her* decision."

Silence fell in the kitchen.

Rhona swallowed before shifting her gaze to Adaira. Staring into her elder sister's storm-grey eyes, Adaira glimpsed her hurt, her confusion. Rhona wasn't being malicious. She truly was at a loss. "Is this really what ye want?" Rhona asked finally, her voice catching.

Adaira leaned into Lachlann, finding solace in the warm heat of his body pressed into her side. However, her gaze never left Rhona's. "Aye," she whispered.

Chapter Twenty-seven

Blood of My Blood

"WHAT ARE YE doing today, daughter?"

Caitrin glanced up from buttering a piece of bannock and favored her father with what she hoped was a serene smile. "I always take bread and sweet buns down to the villagers on Wednesdays," she replied.

He huffed. "Can't they make their own bread?"

Caitrin's smile widened. "Aye, Da ... but it's a tradition that Baltair's father began years ago. I like to continue it. It's good for me to talk with the folk here, to learn what they need from me."

Una gave a soft snort. She'd been daintily nibbling a bannock, but now lowered it. She viewed Caitrin with a shrewd look. "Ye think yerself a chieftain now, do ye, Caitrin?"

Malcolm MacLeod chortled at this, although Caitrin stiffened. "No ... I'm chatelaine."

"Aye, that's right," her father rumbled, his grey eyes still shining with mirth. "And soon Duntulm will have a new chieftain, and ye will be wed again."

Caitrin's pulse quickened. She hated her father discussing her future like this. She'd thought once she became Baltair's wife that her father's interference in her affairs was over, but now she was a widow he'd made her his business once more.

Her fingers tightened around the hilt of the knife she was using. She was so tired of men deciding her fate.

Glancing right, she caught Rhona's eye. Her sister watched her with a knowing look. Few understood how she felt, but Rhona and Adaira did, for both their lives had nearly been ruined by Malcolm MacLeod's controlling ways.

"Taran and I are taking a ride along the coast this morning," Rhona announced lightly. "We thought we'd make the most of the sun before it leaves us again."

"Ye are *all* abandoning me," Malcolm MacLeod grumbled. "What am I supposed to do this morning while ye are out?"

It was Caitrin's turn to utter a soft laugh. "Ye will hardly notice our absence, father. Put yer feet up in Baltair's solar and take a well-earned rest. I'm sure Una can entertain ye." She cast her stepmother a look as she spoke, enjoying the way Una's mouth pursed, before continuing. "Later, we'll eat together."

Duntulm village kirk was a stone building with a steep gable roof and a tiny belfry. Constructed of local basalt, the kirk squatted at the southern edge of the village.

Its silhouette, set against a cornflower-blue sky, was a welcoming sight to Adaira. She and Lachlann hurried toward it, cutting through the windswept kirk-yard and the rows of tombstones that surrounded the building.

Lachlann squeezed her hand as they approached the heavy wooden doors. "Nervous?"

"Aye," she admitted, glancing across at his hooded face. He'd pulled the cowl forward so his face was cast completely in shadow; it was impossible to read his expression. "I can't believe this is happening," she murmured. "What about ye?"

He gave her hand another squeeze before reaching out to push open the door. "My guts are in knots."

Adaira smiled. It gave her solace to know he was as nervous as she was.

The awful scene with Rhona and Taran yesterday evening had put her on edge. The conflict had been resolved, but the memory of it had cast a shadow over Adaira's mood. There had been a moment when Adaira had felt despair touch her heart. She didn't want her union with Lachlann to cause a rift between her and her sisters.

And not only that, but her father perched up in Duntulm keep like a giant vulture ready to swoop.

Adaira hadn't been able to sleep for the worry that he'd ruin everything.

But he hadn't. Here they were, entering Dunvegan kirk, and beginning a new life together. The worst was behind them.

Stepping inside the kirk, Lachlann heaved his shoulder against the heavy door and pushed it shut at his back.

A gentle silence greeted the couple, as did the scent of incense and the faint whiff of tallow from the banks of candles lining the walls. Two rows of wooden benches led up to a raised altar. A small party stood beneath it: Caitrin, Rhona, and Taran—and a man Adaira had never seen before. Small and balding, and wearing dark robes, the priest watched them approach.

Adaira's slippered feet whispered on the flagstones. Above her rose a ceiling of wooden beams, and at each end of the kirk, high tear-drop-shaped windows let in the morning sun.

Adaira and Lachlann stopped before the altar and pushed back their hoods. Meeting Caitrin's eye, Adaira flashed her a smile. She had much to thank her eldest sister for. Caitrin was still dressed in mourning black, although her expression was soft this morning; she almost looked like the girl she'd once been. Back before Baltair MacDonald wed her.

Adaira's attention shifted to Rhona. She hadn't been sure her sister—or Taran—would attend the handfasting. Yet they'd both promised, and here they were. And unlike the day before, Adaira could see no anger in their faces or wariness in their eyes.

Dressed in flowing green, her fiery hair pulled back in a long braid, Rhona favored Adaira with a soft smile. Beside her, Taran nodded at Adaira. However, he cast Lachlann a cool, assessing look.

Adaira suppressed a sigh. Lachlann and Taran weren't likely to be fast friends, but at least they were no longer enemies.

Wordlessly, Adaira and Lachlann shrugged off the heavy cloaks they'd worn for the walk down from the castle. The clothing they wore underneath was quite plain for a handfasting. Lachlann wore leather braies and a clean white léine and Adaira a simple green kirtle. However, this morning Caitrin had woven some wildflowers into her hair.

Lachlann looked down at her, favoring her with a soft smile. "Ye look bonny, Adaira."

She smiled back, suddenly shy.

"Are ye ready?" The priest's gentle voice interrupted them.

Adaira shifted her attention to him, studying the man who would wed them. He had a harried yet kind face, and a heavy wooden crucifix hung around his neck.

"Aye, Father," Lachlann spoke up. "Je suis prest." He broke off here and winked at Adaira. "We're *both* ready."

"Please step forward then and join hands."

Adaira and Lachlann did as bid. The feel of Lachlann's fingers entwining through hers, the heat and strength of his touch, caused the thudding of her heart to calm slightly.

The priest stepped close. He held a length of plaid in his hands, MacDonald colors: green and blue threaded with white and red. He began to wind the plaid around their joined hands while he spoke the words that would join them.

Adaira's vision misted as she listened to him. And when it came to the part where they had to recite their vows to each other, she gave up trying to stem her tears. They flowed silently down her cheeks, as Lachlann recited the words, his gaze upon hers.

"Ye are Blood of my Blood, and Bone of my Bone.
I give ye my Body, that we Two might be One.
I give ye my Spirit, 'til our Life shall be Done."

When the vows were completed, the priest unwrapped the plaid that joined them. "Ye are now man and wife," he said with a smile that made the corners of his eyes crinkle. "May yer union be blessed."

Lachlann pulled Adaira into his arms and kissed her soundly. When they drew apart, they were both breathless, and Adaira's pulse beat like a drum in her ears. Still in the cradle of Lachlann's arms, she turned her head back to where her sisters stood. She hadn't looked at them once since the ceremony had begun, for her entire attention had been upon Lachlann.

Rhona was weeping openly, tears streaming down her face. She clutched Taran's arm, as if for support. Caitrin stood quietly next to her. She too wept, but in a gentle, reserved way.

When Adaira and Caitrin's gazes met, her sister's mouth curved in a tremulous smile. "That was beautiful," Caitrin said huskily. "Thank ye for letting me be part—"

Boom.

The kirk doors flew open, crashing against the wall. The entire building shuddered in the impact.

Adaira gasped. She went rigid in Lachlann's arms. His embrace tightened as their gazes swung back to the doors.

A heavy-set figure with wild auburn hair, and an even wilder expression, limped into the kirk, followed by four burly warriors. Una hurried into the kirk behind them.

"Stop this handfasting!" Malcolm MacLeod roared, his voice echoing high into the rafters. "I forbid it!"

Chapter Twenty-eight
The Heart Decides

"YE CAN'T FORBID it," Lachlann replied, his voice ringing out across the kirk. "It's already done. We're now husband and wife."

The sight of Malcolm MacLeod, the man who'd thrown him down into the dungeon to die, and who was now trying to ruin his life once more, made fury rise within Lachlann. How had MacLeod learned of this ceremony?

However, it didn't matter—he was too late.

"Bastard Fraser whelp!" MacLeod limped up to the altar and stopped before them, meaty hands clenched at his side. "How dare ye. No Fraser is wedding one of my daughters—not now, not *ever*."

"I'm sorry ... but they are wed in the sight of God," the priest spoke up timidly. "Ye cannot undo it."

The look the MacLeod clan-chief bestowed upon the priest was so venomous that the small man wilted. His throat bobbed, and he cast Lachlann a pleading look.

Lachlann kept his arm firmly around Adaira as he faced her father. He could feel her fear, the rigidity of her body.

"Da," Rhona spoke up. "Please don't—"

"Silence!" Spittle flew as MacLeod roared. "I'll deal with ye and Taran later. Do ye think the windows of Duntulm keep are blind? Una saw ye two ride off earlier. Only ye didn't take the coast road as ye said. Instead, ye rode directly here." His gaze swiveled to Caitrin, pinning her to the spot. "And ye, lying vixen. Ye carry no basket of bread. Ye hurried straight through the village to the kirk. Una saw it all."

Lachlann drew in a long breath. So, it was his former stepmother who had betrayed them.

Una MacLeod was staring at him, a look of naked victory upon her face. He hadn't seen her in a few years. There were no signs of age upon her; she looked exactly as she had when she'd lived at Talasgair. She was small and dark, with elfin looks. Her eyes were just as sly as he remembered too.

"Stop it, Da," Adaira finally gasped. "None of this matters. Lachlann and I have pledged our lives to each other. Ye can't change it now."

Adaira's words impressed Lachlann. The lass had courage. She was terrified of her father, and yet she faced him.

Malcolm MacLeod hadn't been expecting such a proclamation. He jerked back as if she'd just struck him across the face. Even Una's smirk faded. However, the shock only lasted a moment. MacLeod recovered swiftly.

"Lachlann Fraser is my prisoner," he snarled, his neck stretching out as he glared at her. "And ye are my daughter and will do as ye are bid. Both of ye are coming back to Dunvegan."

Lachlann let go of Adaira and stepped forward, going toe-to-toe with MacLeod. "Yer daughter freed me because she was desperate," he growled. "What kind of father promises a lass like Adaira to the likes of Aonghus Budge?"

MacLeod's heavy-featured face screwed up. "Don't tell me what—"

"I'll tell ye what kind," Lachlann cut in savagely. How he longed to lash out at this man. They were standing so close he could smell the wine on the clan-chief's breath.

"A tyrant who thinks nothing of sacrificing his youngest daughter."

The clan-chief roared and lunged for him.

Lachlann had been anticipating the attack. Even so, he hadn't expected such an overweight man to move so fast.

MacLeod's knuckles grazed Lachlann's ear as he ducked.

Lachlann brought up his arm and caught the chieftain's wrist, holding him fast. He barely managed; the man had fearsome strength. He had wrists twice the width of Lachlann's own.

MacLeod snarled a curse and threw his entire weight at Lachlann, slamming into him. They went down on the flagstone floor of the kirk.

Adaira's scream echoed through the building, but neither man paid her any attention. Lachlann was locked in a fight for his life; he didn't dare spare her a glance. Yesterday, when Taran had attacked him, Lachlann had been impressed by the warrior's brute strength. Yet it appeared insignificant to that of Malcolm MacLeod.

Incensed, MacLeod pummeled at him with huge fists, his bulk pinning Lachlann to the floor.

"Stop this," the priest cried, panicked. "This is a house of God. There can be no violence here!"

MacLeod ignored him. Bellowing curses, he slammed his fist into Lachlann's jaw.

Lachlann managed to get his legs free. He drove his knee up into MacLeod's gut. The big man gave a choking gasp and fell sideways. It was an instant's distraction, but all Lachlann needed. He reared up and head-butted the clan-chief in the nose.

MacLeod roared, blood spurting. But instead of quieting him, the blow seemed to drive him to madness. He came at Lachlann, grabbed him around the throat, and threw him backward.

The back of Lachlann's skull hit the flagstones with a crack. His vision darkened for an instant. But when MacLeod's fingers started to tighten around his throat, Lachlann fought him. The madness in the clan-chief's grey eyes, as he loomed above Lachlann, warned him that MacLeod was intent on killing him.

He grappled with the hands around his throat, grabbed hold of the little finger of MacLeod's right hand, and yanked it back.

The crack of breaking bone sliced through the air.

Malcolm MacLeod gave a shout of agony and let go of him. Lachlann rolled away, choking, before bouncing up into a crouching position. The back of his skull ached, as did his throat, but he was ready for the bastard, should he come at him again.

MacLeod glowered at him, tears of pain glittering in his eyes. Then he drew his dirk with his left hand. "I'm going to gut ye, Fraser."

"No!"

A small body hurtled in between them.

"Adaira!"

Lachlann reached for her arm, but she ducked out of his grasp. Instead, she faced her father, stepping forward so that the sharp tip of his dirk nearly touched her breast.

"Get back, Adaira," MacLeod ordered, biting out the words. "Don't interfere."

She shook her head, her gaze never leaving his. "No, Da. Not until ye promise to let Lachlann be."

"Foolish lass." His voice was a low, threatening growl. "Don't ever stand in my way. Once I deal with Fraser, I'll find a suitable punishment for ye."

"No!" Her voice lashed across the kirk. Lachlann saw the high spots of color that had appeared on her cheeks. She wasn't just upset, she was incensed. "I can't live the life ye have chosen for me. Let me be free ... let me be happy with the man I love."

Lachlann's breathing hitched. He stepped forward, reaching for Adaira's arm, but a strong hand clasped around his shoulder and hauled him back. He twisted to see Taran behind him. The warrior's scarred face was grim. "Leave her," he warned, his voice low. "Let Adaira finish this."

Malcolm MacLeod's slate-grey gaze narrowed. "He's a *Fraser*," he spat. "Why did ye have to fall in love with one of them?"

Did Lachlann imagine it, or was there a quaver to the man's voice? The madness was gone from his eyes. They now glittered. From the pain of his broken finger, or something else?

Adaira's throat bobbed. "The heart decides," she whispered. "It doesn't care for feuds or reckoning." She paused here, and father and daughter shared a long silent look.

Malcolm MacLeod's face tensed, still fighting his outrage. "Morgan Fraser will crow over this ... to know his son has wed a MacLeod."

No, he won't, Lachlann thought grimly.

Adaira shook her head. "Lachlann has broken with his father. We will leave Skye and start a new life elsewhere."

MacLeod stared at her. His mouth tightened, a nerve flickering in his cheek.

When the clan-chief spoke, his voice was barely above a whisper, although there was a raw edge to it. "I've failed ye, lass. Ye look at me as if I'm a beast."

Lachlann grew still as he watched. It was painful to see a proud man struggle so. He saw then that despite his foul temper and controlling ways, MacLeod did indeed love his daughters.

"Let us be then," Adaira's voice, although quiet, carried across the silent kirk. "Let me love whomever I choose."

The priest stood a few feet away, his face ashen, while Rhona and Caitrin stood beside him, arms clasped around each other. The sisters' faces were stricken.

A long pause stretched out.

"Da." The pain in Adaira's voice made Lachlann's chest constrict. "Will ye give us yer blessing?"

Another silence fell, this one heavy with tension. Lachlann watched MacLeod's face and witnessed the struggle there. The man was fighting a war within. Pride and anger against a fierce love for his youngest daughter.

The clan-chief closed his eyes and dropped his chin to his chest. His answer came in a whisper. "Aye, lass, I do."

Chapter Twenty-nine

Ten Lifetimes

LACHLANN HELD ADAIRA close and buried his face in her hair. "Promise me that ye will never take such a risk again." His voice held a raw edge. "Ye could have been injured ... or worse."

Adaira squeezed her eyes shut. She buried her face in his chest, finding solace in the heat and strength of his body. "I promise," she whispered back.

She hadn't wanted to intervene. But as she'd watched her father draw his dirk, she'd known he meant to slay Lachlann. Initially, he'd wanted to take him prisoner again, which would have been bad enough. But she couldn't bear the thought of seeing her father kill him.

Lachlann could hold his own, she'd seen that. Yet he didn't possess her father's murderous rage. Few withstood it.

She'd acted on instinct then.

Lachlann pulled back and hooked a finger under her chin, raising her face so that their gazes met. His mouth quirked. "So ye love me, Aingeal?"

Adaira huffed. "I was wondering when ye would bring that up."

"So ... it isn't true then?"

They stood alone in the kirk. The others, including the priest, had left. Lachlann was watching her with a tender look that made a lump rise in Adaira's throat.

"Of course it's true," she whispered. "Do ye think I'd say such a thing if I didn't mean it?"

Lachlann smiled, his eyes crinkling at the corners. "It was a difficult situation ... desperation might have driven ye to it."

Adaira swallowed, suddenly shy. "No," she replied softly. "It just made me brave enough to say what was in my heart."

They left the Duntulm village kirk and walked, hand-in-hand, through the crofters' hamlet beyond. The nooning meal approached. The aroma of baking bread and stew wafted out of the cottages' open doors.

Children, playing outdoors while their mothers readied the meal, called out to the couple.

Adaira raised a hand and waved at them, although she couldn't summon the energy to call out a greeting.

After what she'd just endured, she felt utterly exhausted.

Caitrin was putting on a special nooning meal for their father's visit. They would all be gathering in the Great Hall for it soon. Adaira was tempted to retire to her chamber and hide away, yet she knew she and Lachlann would have to join them for the feast.

Her father had swallowed his pride and given them his blessing. But his acceptance was brittle. She couldn't risk offending him.

Adaira glanced across at Lachlann. "Are ye happy to join the others in the Great Hall now?"

He made a face. "As long as ye are sure yer father won't try to gut me with a carving knife."

Adaira favored him with an arch look. "Not today, he won't."

"Then, aye, I'll join yer kin for the feast, although I can't say I've much appetite."

Adaira linked her arm through his. "Me neither."

He placed a hand over hers and squeezed gently. "I wanted today to be special for ye. I'm sorry it wasn't."

She glanced up at him. "It *was* special."

Lachlann snorted. "Until yer father barged in."

"Thank the Lord, Da didn't interrupt us sooner."

He smiled, and the expression released the last of the lingering tension within Adaira. Lachlann Fraser had a smile that could warm the coldest day of winter.

The smile turned wicked then. "Does this mean ye promise to obey me from now on ... *wife*?"

She jabbed him in the ribs with a sharp elbow. "Not at all ... *husband*."

The aroma of rich boar stew filled the Great Hall. Lachlann dug a spoon into the dumpling that floated in the wooden bowl before him. The meal smelled incredible; a pity then that with Malcolm MacLeod glowering at him at the head of the table, he didn't feel like eating. The healer had splinted MacLeod's broken finger, and his right arm now hung in a sling.

The table before them groaned under the weight of the feast Caitrin had put on for them. There were huge tureens of stew and dumplings, baskets of breads studded with walnuts, wheels of cheese, and a divine-smelling apple pudding. MacLeod had the look of a man who enjoyed such fare regularly. However, he ate soberly, his storm-grey gaze never leaving Lachlann.

A lilting harp melody accompanied the meal. A young woman with dark hair sat by the nearby hearth, a serene expression on her face as she played a soft tune.

It did little to ease the tension in the Great Hall.

Lachlann raised his cup of ale to his lips and glanced at Adaira. She sat beside him, silent and watchful. Like him, she ate slowly.

"A delicious meal, Caitrin." Rhona broke the ponderous silence with a forced smile. "Yer cook could teach Fiona and Greer a trick or two."

"Don't ever mention such to them," Taran replied with an arched eyebrow. "Fiona prides herself as Skye's best cook."

Una huffed at that. Seated at MacLeod's side, the woman wore a petulant expression. "She over-salts her stews, and her bannocks are too heavy," Una said sourly.

The comment earned her a dark look from her husband. "Fiona serves me well, wife," he grumbled. "If ye think ye can do better, maybe I should send *ye* to toil in the kitchen."

Lachlann hid a smile behind his cup. Although he bore his father little goodwill these days, he knew that Una had been the cause of much of Morgan Fraser's bitterness and hate. She sailed through life, taking what she wanted and leaving wrecks behind her. Una had broken off a long-standing betrothal to wed Morgan Fraser. But she'd met her match in Malcolm MacLeod.

The clan-chief shifted his gaze to Lachlann then, pinning him with a hard stare. "How is it ye managed to escape Dunvegan?" His voice was low with a threatening edge. "The guards at the Sea-gate swear they never saw ye."

"Do ye remember how I loved to explore when I was a bairn?" Adaira spoke up before Lachlann had time to ready a suitable reply. "Ye were forever telling me off for wandering through the dungeon?"

Her father nodded, his expression wary.

"Well, one day I discovered a hidden passage there ... it leads out to the woods northeast of Dunvegan."

MacLeod tensed, his gaze narrowing. "What?"

"After I drugged the guards and freed Lachlann, we escaped through it."

A nerve ticked in the clan-chief's cheek. "Why didn't ye ever tell me of this passage?"

Adaira lowered her gaze, chastened. "I liked having a secret ... I'm sorry, Da."

"And ye are the only one who knows of it? No one else was involved in this plan of yours?" MacLeod cut a hard glance toward Rhona. His voice was flinty now.

Adaira shook her head.

Lachlann drew in a slow breath, resisting the urge to look Rhona and Taran's way. Wisely, Adaira had left them out of it.

A brittle silence settled over the table.

Lachlann let his gaze rest fully upon his father-in-law. Feeling the weight of his stare, MacLeod met his eye. He could see the resentment, the simmering anger that needed very little to ignite it.

Although it galled him to do so, Lachlann knew his next words needed to weave peace, not antagonize.

"I love yer daughter," he said, his gaze never wavering. "And I will work for the rest of my life to prove myself worthy of her."

MacLeod's mouth twisted, and he snorted, although the dislike in his eyes dimmed a little. "Ye would need ten lifetimes for that, Fraser."

Lachlann stood by the hearth in the Great Hall, nursing a goblet of wine. MacLeod and Una had retired to their chamber, while Adaira had gone off with her sisters. They would help her prepare for her wedding night.

The emptiness of the hall soothed Lachlann. The crackle of the hearth and the richness of the wine eased the tension in his shoulders.

This was a day he'd never forget. He'd wed the woman he loved, but MacLeod had almost ruined everything. The man was as tenacious as a maddened boar, and just as difficult to fight. He wasn't sure how he'd have handled things if MacLeod had actually come at him with that dirk.

All the same, he hated that Adaira had put herself in danger to save him.

Lachlann ran a hand down his face. He had to do a better job of protecting her in future.

"I misjudged ye, it seems." Lachlann tore himself from his brooding and glanced up to see Taran MacKinnon standing next to him. "Ye aren't the feckless bastard I took ye for."

The warrior wasn't looking at him. Instead, he was staring into the fire, his expression reflective. The firelight played over the two scars that slashed across his features. They were deep and ugly, and Lachlann wondered how he'd gotten them.

Lachlann huffed, his fingers tightening around the goblet. "Ye seem like a good judge of character to me, MacKinnon."

Taran grunted. He glanced over at Lachlann, studying him. "Ye have balls, I'll give ye that ... few men stand up to MacLeod and live."

Lachlann's mouth twisted. "I don't think he appreciated what I had to say."

Taran laughed, a low rumble in his chest. "Maybe not ... but he'll never forget it. Ye didn't just defend Adaira in that kirk, but her sisters as well. Ye told him what he should have heard years ago."

Their gazes met, and for the first time since their meeting in Dunvegan dungeon, the flinty chill in the man's eyes was gone. With a jolt, Lachlann understood that Taran MacKinnon was very different to how he appeared. Beneath that scarred, forbidding appearance lay a kind, big-hearted soul.

He'd helped Adaira escape Dunvegan after all.

Lachlann frowned, recalling the tense discussion during the feast earlier in the day. MacLeod was shrewd; he knew he'd not been told the full story. Lachlann had seen the naked suspicion in his eyes.

"He doesn't know about what happened after Adaira and I left Dunvegan, does he?" Lachlann asked. "About Talasgair ... and my father?"

"No ... ye wouldn't be drawing breath right now if he did." Taran paused here, his gaze shadowing. "MacLeod doesn't know Rhona and I helped Adaira either ... and it's best he never does."

Chapter Thirty

Here We Are

"YE HAVE ALREADY lain with him?" Rhona stared at Adaira, aghast.

Adaira nodded.

"When did this happen?" Rhona demanded. She placed her goblet of wine down on the table beside her with a thud. They sat in Caitrin's solar, in high-backed chairs before the hearth.

"On the journey here," Adaira replied, her mouth quirking. Rhona's shock was almost comical. "In a forest glade on the eve of Samhuinn."

Rhona swung her gaze around to Caitrin. Their eldest sister was looking down at her wine, a smile curving her lips. "Ye knew?"

"Aye." Caitrin glanced up, her smile widening. "Why do ye think I was so keen to see them wed? I had to make sure Fraser made an honest woman of her."

Adaira snorted.

Rhona picked up her goblet once more and took a gulp of wine. She then fixed Adaira with an appraising look. "So ... what was it like?"

Adaira's cheeks warmed. Her mind went blank as she struggled for a response that wouldn't embarrass her or reveal too much. She couldn't think of one.

Rhona was smirking now. Her sister was giving her a knowing look that made her squirm. "I see," she murmured, raising an eyebrow. "Words fail ye, do they?"

Adaira make a small choking sound—rescued when Caitrin cleared her throat and cast Rhona a look of censure. "Stop teasing her."

"I only asked a simple question," Rhona replied, all innocence.

Caitrin then turned her attention back to Adaira. "Was he gentle with ye?" she asked. She wore a tense, pained expression. "A woman's first time can be ... traumatic."

Adaira met her gaze, her chest constricting when she saw that her sister's blue eyes were shadowed. She knew then with certainty that Caitrin had never found any pleasure in Baltair MacDonald's bed.

Adaira's heart ached for her. She wished her sister could know passion, tenderness, and trust in a man's arms. She wished her to experience what she had with Lachlann.

"Aye," she said softly. "He was gentle."

Caitrin smiled, although the expression held a melancholy edge. "I'm glad ... I only want ye to be happy, Adi."

Adaira smiled back, her vision misting. "And I wish the same for ye."

Caitrin glanced away. "I am content now. I like feeling useful, having a purpose that goes beyond being a wife and a mother." Her features tensed then. "I just hope Da doesn't interfere."

"After today he might rethink the way he treats us," Rhona replied.

Caitrin looked up. "I can't believe what Lachlann said to him."

"Or that he's still breathing after saying it," Rhona quipped.

Adaira's mouth curved. "Why do ye think I had to step in?"

Rhona took a sip of wine, her expression turning wistful. "Do ye remember how we three used to sit in Ma's solar and speculate about the men we'd one day marry?"

Caitrin rolled her eyes. "Ye used to scoff at us. Ye were adamant that ye would wed no one."

"I was," Rhona replied with a wry smile. "But fate had other plans for me." Her gaze shifted to Adaira. "Ye were forever going on about how the man who'd one day win yer heart would be strong, valiant, and handsome. Have ye wed the man ye dreamed of?"

Adaira took a measured sip from her own goblet. She knew Rhona was teasing her again, but she didn't mind. The question made her think. "Lachlann is all those things," she said quietly after a long pause. "But he's also real. He can be impatient, arrogant—and infuriatingly stubborn. No one makes me as angry as him."

Caitrin huffed a laugh. "I'm glad to see ye aren't blind to his faults."

Adaira shook her head, smiling. "I'm not perfect either. Lachlann exists in this world, not in my dreams ... I prefer it that way."

"Aye, perfection is boring." Rhona's gaze met hers before a wicked gleam lit in her eyes. "But seducing yer husband isn't. Let's talk about more pressing matters. What are ye going to wear to bed?"

A chill night settled over Duntulm, bringing with it a seeking wind that shrieked across the bare hills outside, rattled the shutters, and moaned against the walls. Despite the keep's thick exterior, the wind still managed to push its way inside. A draft feathered across

Lachlann's face as he mounted the stairs to the chamber that he and Adaira would share tonight.

As man and wife.

He opened the heavy wooden door and stepped inside. Adaira was there, awaiting him. She stood before the fire, dressed in a sheer léine that reached her ankles. He could see the outline of her lithe form against the orange glow of the flames behind her. Adaira's long brown hair was unbound and brushed. It fell in heavy waves down her back.

Wordlessly, she turned from the fire, her gaze meeting his.

Lachlann pushed the door closed and leaned against it, drinking her in.

Adaira's loveliness took his breath away. He noticed then the large bed that dominated the chamber; he'd not even seen it when he opened the door, for his attention had been wholly upon Adaira. A bank of candles burned in one corner of the room, bathing the space in golden light.

"The Devil take me ... ye are a bonny sight," Lachlann murmured finally. His gaze left her face, noting the sensual smile that curved her lips, and moved down her body. He could see the outline of her nipples through the léine's thin fabric.

"Come here, Aingeal," he rasped.

Her smile widened, her eyes glowing in the firelight. Still not speaking, Adaira padded barefoot across the flagstones toward him. Lachlann noted then that someone had scattered rose petals over the floor.

When she drew close, Lachlann reached out and hauled her into his arms. His mouth slanted over hers in a deep, possessive kiss. One hand slid up her neck, tangling in her hair, while the other splayed across the small of her back.

Adaira moaned against his mouth. Her fingers dug into his chest through his léine, and she kissed him back with abandon.

Lachlann spun Adaira around and pressed her up against the door. Then he reached down and grabbed the hem of her léine, yanking it up, and stripping it from her. His mouth never leaving hers, he ripped off his own clothing.

Adaira's fingers fumbled as she aided him. And then they were both naked, pressed up against the door, savaging each other's mouths as if they'd been separated for weeks. Need pulsed through Lachlann, made his blood catch fire. His ache for her drove all other thought from his mind.

Their first coupling on the journey here had ignited a hunger within him that he felt would never be sated.

He could never get enough of this woman.

Adaira trailed kisses across his face before gently biting his earlobe. A thrill of pleasure knifed through Lachlann's groin, intensifying the ache there till it was almost unbearable.

Lachlann's hands explored her nakedness: the long length of her back, the plane of her belly, and her lush high breasts that strained toward him.

Slipping his hands under Adaira's buttocks, Lachlann picked her up and stepped away from the door. Then he turned and carried her over to the bed before lowering her down onto it.

Positioning himself between her legs, he parted her trembling thighs and thrust deep, seating himself fully inside her. Adaira gave a hoarse cry, bucking hard against him as she wrapped her legs around his hips and drew him closer still. The sensation, the heat of her, almost undid him; he threw back his head and groaned.

Slow down.

He needed to pace himself or this would be over too quickly. He wanted to savor this moment, their first coupling as man and wife.

Adaira arched back, her lips parting. "This feels too good," she moaned. "My heart could stop from it."

He laughed softly. "I hope not, Aingeal, for I have plans for ye."

He gazed down at Adaira as she lay upon the soft woolen coverlet. Her hair fanned out like a cloud around her, and she stared up at him with such naked want in her eyes that Lachlann almost forgot his resolve to go slowly.

He took hold of both her legs now and raised them so she could hook her knees over his shoulders. Then he rocked against her, taking Adaira in long, slow thrusts, and watching her face as he did so.

Adaira's chest heaved with each movement. Her high pink-tipped breasts, full for such a slender woman, bounced with each thrust, straining toward him. Later, he'd suckle them until she begged for mercy, but right now he just wanted to watch the pleasure that dilated her pupils and made her cheeks flush.

He wanted to make her lose control and cry his name as she did so.

"Lachlann!" Adaira arched up against him and brought him deeper still. Her mouth opened in shock as the angle touched a sensitive place deep inside her. Lachlann watched, drinking her in as her body shook from the force of it. Heat enveloped his shaft, and he felt her contract against him.

Pleasure slammed into him. It was too much. He'd tried to hold back, but he wasn't made of stone. Lachlann gave a hoarse cry and drove into Adaira once more, giving himself up to it.

Adaira sighed and rolled onto her side. She reached out, her hand sliding down Lachlann's sweat-slicked torso. That was the third time they'd made love that night, but it had barely taken the edge off the hunger she felt for him.

She rested her head upon his chest and listened to the thunder of his heart. She stroked the hard planes of his chest and belly, her breath catching as she did so.

Was this what Rhona felt for Taran?

She remembered their kisses, the heated looks she'd seen pass between them when they thought no one was looking, and the expression on Rhona's face the day after their wedding: a blend of serenity and excitement.

Adaira had never known such pleasure could exist; magic lived after all.

"Are ye well, Adaira?" Lachlann asked.

Adaira heard the rasp of exhaustion in his voice and smiled, lifting her head so she could meet his gaze. "Aye, very … but are ye? I haven't worn ye out already have I?"

He huffed, feigning offense. "*Already*. Just let me have a breather, ye saucy vixen, and we'll see who's worn out."

Adaira laughed. "It was an innocent question." She reached up and stroked his chin. He'd shaved that morning, but she could feel the rasp of new stubble under her fingertips. Continuing her exploration, she traced the sculpted lines of his face: his straight nose, full mouth, and high cheekbones. The first time she'd ever set eyes on him, she'd been struck by Lachlann Fraser's comeliness. Now her attraction to him went far deeper than that.

"I'm so happy," she whispered. "I never thought such happiness was possible."

His green eyes darkened, gleaming as he stared back at her. "I never thought so either … but here we are." His voice turned husky. "I've never been in love before … but that all changed with ye, Aingeal."

Adaira smiled. She'd once hated him calling her his 'Aingeal'. She'd found the name mocking. She no longer thought so. The endearment was sweet, heartfelt.

He reached out and cupped her cheek tenderly. "There is nothing I wouldn't do for ye, my darling Adaira."

Tears pricked at Adaira's eyes, and her vision swam. The intensity in his face as he spoke, the way his voice shook slightly, filled her with a surge of love so fierce that she was momentarily struck speechless by it. A surge of protectiveness filled her; the bond they shared went both ways.

When she finally found her voice, it trembled from the force of her feelings. "I know," she whispered.

Chapter Thirty-one

Secrets

LACHLANN WAS SHOEING a horse when he saw Malcolm MacLeod lumber across the bailey toward him.

Letting down the horse's hind leg, Lachlann straightened up. The grim look on the clan-chief's face made him wary. A couple of days had passed since Lachlann and Adaira's handfasting, and although MacLeod had been civil to Lachlann, relations between them were still strained.

"Afternoon, MacLeod," Lachlann greeted him. He kept hold of the iron file he'd been using. Surrounded by MacLeods and MacDonalds at Duntulm, he liked having a weapon in his hand.

Frasers weren't well-liked here.

Malcolm MacLeod stopped, his iron-grey eyes narrowing. "I've just received word from the south. Yer father's men have been searching my lands."

Lachlann tensed. He shouldn't be surprised, for he knew his father wouldn't let things lie, but he still didn't welcome the news. "And?"

MacLeod's frown deepened to a scowl. "We've sent them back across the border with their tails between their legs." He folded his thick arms across his chest. "Now ... why would Frasers be riding across my lands?"

Lachlann shrugged, feigning confusion even as his pulse quickened. "Maybe they've heard I escaped Dunvegan dungeon and have come looking for me."

"And how would they learn that?"

"It's been two months ... folk travel and tongues wag. News could have reached Talasgair."

MacLeod snorted, although the suspicious look in his eyes ebbed.

"Was my father with them?" Lachlann asked, keen to steer MacLeod onto a safer topic.

The clan-chief's heavy-featured face screwed up. "After the wound I dealt him, I'd be surprised if he still breathes, and he certainly won't be traveling far again."

Lachlann swallowed the impulse to tell MacLeod that the last time he'd seen Morgan Fraser the man could ride a horse and was about to wed. He wisely held his tongue. There were some facts it was best Adaira's father remained ignorant of.

Instead, Lachlann frowned. "So ye think he's dead?"

MacLeod's lips compressed. "I hope so. I skewered the bastard like a boar."

Lachlann let out a slow, measured breath, fighting annoyance. Despite that he'd broken with his kin, he didn't appreciate MacLeod's insults. Blood was still blood after all. He wondered if MacLeod was deliberately baiting him.

The cunning light in the clan-chief's eyes confirmed his suspicions. "I don't understand why ye didn't return to Talasgair after ye left Dunvegan," he said after a pause. "My daughter must have wielded quite an influence on ye."

"She did," Lachlann replied. He didn't like the turn the conversation had taken again; they were now skirting the truth MacLeod could never learn.

"I'd heard that Morgan Fraser's eldest was as ambitious as his sire," MacLeod continued. "But ye gave it all up ... for a woman?"

Lachlann could hear the genuine puzzlement in the older man's voice. He resisted the urge to smile. "I did."

"Why?"

Lachlann held Malcolm MacLeod's gaze, his own steady. "Because some things are worth more than land and titles. Yer daughter is more valuable to me than my inheritance."

It had taken Lachlann a while to learn that—so long he'd nearly condemned Adaira to a miserable life—but her father didn't need to know that either.

MacLeod snorted. However, his expression had softened, his gaze gleaming with pride. "Aye, she is."

"The wind is getting up. Shall I take Eoghan indoors, milady?"

"Aye, thank ye, Sorcha. We'll follow shortly."

Adaira watched the dark-haired hand-maid relieve Caitrin of the bairn and carry him away, leaving the three sisters alone on the shore. A fresh wind gusted in off The Minch, foaming the water. Adaira drew her cloak around her, her feet crunching on fine pebbles as she followed Rhona and Caitrin along the strand. The weather was definitely getting cooler; it reminded her that she wouldn't be able to stay at Duntulm much longer.

"When will ye leave for the mainland?" Rhona asked as if reading her thoughts. Her sister's wild auburn hair blew into her eyes, and she pushed it aside impatiently.

"I don't know," Adaira replied. Her belly contracted as she spoke these words. Although she was ready to confront an uncertain future, she was also nervous about it. Where would she and Lachlann end up?

"Ye can go to Argyle as ye had first planned," Caitrin spoke up. Unlike Rhona, who let her long hair fly free in the wind, Caitrin's hair was tightly braided and wound around the crown of her head. She regarded Adaira with a gleam in her eye. "Ye didn't hear it from me, but Da has sent word to our uncle and given his blessing for ye and Lachlann to reside at Gylen Castle."

Adaira halted abruptly, turning to her sister. "Really?"

Caitrin smiled. "Aye ... he's planning to tell ye soon, and ye are to act surprised when he does."

Rhona snorted. "It's not like ye to spill a secret, Caitrin. Remind me never to tell ye any of mine."

"I could see that Adaira was worried about the future," Caitrin replied with an irritated look at Rhona. "I wanted to allay her fears."

Adaira reached out and took Caitrin's hands, squeezing. "And I appreciate it." She frowned then, as something occurred to her. "Morgan Fraser knows I intended to go to Gylen Castle ... what if his men come asking questions?"

"Our uncle won't say anything," Caitrin assured her with a smile. "But if ye are worried, ye can have a quiet word to him after ye arrive."

Adaira nodded, her brow smoothing. Caitrin was right—her uncle had no reason to betray them.

Relief filtered through her. She felt happier knowing they could go to Gylen Castle, and that her uncle would welcome them and keep Lachlann's identity hidden. Life had been so eventful of late, all she wanted now was a little peace.

"Come on, let's turn around," Caitrin replied, pulling the collar of her fur cloak up. "This wind is unpleasant."

"Aye," Rhona agreed. "My hair will look like a rat's nest by the time we reach the keep."

The sisters began to retrace their steps along the beach before they left the shore and took the road through the village. It was late morning and the aroma of baking bread and stewing vegetables greeted them.

Many villagers called out to them, greeting Caitrin, who waved back.

Adaira cut Caitrin a sidelong glance. "Do ye like living here?"

"Aye," her eldest sister replied. "Much more than I did initially."

"I'm glad Baltair's dead," Rhona spoke up. Never one to mince her words, Rhona wore a fierce expression now. "He was a tyrant."

Caitrin loosed a sigh. "I know a wife shouldn't wish her husband dead … but I did. I felt nothing but relief when I saw him laid out in Dunvegan's chapel. When we buried him in the kirkyard here," Caitrin motioned to the peaked roof of the kirk rising to the south. "I stood there dry-eyed and feared the folk of Duntulm would judge me for not weeping."

"And did they?" Rhona asked.

Caitrin shook her head. "They're good people," she said softly, "and have made me feel very welcome here."

Adaira studied Caitrin's face and saw that her expression was suddenly shuttered. Even with her sisters, she didn't often speak openly. Adaira sensed she was pulling back from them, putting her shields back in place.

Caitrin hadn't always been this way. Before wedding Baltair, she'd been a carefree lass with a sharp wit. But looking at her now, Adaira realized that lass was gone forever.

Perhaps she just grew up, Adaira reflected, *like I had to*. She glanced over at Rhona then and saw that she looked thoughtful. Rhona was easily the most resilient of the three of them. Even as a young lass she'd had a knowing edge to her, an understanding about the ways of the world, that both Adaira and Caitrin had lacked. Yet she'd changed too in the past months. Taran had tempered her wildness.

The three sisters fell silent and made their way up the incline to the keep. The walls of Duntulm rose against the windswept sky, the MacDonald pennant snapping and billowing.

They crossed the drawbridge and entered the bailey to find a large mob of men amassed in the center of it. They were jostling to get a view of something occurring in the heart of the crowd.

Caitrin turned to one of the guards at the gate. "What's going on here?" she demanded, her gaze narrowing.

"Fraser and MacKinnon are going at it, milady," he answered her. "Sounds like a great fight ... I'm sorry to miss it."

A loud grunt echoed across the yard then, followed by a man's curse.

Adaira's breathing hitched. *Lachlann.*

Picking up her skirts, Adaira rushed to the edge of the crowd. She went up on tip-toe, straining to see over the broad shoulders of the men in front of her. Yet it was impossible—they were all much taller than her.

"Let me through!" She elbowed her way through the fray, Rhona and Caitrin close behind her. The men gave way reluctantly, their attention focused on the fight before them.

Adaira reached the edge of the crowd to see Lachlann and Taran, both naked to the waist, battling with blades.

She let out the breath she'd been holding, relief flooding through her. It wasn't a fight to the death—they were sparring with wooden swords.

As the panic drained from Adaira, she found herself studying her husband with frank admiration. He moved with a dancer's grace, easily holding his own against Dunvegan's best swordsman. Adaira had watched Taran fight many times over the years in the practice yard of her father's keep. He was a big man, but he was light on his feet. His scarred face was tense with concentration as he fought.

"Get under his guard, MacKinnon!" Malcolm MacLeod bellowed. The clan-chief stood a few feet away, at the edge of the crowd, his gaze tracking the fight with predatory intensity. "Beat the bastard into the dirt! Wipe that smirk off his face!"

"Da!" Adaira put her hands on her hips, her anger rising. "Don't say such things!"

MacLeod spared his youngest daughter a glance before grinning. "Don't look so fierce, lass. It's just a bit of fun."

Indeed, Lachlann looked like he was enjoying himself. His eyes gleamed and a smile stretched his face. However, his attention didn't shift from his opponent. Sweat poured down his naked chest, the muscles in his shoulders flexing as he lunged for Taran.

His opponent parried, bringing up his blade to block the attack. He then swiftly followed it up with a feint. Lachlann jumped to one side, narrowly avoiding the trap.

The two men moved fast, circling each other as they lunged, attacked, feinted, and parried. Their wooden blades became a blur.

Lachlann managed a circle parry, catching the tip of Taran's sword with his own and deflecting it. He followed up with a swipe at Taran's ribs, slamming into him with the flat of his blade. Taran's hiss echoed across the bailey.

Adaira held her breath. She'd seen few men beat Taran MacKinnon, but Lachlann was close to doing so.

It was then that Lachlann realized Adaira was among the crowd.

His gaze snapped her way, and he grinned.

That was when Taran made his move; one moment of distraction was all he needed.

He lunged and brought his blade down across the hilt of Lachlann's wooden sword, where his fingers grasped. Lachlann reeled back, but Taran was still moving. He ducked past him and slammed his sword into Lachlann's belly.

Lachlann wheezed, as the breath gusted out of him, and sprawled backward onto the dirt.

Adaira gasped, her hand flying to her mouth, while around her the surrounding MacLeod and MacDonald warriors roared with approval.

Standing over Lachlann, breathing hard, Taran grinned. "Novice's mistake that ... letting a woman distract ye."

Lachlann winced, propping himself up onto an elbow. He rubbed the fingers of his right hand. "Aye." His gaze traveled back to Adaira again. Relief flooded through her when his mouth curved into a smile, swiftly followed by frustration. The man was irrepressible.

Lachlann tore his attention from his wife and shot Taran a challenging look. "That's round one to ye, MacKinnon. Best of three?"

Chapter Thirty-two

My North Star

"RAIN'S ON ITS way ... mark my words."

Adaira huffed in frustration and glanced up at the sky. "Nonsense. There's hardly a cloud in the sky."

"Ye obviously haven't looked north then," Lachlann replied with a raised eyebrow, "at the enormous bank of rain clouds rolling toward us." His brow furrowed then. "God's bones, where are ye taking me, woman? We've been walking for hours."

"Oh, do stop complaining," Adaira shot back, striding up the grassy hill. "We're almost there."

The picnic had been her idea. Since their handfasting, they'd hardly had a quiet moment alone together. Her father's presence at Duntulm dominated the whole keep. Their only refuge was their bed-chamber.

Reaching the brow of the hill, Adaira smiled. Ahead, the boughs of tall trees beckoned, but before the woodland ran a glittering burn. Caitrin had told her of this place and had suggested it was the ideal location for a husband and wife to spend a private afternoon together.

"This is the spot!" She glanced over her shoulder at Lachlann. He carried a rolled-up blanket under one arm and a basket in the other hand.

"Thank Christ," he muttered. "What did ye put in this basket—rocks?"

Adaira relieved him of it with a sweet smile. The walk from Duntulm had been longer than she'd realized, and she'd packed rather a lot for their noon meal.

"The effort will be worth it, my love," she told him, stretching up on tip-toe to kiss him. "Ye shall see."

Lachlann smiled, his gaze gleaming as he took in his surroundings. "It's a pretty spot … I'll give ye that."

"Put down the blanket," Adaira instructed. "I don't know about ye, but I'm starving."

With a grin, Lachlann did as bid. Adaira settled down next to him and produced a large clay bottle from the basket. "Newly pressed cider."

His gaze widened. "No wonder that basket was so heavy … how did ye manage to get yer hands on that?"

Adaira favored him with a conspirator's grin. "I made a plea to Caitrin."

"Generous lass." Lachlann took the bottle from her and poured out two cups of cider. "She comes across a bit stern at times, but it's good to see there's a heart in there."

"Caitrin hasn't had an easy time of it," Adaira murmured, her buoyant mood ebbing as it sometimes did when she thought of what her sister had endured. "Baltair MacDonald was a cruel man," she added with a shudder.

Lachlann's gaze narrowed. "A shadow passed over yer face when ye said his name … did he do something to ye?"

Adaira paused, considering whether to tell him. Lachlann was her husband; there shouldn't be any secrets between them. "He started taking a liking to me during his visits to Dunvegan," she admitted. "I didn't notice at first, but then I caught him staring at me at mealtimes. The day after Caitrin gave birth, he cornered me and tried to kiss me. Rhona interrupted him, thankfully."

Lachlann's expression turned thunderous, and Adaira was glad that Baltair MacDonald was dead. Even so, his protectiveness, his concern, warmed her. "Worry not," she assured him softly. "Baltair never had the opportunity to corner me again." She paused then and took a sip of cider. It was light and fruity. "Before ye met me, I could be a bit silly. Both Rhona and Caitrin warned me that I trusted too readily and always thought the best of folk ... even when they'd done nothing to merit it."

Lachlann watched her, his expression softening. "I cured ye of that, didn't I?"

"Ye did."

He glanced away. "I destroyed something in ye, Adaira. I'll always be sorry for that."

"No, ye didn't," she replied, reaching out a hand and placing it on his arm. "Ye forged me."

He looked up, surprised. "What?"

"I was a bit helpless before we met. I'd never have escaped Dunvegan if it weren't for Rhona and Taran. Ye forced me to see the world as it really is. Ye made me strong, like a tempered blade."

His mouth compressed. "Aye, but it was a high price to pay, Aingeal."

"A price we both paid," she said softly, holding his gaze. "We gave up different things, but in the end, it was the making of us."

Lachlann inhaled slowly, his moss-green eyes darkening. "Ye are my north star, Adaira. Every time I look at ye, I'm reminded of what really matters."

Their gazes held for a long moment before Adaira smiled. "Aye, that's why I wanted us to come here today. I never see my husband."

He gave her an arch look. "The Lady of Duntulm likes to keep me busy. I shoed half the horses in her stable yesterday. She wants me to do the other half tomorrow."

Adaira laughed before leaning back and retrieving a cloth-wrapped parcel from the basket. "I think that's why she let me bring these." She pulled back the cloth to reveal a pile of pork and egg pies.

A smile spread over Lachlann's face. "As I said before—she's a generous lass."

Seated on the banks of the burn, they ate their meal and shared the bottle of cider. The day had started unseasonably warm, but it grew chiller as the afternoon wore on. A wind sprang up, driving in from the north, and to Adaira's chagrin, she noted the dark clouds Lachlann had spied on the way here were now looming close.

Presently, fat drops of rain started to patter across the ground.

Adaira, who'd been lying on her side next to her husband, sat up and cursed.

"What did I tell ye?" he said smugly.

"No one likes a 'know-it-all'," she replied tartly. "Come on, help me pack up."

They'd just cleared away the remnants of their meal, and were rolling up the blanket, when the heavens opened. Heavy sheets of rain sluiced across the hillside, battering them.

"We're going to get soaked," Adaira cried, clutching the basket to her.

"Come on." Lachlann took hold of her arm and steered her toward the trees. "Let's see if we can find shelter in the woods."

They dove for the tree line, ducking their heads under the pelting rain. Inside the woods they found a spreading oak to hide under. The tree had lost half its leaves, but it still provided some shelter. Shaking the rain from her hair, Adaira glanced over at Lachlann to find him grinning at her. "Don't say a word," she growled. "Ye insufferable man."

Lachlann's grin turned wicked. "Insufferable, am I?"

"Aye, ye love to be proved right."

He laughed and grabbed hold of Adaira, catching her so suddenly that she squealed and dropped her basket. Then, he pressed her up against the tree trunk and kissed her breathless. Around them, the rain drummed down and thunder rumbled overhead.

Eventually, tearing his mouth from hers, Lachlann trailed a burning line down her neck. "I took ye for the first time against an old oak like this one," he murmured, his voice husky.

Adaira sighed, arching her neck back to encourage his questing lips. She'd never forget that night. It had changed her life forever.

"Shall I take ye again?" Lachlann whispered. He ran his hands down her back and rucked up her damp skirts. "Here in the rain?"

Adaira's breathing hitched, fire surging through her veins. "Aye," she breathed.

Lachlann raised his head from her. "I didn't hear ye, wife." His hand slid up the bare skin of her thigh. "Do ye want me to stop?"

"No," she gasped. She tangled her fingers through his wet hair, pushing his face back down to her exposed neck. "But ye can cease talking now."

Epilogue

Always

ADAIRA HATED GOODBYES.

She knew it was cowardly, but she would have preferred to have stolen away under the cover of darkness than to have to bid her family farewell. Despite her happiness with Lachlann, and her excitement for their future together, she'd been dreading this moment.

Two weeks had passed since their wedding. Malcolm MacLeod had continued to remain at Duntulm, as had Rhona and Taran. Caitrin seemed pleased to have the company and now that she'd made peace with her father, Adaira was relieved too. However, they all knew the moment to say goodbye was looming.

The cool weather was setting in—Lachlann and Adaira needed to travel to the mainland before the first of the winter storms made the crossing treacherous. Adaira had put off naming their departure date, for she'd loved seeing her sisters again, spending long afternoons talking to them as they sewed, spun, or embroidered in Caitrin's solar.

But now, here they all were, standing upon the jetty on the shore to the north of Duntulm village. She couldn't put off the inevitable any longer.

A brisk breeze blew in off the water, bringing with it a chill that drilled into Adaira's bones. They'd delayed longer than they should have. Beside her, Lachlann cast Adaira a smile.

"The boat's ready, Aingeal. It's time to go."

Adaira nodded, turning to the four figures standing behind her: Caitrin, Rhona, Taran, and Malcolm MacLeod. Her stepmother hung back, deliberately keeping her distance. Relations had been cool between Una and her step-daughters during the past two weeks. Adaira would shed no tears over leaving Una behind.

Caitrin was weeping as she stepped forward and threw her arms around Adaira. "I'll miss ye."

Adaira hugged her back, squeezing her eyes shut as tears leaked out. There wasn't any point trying to stem them. It would only make saying goodbye harder. "Once we're settled, come visit us."

"I will," Caitrin replied, her voice husky. "I promise."

Caitrin stepped back, not bothering to wipe her wet cheeks. Even upset, there was a dignity to her sister, a regalness that Adaira knew *she'd* never possess. Caitrin could rule Duntulm as well as any man could.

"Take care, lass." Taran stepped forward and embraced her. The gruffness in his voice belied the warmth in his eyes. His gaze shifted to Lachlann. A look passed between the two men. Adaira had been surprised to discover that they'd become friends of late. They'd taken to sparring every morning in the practice yard and had gone out hunting together two days earlier. "Ye too, Fraser."

Lachlann nodded before smiling. "Keep working on yer feints. Ye often go to the left and give yerself away."

Taran snorted. "And ye are overconfident to a fault. I'd watch that."

Lachlann laughed.

Rhona choked back a sob as she threw her arms around Adaira. "What will I do without ye?" The two of them had spent so much time together over the past fortnight that it had felt as if they'd gone back in time, to the days when neither had been wedded, to when their lives had followed the same path. But those days were gone now; this short period together had been a blessing—one that would always come to an end.

"Ye will be fine," Adaira whispered back. "I'm a nuisance anyway. I prattle too much and get on yer nerves."

"I'll never complain about yer prattling again ... I promise." Rhona pulled away and scrubbed at her tears. Her cheeks had gone blotchy, and her eyes were red-rimmed, yet she was still beautiful.

"Ye will visit me too?" Adaira asked, her gaze flicking between Rhona and Taran.

Taran nodded. "As soon as we can."

Heaving a deep breath, Adaira turned to the last person who waited to say goodbye to her.

Malcolm MacLeod had stood quietly, awaiting his turn. He watched Adaira, his grey eyes gleaming.

"Goodbye, Da," Adaira said softly. "I'll miss ye too."

His throat bobbed. "Will ye, lass?"

"Aye." Adaira stepped close. She meant it too. They'd been through much of late, and there had been times when she'd hated her father. But all that was behind them now. Since their wedding day, MacLeod had slowly thawed toward Lachlann, to the point where he could now look at him without glowering. However, when she looked into her father's eyes now, all Adaira could see was love.

"Thank ye for sending word to Gylen Castle," she whispered. "Yer blessing means a lot to me." She stepped close to her father then and threw her arms about him. His girth made him difficult to embrace, and for a moment, MacLeod just stood there, stone still. Adaira was about to pull back, disappointed that he had not responded, when his arms went about her and squeezed tight.

"Ye are a good girl," he rumbled, his voice thick with emotion. "Ye have yer mother's pure spirit and soft heart. She'd be proud to see ye now."

Adaira swallowed as more tears flowed, burning down her cheeks. Her father had never before said such a thing. He had no idea what his words meant to her.

When she pulled away, she saw that his eyes glittered with tears. However, a moment later, he shifted his gaze to Lachlann and his mouth compressed. "Make sure ye look after my daughter, Fraser."

Lachlann inclined his head. "With my life."

Adaira waved until her arm ached, until the four figures on the jetty were mere specks in the distance. Even then she continued to watch, her gaze upon Duntulm's lonely silhouette, perched upon the cliff edge.

The wind bit and clawed at her, stinging her wet cheeks. She pulled her fur mantle close and tried to ignore the emptiness in her chest. Lachlann sat next to her, but remained silent, giving her the time she needed. Meanwhile, the screech of gulls and the rhythmic splash of the oarsmen were the only sounds. Caitrin had asked four of her men to escort Adaira and Lachlann across the water and ensure they reached Argyle safely.

Eventually, Adaira sniffed and withdrew a scrap of linen. Embroidered and scented with rose, it had been a gift from Caitrin that morning. Adaira dried her face and turned to her husband. "I hated that," she whispered. "It feels as if someone just tore my heart out."

His gaze was soft as it met hers. "That's because ye love more deeply and true than anyone I've ever met," he replied, reaching out and brushing the last teardrops from her eyelashes. "There's no shame in it. It's why we all adore ye. A woman with yer capacity to love will never be alone."

A smile curved her mouth at his words. He spoke them with gruff sincerity.

"Thank ye for understanding," she whispered. "For putting up with my bossy sisters."

He huffed a laugh. "I'm glad ye had the chance to mend things with yer kin before ye went."

Adaira watched him, noting how his eyes shadowed then. Lachlann would not have such an opportunity with his brothers or father. He was dead to them now, or as good as dead if his path should ever cross theirs again.

"I'm sorry yer family is lost to ye," she murmured.

He shook his head, flashed her a smile, and put his arm around Adaira's shoulders, drawing her close. "Ye are my family now, Aingeal," he replied softly. "The only one I'll ever need."

The End

From the author

I hope you enjoyed the second installment of THE BRIDES OF SKYE.

THE OUTLAW'S BRIDE combines a few of my favorite things. It's an 'on the road story' (I love road trips!) with a bit of adventure thrown in. The story is a twist on the 'savior/protector' theme. Lachlann Fraser was a great character to unravel. Initially I was going to have him as the 'baby of the family' (like Adaira) but then I decided I'd make him a bit more alpha. At the start of the story he's driven and ruthless, but I enjoyed the influence that Adaira wielded over him. I liked watching him wrestle with himself and choose love over ambition—and I wanted them both to have a profound influence on each other.

Adaira was quite a change from Rhona. She starts off an innocent but grows up pretty fast when she realizes that the man she'd trusted has betrayed her. Her peppery temper surprised me (yes, characters do sometimes surprise authors!). Lachlann soon learns that although she's a gentle soul, she's not to be messed with!

I know you all LOVED Taran from Book #1. He was always going to be a hard act to follow for my next two heroes. Lachlann and Taran are nothing alike, but both men had difficult decisions to make. I hope you enjoyed Taran's role in this book—and he'll be appearing in Book #3 too.

Now you'll be wondering what happens to Caitrin. This story is going to be very angsty! There's 'history' between Caitrin and Alasdair so prepare yourself for quite a bit of conflict. Sit tight—Book #3, THE ROGUE'S BRIDE up next!

Jayne x

About the Author

Award-winning author Jayne Castel writes epic Historical and Fantasy Romance. Her vibrant characters, richly researched historical settings, and action-packed adventure romance transport readers to forgotten times and imaginary worlds.

Jayne has published a number of bestselling series. In love with all things Scottish, Jayne also writes romances set in Dark Ages Scotland ... sexy Pict warriors anyone?

When she's not writing, Jayne is reading (and re-reading) her favorite authors, cooking Italian feasts, and going for long walks with her husband. She lives in New Zealand's beautiful South Island.

Connect with Jayne online:
www.jaynecastel.com
www.facebook.com/JayneCastelRomance/
https://www.instagram.com/jaynecastelauthor/
Email: contact@jaynecastel.com